FINAL DEMANDS

By the same author

Novels
Obbligato
The Earlsdon Way
The Limits of Love
A Wild Surmise
The Graduate Wife
The Trouble With England
Lindmann
Darling
Orchestra and Beginners
Like Men Betrayed
Who Were You With Last Night?
April, June and November
Richard's Things
California Time
Fame and Fortune
Heaven and Earth
After the War
The Hidden I
A Double Life
Coast to Coast

Short Stories
Sleeps Six
Oxbridge Blues
Think of England
The Latin Lover

Biographies
Somerset Maugham
Byron

Translations
(with Kenneth McLeish)
The Poems of Catullus
The Plays of Aeschylus (2 vols)
Euripides: Medea, Bacchae
Sophocles: Ajax
Petronius: Satyrica

Essays
Cracks in the Ice
Of Gods and Men
The Necessity of anti-Semitism
The Benefits of Doubt

Autobiography
Eyes Wide Open
A Spoilt Boy

Ancient Greece
Some Talk of Alexander

Notebooks
Personal Terms
Rough Copy
Cuts and Bruises
Ticks and Crosses

Screenplays
Two for the Road
Oxbridge Blues
Eyes Wide Shut

FREDERIC RAPHAEL

FINAL DEMANDS

JR
BOOKS

First published in Great Britain in 2010 by
JR Books, 10 Greenland Street, London NW1 0ND
www.jrbooks.com

A catalogue record for this book is available from the British Library.

ISBN 978-1-906779-84-9

1 3 5 7 9 10 8 6 4 2

Printed by MPG Books, Bodmin, Cornwall

For Beetle,
Paul, Sarah and Stephen

I

Adam Morris stood up, took one more look at the revisions of the screenplay he had written from his novel *Life and Loves*, clicked on 'save', and edged out from behind his walnut partners' desk to go across to the glassed door of his study. He had just stepped out on to the narrow, wisteria-hooded terrace overlooking the patio, when the telephone rang in the house.

'Go away,' Adam said, 'and leave me alone.'

Over in the orchard, he could see Barbara, under her floppy white hat, wheeling a barrow of uprooted vegetation towards the bonfire. She was wearing red gardening gloves. A grey beard of smoke aged the big apple tree. In the valley below *Écoute s'il Pleut*, their neighbour, Norbert Malaurie, was on his tractor, hefting rolls of baled hay on to a rubber-tyred trailer. Somewhere beyond that, Adam could hear, a cow was in labour.

'*Allo, oui?*'

'*Allo*. Dad?'

Adam said, 'You don't have to tell me. He died. I'm so sorry.'

'"Only one thing worse than the unexpected, that's the inevitable." Who said that? You did, didn't you? You said everything, didn't you?'

'Only some of it, Raitch. I'm saving the rest for my old age. Which comes, you will remember, on silent foot and somewhat bent. How are you?'

'You become complicit with what you dread. And then you dread your complicity.'

'I can imagine. Just. No, easily. When did it happen?'

'Last night, as a matter of fact. How's Mummy?'

'Fine. Planting out young cabbages or something Mr McGregorish of that order. Were you with him?'

Rachel said, 'Is this a bad moment?'

'There must have been better, if we rummage in memory's basement. No, of course not, darling. Yes, of course it is. Words break down and then we do. Actually, I didn't know that I cared all that much about Bill. Until you started to. If then. Do you want to talk about it or shall I busk on in the manner so sadly habitual among English-type persons when faced with the unspeakable? Was it . . . what was it? How, and when did it – ?'

'This time yesterday, more or . . . less actually, he gave his last seminar. On Petronius. He had almost no voice left, but everyone was there, pretty well, to listen to it. One or two people couldn't take it, had to leave. Three. One male, two females. He fainted and they carried him out, isn't that how it goes? Bill'd made a lot of notes and I was able to do . . . sort of subtitles, or do I mean voice-over?'

'Must have been hell.'

'He loved it. Being centre-stage; you wouldn't understand, would you? He even did a Q and A session afterwards. Mind was still . . . busy, busy, and funny, funny sometimes!'

'Hell for you, I meant.'

'Actually, I was rather – short pause for finding suitably disreputable word – how about . . . exhilarated? I was rather. Kicking against the pricks. Bill too. He was . . . like he was . . . whenever he was like that: the naughty little Liverpudlian who'd got away with something, for the last time. Still alive, very, the eyes. And then last night, the same night, he couldn't speak at all. And the pain . . . beat the morphine barrier. He could still smile though, because it was all so . . . Petronian, I suppose. You remember how Petronius died? After Nero ordered him to commit suicide.'

'Elegantly, if I remember rightly. With a touch of up yours, great ruler of the known world.'

'It isn't living well that's the best revenge, it's dying as if we had better things to do. That's what Bill told his seminar. Just about the last thing he did, in public. The last thing he ever said at all was, when he whispered to me . . .'

'You don't have to do this.'

'Of course I damn well do.'

'Right. The last thing, what was it . . . ?'

'"Shit, I think I'm turning into a god."'

Adam said, 'Trust Bill to quote Vespasian as an exit line. What . . . happened exactly?'

'Nothing messy. He had the stuff ready. Someone in the medical world he knew tooled him up; no prob there, fortunately. He did what Petronius would've if he could've: plugged his "terminal cocktail" into his drip thingy, as if it was champagne and . . . mouthed "Cheers". I said the same. He smiled, just, and closed his eyes.'

'The things we listen to and . . . can't imagine to be true because we know they are!'

Barbara was coming up the four mossy steps from the patio. She took off her floppy hat, shook her hair free and opened the door. 'I was thinking of making some tea, if you can bear to stop . . .' She saw he was on the telephone. Her head went slightly to one side. '*Ici Londres,* I presume.'

Adam covered the receiver. '*Ici* Los Angeles actually.'

Barbara said, 'Oh, nice! So who wants to make a whore of you today, only you're not going to let them . . . until tomorrow?'

'It's Rachel. Bill died.' He uncovered the receiver. 'Your mum just came in and I was . . . would you like to talk to her?'

Barbara said, 'Not now. She wants to talk to you. I'll go and . . . see you later. Give her my love and . . . Take your time.'

Adam said, 'Ba sends her love. She'll talk to you later. So that was that, was it?'

'Not quite. Useful to know I imagine, this, isn't it, for you?'

'*Raitch* . . .'

'He indicated to me to lie down with him. He was shorter than me. He mumbled things about his childhood. He didn't really have a voice left. I held him against me, like a little boy. I guess I fell asleep at some point, because when I woke up, I knew he'd . . . taken the chance to slip out, is how I thought about it. Like he did with his mother when she asked, "Where are you going?"'

3

'And he said, "Out!" I remember him saying it in his first year, with an exaggeratedly Scouse accent. Which he soon lost except for comic purposes.'

Rachel said, 'This time he was gone for good. Little bastard, is what else I thought. You think you know what dead is, don't you? But you never do.'

'Death is not an experience of life. It is not lived through. Didn't someone say that?'

'He was wrong though, Ludwig. You do: live through it. He was even smaller when he was dead, Bill. He wasn't there any more, and there he was. So here's the thing, dad.'

'That wasn't the thing?'

Adam had sat down again behind his desk. A page of *Life and Loves* was still up there, white on a blue field, on the screen of his computer.

'Not all of it. Because . . . OK, could you come out here possibly?'

Adam saw that one of the lines of dialogue in his script was superfluous; no, actually, two were. 'I thought . . . there were people . . .' He deleted the lines and nodded to himself. 'You told me . . .'

'That was then,' Rachel said. 'And then can be a long time ago. The thing has a . . . kicker to it I'd really like to . . . see you about, face to face. And . . . above and beyond that, no, before it actually . . . some people had already asked me if I could persuade you to come and do a week out here. Knowing it all as you do, and pass on some of it to a bunch of the students in the writing programme. They've got a small bouquet of money all ready to throw at you. So it wouldn't have to cost you anything or anything.'

Adam said, 'Rachel, I know you're . . .'

'You won't say discombobulated, will you, dad? Because of course I am. But will you? Come. The point is . . . You know what the point is. It's what people never come to and when they do . . . it's not what you want to hear. I want to see you. Very much. Nothing to worry about. But . . .'

4

Adam said, '"But" is the part I'll worry about.' He could see that another line of dialogue, lower down on his text, related to one of those he had cut; it too would have to be changed. 'Of course I'll come.'

'It'd be *such* a favour, to me. Not right away. Not till after . . . you know. How about in two weeks' time? The invitation comes from someone who's been very . . . can you bear "supportive"? Will it mean doing a lot of . . . re-jigging?'

Adam said, 'I don't jig all that much these days.'

'Am I imagining it or do you sound . . . ?'

'You're imagining it,' Adam said.

'While you're here, if you're coming, there's going to be a special thing for Bill. Faculty . . . memorial brunch. Gathering of the bibulous crocodiles. It would be so great if you'd say something.'

'Anything you like. Bibulous crocodiles. That's a phrase to run with.'

'One of Clifford's,' she said.

'Clifford being . . . ? Do I remember correctly: one of Bill's ex-graduate students? Sounds like a smart guy. Supportive even, could he be?'

'Don't pack the black tie, pops, OK? Or the long face. Bill wouldn't expect you to omit the *scherzo* just because he's gone to the great library in the sky.'

ii

Barbara was sitting at the dark oak table in the kitchen, cutting the stems of the maroon and yellow dahlias which she had brought in from the garden.

Adam said, 'Shall I put the kettle on?'

'It's already boiled. Have I guessed already? Rachel wants you to go to California.'

Adam said, 'I think she'd like us both to.'

'But she prefer it if you did.'

5

'Not exactly what I want to do, God knows.'

'That should get you doing it,' Barbara said.

'Why do I love you?' Adam said.

'The back of my neck got all the notices last time.'

'It's a sort of two for one offer. They'd like me to speak at this . . . wake thing they're doing for Bill. And they've also got this creative writing class one of her friends would like me to guest at. Tell the kids how easily it's done. Novels. Stories. I lie: *they* lie: they only truly ever want to know how to write screenplays and win awards. Which would . . . pay the fare and leave something for a Venice beach T-shirt or two.'

'Well, there you are then,' Barbara said, 'and there I'm not. Do you want some tea? Why are you looking like that?'

'I always want some tea. Or do I only always say I do? That's what I look like.' He watched her make the tea. 'Do you remember when it wasn't done to use tea-bags? I know: I swore I'd never go to L.A. again. I told you that when I came back last time.'

'And you may very well say the same thing next time. Rachel wants you there, you should go.' She sat there not looking at him. 'Must we have a drama?'

'Exactly what a surprisingly large percentage of Athenians said when Oedipus put his eyes out. Listen, come with me. We can . . . go down to Baja California afterwards and count the pelicans again and stone the crows and – '

' – discover, yet again, that all our luggage has been sent on to Rio. I'll be fine here. I'll be very happy with my own company for a change. I don't get to see all that much of myself.'

'Probably what I'm afraid of.'

Barbara was bending down to the lowest shelf of the *armoire* at the foot of a twist of stairs that went up to the *grenier* where the television was. She brought out a tall blue vase, which they had bought in a pottery outside Figueras, and carried it to the end of the table where the cropped dahlias lay. 'Bill Bourne was your friend,' she said. 'He was never mine. They want you to tell the children how to write, not me. At least it's not Mike Clode.'

6

'What isn't? Dead, you mean?'

'Wanting you to go to Calif.'

'I wouldn't in that case.'

'No?'

'What made you think of Mike?'

'Never going to be lust,' she said. 'Promise you that.'

Adam poured more tea, as if he were thirsty. 'I sometimes think – '

'You sometimes think everything,' she said. 'Time you eased up.'

'As if easing up were ever easy. Talking of Mike, the hell of it is, Bruno still wants the bastard to direct *Life and Loves*.'

'And the heaven of it is: so do you. Why do you think she's changed her mind? Rachel. About you going out there. The last thing I remember is her saying it was much better if you didn't.'

'How about while Bill was still alive, she thought she could cope and now . . . she's feeling whatever she's feeling and she . . . ?'

'You may be right.'

'Sounds as if I'm wrong,' Adam said. 'Am I?'

'Tell me when you get back,' Barbara said. 'Meanwhile, you'd better answer that *bloody* phone, because I'm not going to.'

'*Merde. Merde. Allo. Oui?*'

'Adam?'

'Who is this?'

'Jason, of course. Why do you use that strange accent when you answer the phone?'

'I'm in France,' Adam said. 'A lot of people around here have it, more or less. Must be the climate. What's happening, Jace?'

'I've had Connie Simpson on the telephone.'

'You'll never make the gossip columns that way,' Adam said. 'Try having her on the kitchen floor. Many have apparently.'

'She loves it. Second time and she still loves it.'

'So her many admirers have led us to believe.'

'The novel. They want *Into Africa* to be their big one for next year. It could be mega, Connie thinks. And she does have a nose.'

'But you do tend to notice the tits first, don't you?' Adam had his back to Barbara as he leaned against the white work-surface. 'Come to the point, Jason. I suspect it may be blunt. Is it?'

'This Winston Churchill character of yours. The West African Caligula, isn't that what you call him?'

'That's what the about-to-retire British ambassador calls him. He read Greats, and likes to prove it. Any objection?'

'Not to the Caligula bit.'

'Winston Churchill Abrahams is his name. I'm not changing it.'

'No one minds his name; it's his diet. Connie thinks it's needlessly provocative. Imagine if you read about a Jew eating people's brains.'

'Instead of living off them, you mean?'

'Adam, you say things to me that you wouldn't say to anyone else in the world, don't you? Why is that?'

'Because I know you can take it,' Adam said. 'Ten per cent of it anyway.'

'A lot of the new agents are going for fifteen per cent these days,' Jason Singer said, 'and getting it. Will you at least take a look at the scene? See if you can't – '

'And meanwhile tell Connie to read *Heart of Darkness*. At least the title. And then maybe she'll see the exquisite irony. Alternatively – '

'Exquisite irony sells three copies. Tops. Plus, you're laying yourself open to all kinds of accusations, Adam. Racism, frankly.'

'Winston is a blood-sucking cannibal dictator with a Savile Row pinstriped wardrobe who's busy murdering thousands of his own people with the support of right-thinking pinkish folk in the oil business – '

'I read the bloody thing, Ad, OK? I read it. Only this isn't literature time, this is major success time; conceivably. Connie wants this to be their Dickens Prize entry for next year. Possibly. Do you actually have to *specify* what Winston's got in his deep freeze?'

Adam palmed himself on to the work surface and dangled his legs. 'No, and I don't: *he* does. In the dialogue, if you look closely – that's the bits in inverted commas if you know what those are – '

'Why do I put up with this stuff from you? Seriously, why?'

'Because one day it may not be raining rain you know, it just may be raining daffodils. As far as Connie's concerned, "the horror, the horror" is lost sales in the sunset. Winston *tells* Saul Nathan that he's got a deep freeze full of appetising parts of people who tried to stop him from being de friend of de West. People like Guy Fielden, who – do I need to go on? – come and make trouble in parry-dies.'

'You need to stop,' Jason Singer. 'Beating on me.'

'What else are tom-toms for? Ask Winston. Ask Connie. I only write novels to stick it to the punters before de lights go out.'

'I know you won't take my advice, so I won't give it. But she has had one of her editors do some notes on *Into Africa* for her.'

'And I'll bet it's the one who studied creative creating at East Anglia and knows how novels ought to be composed, not to say confected, if they're going to be at once salacious and subtle, hard-hitting and soft-soaping, outspoken and reticent, in a word, thinking man's pap. And this right-hand person has – out of the goodness of his or her heart; my bet would be "his" – sketched out a version of the scene in which Saul goes to see Winston Churchill Abrahams and doesn't get shown the deep freeze or have its gore-may contents listed to him, but . . . Got it! Winston, with a smile, accuses Saul of *thinking* that he's a cannibal monster when in truth . . . he's a – how about? – vegetarian. Bingo?'

Jason said, 'You might have told me.'

'I did tell you.'

'That she's already sent them to you, the notes.'

'Bingo, bango, bongo, I don't want to leave the Congo. You don't even know what I'm talking about, do you? Danny Kaye means nothing to you. She didn't send them to me and now she needn't bother, tell her.'

'I'm not going to do that.'

'Because you've got your relationship with madame to think about. In that case be good enough to tell Connie that she is underestimating . . . wait for it, Jason . . . underestimating Winston – *my* Winston – if she thinks that he's incapable of a joke, or what might be a joke, about making *carpaccio* out of his enemies just to make Saul realise . . . all the things about himself he thinks he doesn't think. Remember *Black Mischief*? There's another title Connie should read – '

'One day, Adam, you'll start dropping bombs on your enemies instead of your friends.'

'I never drop my friends on my enemies. I don't have enough.' Adam sat sideways to allow Barbara to go past him with the vase of dahlias and up the three steps to the passage leading to the living room. 'Plus, they often fail to explode.'

'You can mock me,' Jason Singer said. 'I'm not allowed to mock you.'

'Deal!'

'This new editor she's got is very bright and he loves your work. Terry Slater. He's written a novel himself I've just sold to Coriander. We're all on your side, Adam. Only it's getting to be time you really thought about – '

'I'm not moving to another level, OK?'

' – becoming . . . laugh if you have to, but I'm going to say it: canonical.'

'You've been talking to Samuel Marcus Cohen. He's getting so canonical his books ought to come complete with dog-collar.'

'Samuel Marcus is only rumoured to be fancied in Stockholm. Nobel time! If not this year then next, or the one after. If his new one is as good as I happen to know it's going to be.'

'It'll have to be better than that,' Adam said. 'How's Tamara?'

Jason said, 'Why do you ask?'

'Um . . . does "common courtesy" sound recklessly self-serving? Why not?'

'I'll fax you these notes that Terry Slater's done. Connie loves the book, Adam. Hold on to that. Put it in your deep freeze even. Tammy's fine.'

Adam was putting the handset back on its rack when it rang again.

Jason said, 'I should've asked you: how's Barbara?'

'She's fine. And probably about to tell me that she agrees with Connie and – what's his name? – Terry.'

'Slater. There you are then.'

Wearing her rimless reading glasses, Barbara was sitting at the marble-topped table comparing cheque books and credit-card receipts with statements. The Mozart clarinet concerto was playing on the sound system.

Adam said, 'Am I right? About you not liking the deep-freeze scene?'

Barbara said, 'Tell me about Rachel and her . . . problems.'

'Sorry about that. Jason Singer and . . . She was very . . . controlled. I don't think it was ever a great love affair, her and Bill.'

Barbara said, 'But you're not sorry he's dead.'

'Sorry, but not sad,' Adam said. He stood by the low table, which now had a vase of dahlias on it, and opened the latest *TLS*, at the letters page. 'I was always surprised when he got in touch. Which he did quite regularly, in an irregular sort of way. Dear God, someone else complaining about how the Jews are ganging up on T.S. Eliot. I suppose Bill must've liked me, not that I ever thought so at the time. And you. He was my age.'

'But with luck you'll soon be older.' Barbara removed her glasses, pinched the top of her nose between two fingers. 'He liked you. And he also wanted you to see how well he had done, despite being an undersized Scouser from the wrong side of the docks. What was the name of that black girl he brought to Upper Addison Gardens that time? Joanna?'

'Joann. The doctor with the blacker than black eye. Are we allowed to say that when two or three are gathered together?'

'Whom he later married, didn't he?'

'And later again unmarried, among others. And still found time to write all those university-pressed books that combined rigorous philology with critical iconoclasm, if I remember the off-putting blurb correctly. Plus footnotes with a kick in them.'

'They had elaborately noisy sex.'

'He wanted you to hear what you were missing. His dark lady

called him "lover", several times, with increasing enthusiasm. And he called her "babe"; worked better than sonnets. Ah the dear dead Fifties!'

Barbara said, 'Those weren't the days; you can certainly say that for them.'

'Are you really going to stay here by yourself when I go to L.A. or . . . do you want to head back to London and . . . hang out there?'

'Turn my back on the garden now, and it'll be all over the house by the time I get back. Don't mention the Thurber cartoon, all right? Because you did that last time. With the creeper coming round and round at full speed. What was the caption again?'

'"Look out, here it comes again," wasn't it? Only it wasn't Thurber actually, was it?'

'*New Yorker* then.'

'*New Yorker* it was. Too well drawn to be Thurber. So who was it? Will you really be OK?'

'I shall be fine, and remarkably unchanged, I look forward to hearing you say, when you get back.'

'We can never get it right,' Adam said, 'can we? Any of it. Whatever it is.'

iii

'Next.'

Adam stepped across the forbidding yellow stripe and went up to the Immigration Officer. His badge said his name was Louis Bilbao.

'What brings you to the U.S., Mr . . . Morris?'

'I'm coming to . . . see my daughter basically. She's teaching here and . . . the guy she was with died, so I . . .'

'Writer, I see. Not figuring to work while you're here, are you?'

'Not if I can help it.'

'What kinda stuff do you write? Movies?'

'Sometimes. And books.'

'Ever come across Chelsea Pellegrino?'

'Not personally. Why, are you a fan?'

'Not too much. I fucked her maid.'

Adam went through the plastic doors into the Arrivals Hall and scanned the people waiting for the London plane. One large woman was jumping up and down as though on a private trampoline. Adam thought, for a moment, that Rachel had not shown up. Then he saw a white placard with ADAM MORRIS on it. When it was lowered, there she was, fairer than in England, and browner. She wore gold-striped sneakers and white pants and a light blue top, gold hooped earrings. He felt the corner of the cardboard against the small of his back as they embraced.

Adam said, 'I brought a suit like a fool. Which I shall almost certainly never wear. Hence my suitcase – what else? – came off the plane two hundred and thirty-third.' He leaned back, still holding her. 'You look . . . wonderful.'

'And aren't I?'

They started to walk across the concourse. 'You were here,' Adam said. 'You did what you did and now it's . . . done. I didn't do anything and so it's still ahead of me, I suppose.'

'Car's over in the where-the-hell-did-I-put-it place. Can I help you with that?'

'No.'

'I didn't ever love him, you know. Bill. Not lerve. I was being a little more . . . um . . . opportunistic than you might care to imagine. He had a lot to teach me. Two-backed beastliness wasn't ever top of the curriculum. Which, oddly enough, made everything more . . . emotional, especially at the end than I . . . But we won't go into it. And now which the hell easy to remember colour-coded aisle did I put the bloody Nissan in?'

They walked up the first ramp, and then the second.

'Where is the damn thing? I thought I was joking. Turns out I wasn't. Can I be your daughter possibly?'

'Any time you're Lambeth way,' Adam said. 'What colour is it?'

'Yellow. Last time I saw it.'

'How about that one?'

'It's not that big.'

'Perhaps it's grown. You have.'

'Put on weight, do you mean?'

'Only your voice,' Adam said.

'Junk food. We all do it. Life is a takeaway. Gotcha! Over there. Just where we were before. Was Barbara upset?'

'For your sake, yes; of course.'

'Not coming with, I mean.'

Adam said, 'She was very understanding.'

'Bad as that, eh? Do you always expect cars to start? I always expect them not to.'

'You never know your parents, Raitch, and you never know your children. And, of course, you never know yourself. Apollo would never have recommended it otherwise. I don't blame the Athenians for getting tired of Socrates, do you?'

'Not my field, as they say over here. What did you mean "Lambeth"?'

'Pre-war song. From a show that was on at the Victoria Palace, with Lupino Lane. "Any evening, any day . . ." It ends "Doing the Lambeth Walk, oy!" The labels that stick to old luggage, no accounting for them.'

Rachel drove out of the airport, a little fast for Adam's comfort, and past the Hilton (and a 'TOTALLY NUDE' live show) towards the San Diego Freeway.

'So: America; California, how do you like it?'

'Totally love it. Are you ashamed of me?'

'The minute I get here I wonder why we don't live here all the time. And a minute later . . . That's not true. What's truer is, I never quite had the nerve to stay, even when I was A-listed in this town. England's an obstacle race where you end up believing that the obstacles are what prevent you falling over. You maybe do. Have the nerve.'

14

'People're very pleased you're here. That Oscar of yours – '

' – that now very ancient Oscar of mine, it says in my book; which avoids them having to read anything I've written that I actually care about. What's wrong with the freeway?'

Rachel had no sooner reached the San Diego Freeway than she eased off to the right to get down to Sepulveda Boulevard. 'Too many people going north, this time of day. You're wrong, in Clifford's case at least. He's read *An Early Life* and *The Vulture's Portion*. And recently I found him a copy of *The Disappearance* in a second-hand shop on Hollywood Boulevard. So, he's how about . . . primed?'

'Not to say force-fed! Is he a full professor?'

'Associate. No money, no tenure, and not a lot of kudos; but he's very smart and full of . . . energy, so: could happen. If it's cool with you, I said he could drop by later. Literally: he has this bunch of stories and work in progress from his fiction class to wish on you; give you an idea of what kind of students have the itch to write.'

'And the scratch to go with it, presumably.'

'Excuse me?'

'Money. Nineteen-thirties race-track slang, I think. A term I never used until today. That's what jet lag does for you; plumbs the dusty recesses of the vocabulary and trawls up nothing worth having. See under psychoanalysis. Not that it's easy; very dark down there. And it's not just cheese it smells of.'

'Take your foot off the pedal, dad. Relax. Some of the students are quite mature, like in their thirties, looking for a change of orientation, and a whole shoal of them work to pay for their courses, wait tables and stuff. So what I thought was, we'll swing by the apartment and – if you're still awake – '

'And I mean to stay that way; till at least ten, ten-thirty or I'll be jet-lagged all week.'

' – we'll grab something to eat and I can run you to the hotel. They booked you in at the Westwood Mausoleum; can you live with that? Convenient for the campus. I figured you'd like some privacy. Besides, they offered and – '

'I like it there. Good breakfast. Stop-light's green; you can go.'

'Don't drive when you're drunk, dad, OK? Tomorrow, we have this thing the faculty is doing at Frank Skipton's house; celebration for Bill? What's to smile at?'

'The plethora of semi-question marks you've acquired.'

'Yeah? Drinks and dips followed by drinks and drinks. But also with a few words from, well, they all hope you among other people. What Bill was like before they were born and stuff like that. Can you handle it?'

'Why else am I here?'

'We'll get to that.'

'People used to say "presently". When did they stop, I wonder? In England. Once it meant "now" and then it meant "later" and now it's obs.' As Rachel turned right on Wilshire, Adam looked up at the tall buildings which were not there when he first came to the Coast. The traffic was never as thick either. 'Time was, you never had to slow down as long as you went a steady twenty. And you rarely heard a horn either. You're right: who cares?'

'How many black people did you ever have anything to do with, dad, in your life?'

'Black people. Not a lot. I knew a guy at Cambridge, later became a judge in Ghana; he sang in the Footlights, but he didn't take part in any sketches that I can remember. We thought we were being a little bit noble having him in the cast. Instead of no room at the inn, one room at the inn. And then – fifty-seven, fifty-eight – I got to know some of the Caribbean writers when they first came to London. I did some talks with them on the B.B.C., now you ask. Why are you smiling? After that, frankly . . .'

'Very full answer. I didn't mean to put you on oath.' Rachel turned off Wilshire into Veteran Avenue and pulled into the RESIDENTS ONLY parking area of a compound of half-timbered apartments faced with stippled fawn stucco. 'You'll understand, *presently*, why I didn't press too hard to get you to stay in the apartment.'

The tight, low-ceilinged living room was brimming with

books, many of them flagged with post-its of differing colours. The lowered flap of Bill's desk still had papers and letters on it. A notebook with an unfinished paragraph in broad-nibbed blue handwriting was held open by a tub ballasted with sand which had a quiver of pens and pencils stuck in it.

Adam said, 'Bill'll be back in a minute, right?'

'You expected more emotion. From me. I've embarrassed you. Again.'

'Where do you work? I didn't have too many expectations. Fears, yes. I wouldn't say "embarrassed". As for "again" . . .'

'In the back room. I also have an office on campus. Small but . . . OK, so: it's not that I didn't want her to come, Mum, but . . . Is the again part.'

'She guessed. And even then she didn't mind. You don't know her that well.'

'How about you're easier to work on?'

'Is what she guessed. What's wrong?'

'Who said anything was?'

'What's right?'

'Could well be the question. I've pretty well finished my Catullus book. Bill did a bunch of brilliant notes that I'm working through. I said I didn't love him. That was . . . being a big girl. Or a little one. But I did. The way he worked. Totally concentrated. In there with the text, squeezing like a bastard. And then he'd look up at me, dip the pen, go again. I was lucky to know him. And at the same time, there was something . . . ironic, I guess, the way he was totally involved and yet . . . not, not – how about solemn? He knew all about Yeats and scholarly dust, and he agreed with him. The lapsed Catholic never quite lets go.'

'Or is never quite let go.'

'Could also be true.' The entry phone was buzzing. Rachel pressed the button. 'Hey! Come on up!'

She stood in the open door. The tall black man came up the stairs three at a time and was right there, without seeming to have hurried. He had on red and white sneakers, wrap-around shades, a black FCUK tank top and camouflage pants with unloaded pouch-pockets in the flanks and beside the shins. He was carrying a stiff briefcase.

'Hi.' Rachel stood close to him for a moment and then she indicated for him to go on in.

'Clifford Ayres.' He looked taller once he was inside.

'How are you?' Adam shook hands. 'Rachel tells me you've been very . . . the term used was "supportive". Thank you, as if I had anything to do with it!'

'Not a problem. Bill was a helluva guy. You must be exhausted, so what I brought you is just what you need.' He clicked open the briefcase. 'A slew of stories and . . . how about "texts"?, my students selected for you to check out. They're not all as bad as you have every right to fear. But most of 'em almost certainly are.'

'Want some juice or something, Cliff?'

'I'm good. You're some writer, Mr Morris.'

'Adam. "Mr Morris" is older than I want to be.'

'The Vulture's Portion is one tough number for someone's never been to England. You don't spare the horses, do you? Or the donkeys.'

Adam said, 'What kind of things do you write?'

'How about I'm kind of multimedia? I tend to work the interface.'

'If you've got the interface for it, why not? What're you working on at the moment?'

'Right now I'm blocking out a rock musical of Trimalchio's Feast. Petronius Arbiter for people who never heard of him. Blame your daughter, and Bill, for effecting the introduction.'

'Clifford's also a musician.'

'Up to date, would it be, your version?'

'And then some. Set in Palm Beach. Richissimo bastard and his top-of-the-range lowlife friends. Mafia and down. Party of the century time. Ending with them all on a yacht they don't even know it's sinking. Bad idea?'

'All ideas are good,' Adam said. 'And pretty well everything people do with them is . . .' He was turning over some of the printed-out pages which Clifford had handed to him. '. . . what they do with them.'

'He's neat out of the bunkers. You told me he was. You don't have to read those now.'

'Do I have to be careful what I say? When the time comes to talk about them?'

'Tell 'em what they don't want to hear and they'll love/hate you like a father. So listen, I'm very glad you're here. We'll meet up at Frank Skipton's house, right, midday tomorrow? Rachel told you what's going on?'

'Bill Bourne's wake, is this?'

'Bill had some enemies. Did you tell your father? That at least you have to tell him.'

'Enemies? Why? They won't show up tomorrow, will they?'

'Only the ones that liked him. He had some habits that certain people – you've met those before, well, here they are again – didn't necessarily one hundred per cent approve of.'

'Yes? Such as?'

'I was just one of them,' Rachel said.

'You'll recognise the people still have their knives out for him. They're the ones'll be particularly polite to you, until they get to know you better. OK, so listen: see you there. Make sure and be late or it'll seem like forever. And don't let your dad get in Frank's hot tub with Sophie Blow, OK? And . . . thank you for being here, sir. For Rachel. And for me.' He tapped the stack of manuscripts in front of Adam. 'Give 'em hell but give 'em hope. Do I need to say that?'

Clifford stood by Rachel for a moment, looked at her and then at Adam, leaned over with a long arm to collect the empty briefcase from the low table and then he was gone.

Rachel said, 'So now you know.'

Adam said, 'Do I? What is he, six foot four?'

Rachel shrugged. 'Big guy.'

'Handsome. Good hands. I always feel a little surprised at how pale their palms are. Is that something I shouldn't say? Basketball player?'

'Also classical guitar. Those fingers move like . . . dancers. How will you tell her? *What* will you tell her? Mum. When you call her.'

'I'll tell her that . . . you were more worried than you needed to be.'

'About what?'

Adam said, 'Whatever it is you haven't told me yet.'

'There's plenty of time.'

'I rarely find that.'

Rachel said, 'I'm so glad you're here. Because . . . all right: I don't really know what to do.'

'No? About what?'

Rachel patted her stomach.

iv

By the time Rachel and Adam reached Frank Skipton's house, there were so many cars in the neighbourhood that she had to park the Nissan two blocks away. High Crestview was a steep street off Topanga Canyon, north of Santa Monica. The door of 2021 was in at ground level, but the garden at the back was two storeys lower down. The hot tub was on a brick pedestal. Two women and a bearded man were sitting in it, sipping Margaritas. Skipton was a heavily built, semi-bald man with a grey pony-tail. He wore a wide, nicotine-stained moustache. His tartan belly hung over a two-inch wide belt with a big silver buckle. After a while, glass in hand, he climbed to the top of the steep steps that led up to the frame house and stamped one of his cowboy boots on the wooden deck.

'OK, people, this is the moment some of you were dreading, when we have to quit groping the college widow and remember why we're here and who isn't any more. Bill Bourne was a guy you either loved him or you had a pretty damn good opinion of yourself, and he didn't share it. I know that's right, Mitch, that's why I said it. As y'all know, I pick up that Mr Modesty award every year around here so I never had a problem. I loved the guy because he told it like it was, and then some. I liked his courage, I liked his nerve and I liked the don't-look-back thing about him. He brought brains to this campus and he brought cheer and he looked the president of this fine establishment right in the eye and was not turned to stone. Good to see you here, Dorothy. Bill would appreciate your presence. I'm going to keep this short, because we have a guest with us has flown all the way from the little island he lives in, roight next to the one my ancestors grew potatoes in. Mr Adam Morris was at Cambridge with Bill and . . . I guess he's here to tell us what Bill was like before he came out here and settled in Capua.'

'Capua?'

'Where Hannibal's soldiers went soft on him, Elizabeth.'

'Hannibal? In the movie?'

Adam checked his fly, discreetly, and went up the several wooden steps to the deck where Frank Skipton shook his hand and indicated the audience. 'All yours. Do with them what you will. But keep it short, is my advice, because they're fruit flies, most of them, these people. Ladies and gentlemen and who all else, Mr Adam Morris.'

Adam held both hands up, surrendering to the polite applause. 'Thank you. Bill Bourne was pretty well the first person I met when I went up to the college we both went to. We were both classical scholars and, because he had a funny accent and he was shorter than I am, I looked down on him. Very briefly. Because I realised almost at once that he really was a scholar and I was . . . someone who had won a scholarship. The Jesuits had beaten Latin and Greek into him and he was never going to forget it. He soon lost the Faith, but he never lost the grammar. His father was a docker and he was certainly never going to be ashamed to say so. He was also never going to live the life of the working class if he could possibly help it. Scholarship was a passion with him; it was also a ladder. He was a short guy, but he climbed and climbed, rung by rung, and finally he got all the way up to California.'

'Climbed your pretty daughter too, didn't he? Among others.'

'I admired him,' Adam said, 'envied him even, I realise. I admired the way he worked and I admired the way he died. Like an antique Roman. He was a Celt not a Dane and he went, as I would expect, like the Epicurean Stoic he always was.'

'He was also a Eurocentric alcoholic racist bigot.' The voice from the crowd was louder this time. 'Stir that in the mix.'

Adam said, 'He once made me read that James Joyce story, 'A Happy Death', was it called? In which someone in his or her agony calls on God for His mercy, if I remember rightly. Bill didn't, that I know of, ever ask for mercy. He lived to the end. And after it, I hope; in his work. I give you a toast: a scholar and a man! Bill Bourne. *Ave atque vale!'*

Frank Skipton took Adam's hand and held it against his chest and nodded at the people who clapped and whistled, briefly.

'What the hell was . . . ?'

'Doesn't matter, doesn't matter,' Skipton said. 'There's one on every campus. You're lucky if it's one.' They clunked down the stairs towards the barbecue. 'You got Billy right, the little bastard! Rachel probably told you, he ruffled some feathers as faculty chairman. Not the most tactful man who ever raised a gavel. What was worse, he was pretty well always right, and wasn't afraid to come out with what he thought. In the world of the politically correct, that's not always the winning line. Mitchell Ambrose still carries a few bruises is the truth of it.'

Rachel said, 'That was perfect, dad.'

'It was short at least. Are you all right?'

'Don't worry. Everyone knows Mitch Ambrose is out of control crazed.'

'He wasn't the only one. There was a murmur, wasn't there, that was . . . not unfavourable to him?'

'Welcome to today,' Rachel said. 'It's not about me, if that's what's worrying you.'

'So what is it all about?'

'Try Africa invented democracy, throw in Socrates was a black man and the Jews were the prime movers of the slave trade and you're just about a quarter of the way there.'

'Is he a professor?'

'And quite charismatic, as a matter of fact. He's never short of . . . how about acolytes? He can take a lie, turn it into an opinion and then twist it into a theory. Pseudo-scholarly pretzels are his specialty.'

Adam said, 'Big guy?'

'Not too big. But don't even think about it, dad; not if you're thinking what I think you are.'

'I let him get away with it.'

'So let him. You handled it fine. He had a few drinks. He always does. People know that. What else could you do?'

'Sometimes I wish I was a man,' Adam said.

Enough people congratulated him to convince him that he had said the right things; but enough did not for him to realise that Bill Bourne had had other critics apart from Mitchell Ambrose. Dorothy Bishop stopped to shake Adam's hand, but neither she nor the Dean, who was with her, offered any apology for the interruptions. They left promptly enough to leave the impression that they had done their duty and did not care to do more.

'You don't remember me.'

'You and the pluperfect of *histemi* both,' Adam said. 'Or do I? You wouldn't be – '

'Joann.'

'You would. You should've changed a bit and then I might've – '

'You don't have to blow smoke up my ass.'

'My pleasure. We were talking about you last week, Barbara and I. And the time you and Bill came to our flat. How are you?'

'Just fine as a matter of fact.'

'Still doctoring? See? I do remember you, vividly even.'

'Long as I have my licence.'

Adam said, 'Did you see Bill again before he . . . before he died?'

'Quite a few times. We stayed friends right along.'

'That's quite a thing to do. Maybe it happens more in the States than in England.'

'I didn't like England too much. He did. Or had to, at the time. So . . .'

'Simple as that?'

'Absolutely not,' Joann said. 'Still married to the same woman?'

'She still seems very much the same, yes. My good luck. When did you hear Bill was sick?'

'When he called me.'

'I understand. Don't I?'

'If you do, you do.'

'In which case, thank you.'

'*De nada,*' she said. 'Forget it. Please. Soon as you can.'

'Gotcha! Did you marry again at all?'

'Coupla times actually. That bio alarm kept ringing, so I . . . had to find a way to answer it.'

'Bill never wanted to have kids, did he?'

'And couldn't,' Joann said. 'He had some . . . history . . . while he was in the army. Listen, it was good to see you. You were very eloquent in there. Your daughter is a very beautiful woman and very like your wife, isn't she? Straight.'

'But not narrow.'

'Barbara?'

'Barbara.'

Clifford Ayres said, 'Excuse me, but – '

'Gotta go,' Joann said. 'Patients to kill! Good to see you. Thanks for what you said.'

'You too, Joann. Thirty-five years.' He was looking at Clifford. 'Smoke in the wind. You remember Eurydice? She speaks well of you.'

'Orpheus's bitch? Listen, we go way back. Your writing class meets nine o'clock in the morning, if that's OK.'

'Worse things have happened at nine in the morning.'

'And never mind *a las cinco de la tarde,* right? That runs through till noon and then, if you still have the energy, you could maybe lunch in the commissary with the students if – '

' – any of them care to hang in that long.'

'They will. Tenacity is their strong suit. Prehensile is not the

24

half of it. Room 223 in the Samuel and Esther B. Mauser building. I've fixed for you to park. You have a car?'

'I do,' Adam said. 'Ambrose Mitchell.'

'Mitchell Ambrose,' Clifford said. 'He and I also go back a ways. It's nothing you have to think about. And don't worry about Rachel. I'll take good care of her.'

Adam said, 'Are you telling me to butt out?'

'Pretty well.' Clifford offered friendly knuckles. Adam touched them with his. 'Mister!'

v

There were nine students waiting for Adam in room 223. Soon after Clifford had introduced him, a couple more came in, together. They hurried – slightly crouched, as if some movie were being projected over their heads – to their winged desks. Adam told the class that he didn't claim to know how things ought to be written, but that he had acquired a pretty good idea of how they should not; or had better not.

'And what tells you that?'

'You are?'

'Harry Plakeotis.' He was one of the two men with shaved heads.

'Right, so you did the story about the Greek Australian – '

'The Australian Greek.'

'Right. Going back to his grandfather's island. Shades of Orestes. Which I liked, very much. What tells me? To put it simply, eye and ear: does it look right? Does it sound right? Those are the things I rely on. Read your stuff aloud and you can almost always tell: begin to bore yourself and sure as hell you're going to bore other people. It's never a rule, but it sure is an indication.'

The blonde who had her hand up was wearing a white cotton jacket, pockets over both remarkable breasts, and jeans with ragged holes in the knees. Her blue and white striped espadrilles had solid rope heels and ties around the ankles. 'You got me,' she said, 'because I try to read my stuff aloud and then I usually stop.'

'Meaning what? How about you're trying to tell us more than we need to know all at once? How many people have read any Henry James here? No one.'

'All those long words. You want us to write like that?'

'You are?'

'Samantha.'

'OK. He said one thing, twice, Samantha, Mr James, that's worth any number of lectures from fancy English visitors: "Dramatise, dramatise." Promise to swallow that with a glass of water before you start work every morning and I can go on home right now. As I recall it now, you pretty well suffocated your story, Samantha, which was quite – what? – how about daring? – by turning it all into what –' Adam turned pages on the low desk in front of him '– Corinna tells her shrink, am I not right? Does it occur to you that maybe that's a frame you don't need and, what's more, that too many people have used already?'

'Like *millions*,' the other shaven man said.

'How else can I show what her motives were when she – ?'

'Motive is the one thing I try not to get into,' Adam said. 'Why am I here right now? Because of everything in my life until now. Oh yes, and the cheque in my back pocket. Is it still there? It is. I'm never totally sure about why anything. If I have one piece of advice, it's dump the shrinks. No analytic hours in fiction. No therapy.'

'So what can we say about people's . . . characters, what they're really like?'

'Draw him or her right and that *is* their character. Say precisely what happens to people and what they say; not forgetting to imply what they don't. "Why" isn't too interesting; stick to when, what, and how. Their motives come with the right words; the punctuation even. Whenever you're tempted to a comma, pull out a full stop. And here's as near an absolute rule as I can hope to offer you: "He said" and "she said" *never* want an adverb attached to them. Let the reader's imagination supply the adverbs. That way, he or she becomes your accomplice, not your critic; and you pretty well have him, or her, where you want.'

Clifford put his hands together in silent applause, indicated to the class that they were in good hands, mouthed 'see you later', and went on out.

'How do you feel about experimental writing? Don't we need new ways to say new things? "He said, she said," aren't we getting tired of those? With or without adverbs. How do you feel about SciFi. Isn't that the future?'

Adam said, 'I never cared what happened to anybody or anything in any SciFi I ever read in my life, which ain't a lot, did you, Kirie Plakeotis? Honestly? Jamming science into fiction is like jamming jam into it: makes it sticky and hard to turn the pages. Nuts to the twenty-third century, frankly. Marooned on a distant planet? They can stay there. Nothing in the future tense holds my attention for very long. You don't have to write that down.'

'I do too,' Samantha said.

'For me, the old tools still make the best furniture, if you work them with respect. Observe and imagine work in tandem, OK? "Accurate fancy", there's a motto to go in your cracker: imagine it *and* get it right, all in one. Mary-Joe Malinowski, is she here? Good. Because how about you read us your story about waiting tables down at Malibu? Which I suspect you just may have done. Your father didn't produce *In Your Absence* by any chance, did he?'

'That was my uncle.'

'Good answer. What made you choose it?'

'He's my uncle. What do you mean "choose"?'

'Right. But if the answer was something you were writing, you would have choices. For instance, you – the character – could say "My uncle", like that, or "Norman's my uncle" or she might just say "No", which could imply that Uncle Norman is someone she doesn't want to acknowledge and then the story could be about why she doesn't. Or then again, she might just say "*Produce*?" Which would put a handle on what could be a quite different can

27

of beans. Every stroke of the pen has to be like a brush–stroke, if you can work it. But how you work it, that's your problem; likewise "can you?" Ideally, you need to become like a sports star: select your shot and make it all in one motion and with luck you'll hit it right. But you know the old story: the more you practise, the luckier you get. When the truth turns into what you can't help telling, because thought and expression go together, you just may be an artist. Do I believe a word I'm saying? Pretty well actually! Remember the old tennis coach's line? Watch the ball, bend the knees, that'll be ten bucks please. Here's mine: no motives, no emotional states, and keep Virginia Woolf from the door. It may not rhyme, but it just may scan. So now what?'

'Can we maybe talk a little bit about screenwriting?'

vi

'You enjoyed yourself.'

'There's a Shavian answer to that; but I won't give it. I didn't say anything I didn't mean but I felt like I was pretending. Pretending to be something I was. Am.'

'You were right on the money,' Samantha said. 'May I sit with you?'

Adam said, 'You look to have the necessary equipment.'

'What is that, you're eating?'

'They told me it was a Reuben sandwich. Isn't it? We don't have them in England.'

'You have scones, right? What's shaving got to do with it?'

'Not too much,' Adam said.

'Because that was so, so wonderful. Even if you do despise stories with shrinks in them. Like mine.'

'Despise? I wouldn't say that.'

'I thought you were just so . . . how about insightful? Soon as you started talking I wished I'd ripped up that story of mine before you ever got to read it.'

'I wrote one myself, I now realise. About a psychiatrist and his patient; but it was as much about him as about her, only she didn't know that. Proving what? That there are no rules, but that's no reason to break them.'

'I have to tell you: I read *The Disappearance* last night. Blew me away.'

'The work of a very young, over-confident man. Six weeks in Spain and I thought I knew South America.'

'I loved the idea of a guy who deliberately tears up his past; and makes being no one in particular a kind of existential roll of the dice. Chance as master. "Odds are gods." How did you get to that?'

'I stumbled. You stumble and then you have to run to keep your balance. And that boosts you on your way.'

'You're married, aren't you?'

'Very.'

'But she's not with you.'

'And it shows. I'm not myself without her; not that you can tell, I hope.'

'Or care. Particularly.'

Adam said, 'OK. So . . . why do you want to be a writer when you could very well be . . . I don't know?'

'You talked about Antonioni back in there. The way he – what was the word?'

'Dwelt, did I say?'

'Made you look at things and how they sat in the frame longer than maybe you wanted to. "Dwelt" is what you said.'

'You want to be in the movies? Maybe you already have been.'

'None you've seen, I don't imagine. Are you doing anything tonight? Only, while we're talking about Antonioni, they're screening *The Garden of the Finzi-Continis* over at U.S.C.'

'I'm sorry, Samantha, but he didn't direct that. Vittorio de Sica did.'

'But it's set in Ferrara, where Michelangelo came from. He was there when all that was happening to the Jews he was at school with and stuff and nothing in his work ever hints at *anything* about it.'

'Samantha what are you again? You only put your first name on your story. No, I should say: you put only your first name –'

'Sabatini.'

'Any relation? Of the tennis player?'

'Tennis player? It's not really Sabatini as a matter of fact. Or Samantha. How many people want to be Terri Shatz? There's never going to be a line, is there?'

Adam said, 'Terri Shatz. Really?'

'You want it, you can have it.'

'Interesting. To choose another name like that. Brave too. Points up that we none of us have to be what we say we are.'

'Now you know why I liked *The Disappearance*. Was there something you were you didn't want to be that made you write that? Brave? I don't think so.'

'Is she still in there somewhere, Terri?'

'You love to do that, don't you? Look right at people and say things that make them think about what they don't want to think about.'

'You can get served hemlock for doing that kind of thing,' Adam said. 'Ask Harry . . . Plakeotis. If that's really his name.'

'So what do you say?' Samantha said. 'About tonight?'

Adam walked back to the hotel. There were no messages. He went up to his room and dialled his French number.

'Hullo.'

Adam said, 'Not too late, am I?'

'Kitchen's closed, if that's what you mean,' Barbara said. 'I was reading Jane Austen.'

'The new one? What's it like?'

'So how's it going?'

'Slowly. How about you? Lonely, I hope.'

'I met a very nice man, as a matter of fact.'

'I'm sorry to hear that. No, I'm not. Who? How?'

'In the supermarket. A Dutchman. Rejn. Who plays the violin. Really well. Blue eyes, fair hair . . . All the things you aren't.'

'Not my favourite tune, that one,' Adam said, 'necessarily. He fiddles, you burn, is that how it is?'

'He's married and he's older than God.'

'The Father or the Son? Has he . . . played for you already . . .?'

'And other people. He had a concert, at the château at Duras, which I went to. Last night. With his wife. How's Rachel holding up?'

'She seems . . . how about strong? Very.'

'And how about you?'

'I did my duty and showed off for about three hours this morning. My favourite stationery store has closed, which leaves me bereft, likewise the one Westwood bookstore where I once found a copy of my latest. I have another class Friday, when I'm supposed to see what a miraculous difference I've made, and some kind of panel thing with various members of the faculty. Which just might get . . . try inter-disciplinary.'

'What're Rachel's plans now?'

'She's got a seminar tonight, she's teaching. The Catullus book is pretty well done and she's hoping California'll publish it; or maybe Cambridge. She wants me to talk to Sheridan Reece. I'm sure he'd much sooner talk to her.'

'About her life,' Barbara said.

'Her life I'm leaving to her.'

'So what was it all about?'

'I guess she was . . . needing to prove she could make things happen. I was one of them. Payback time for the people who'd been . . .'

'Well, if you're making her feel better . . . Called any movie people yet?'

'Not a one. I'll see you in four days. Less. And I'm not going to.'

'No? Seems a bit of a wasted opportunity.'

'Hey!'

'You too,' Barbara said.

'Morris, party of two.'

Adam and Samantha got up from where they were sitting on the deck outside the California Pizza Kitchen, on Ventura Boulevard, and followed the hostess along behind the people sitting up to the counter. Vietnamese chefs tented thin skins of pizza dough over busy fingers.

Samantha said, 'So what did you think finally? About the movie?'

'Very tasteful. Holocaust *Bolognese*. De Sica at his second best. The book was . . . different. As in better.'

'I better read it sometime.'

'It was maybe too . . . particular, for a movie. If I remember rightly. It had some incest and stuff in there. We don't like all our victims to be flawless, do we? Shatz, were you Jewish in those days, am I allowed to ask?'

'Only Polish, I'm afraid. That's where the hair comes from.'

'And the blue eyes.'

'Incest isn't that big a deal, is it? As sins go.'

'You asking for a quote?'

'You folks ready to order?'

Samantha said, 'I'll have the pizza capricciosa, just a wedge, can I do that? And a mixed salad hold the onions, hold the peppers?'

'I'll have the seafood calzone,' Adam said. 'Should help me not to sleep. And a cappucc'.'

'Excuse me?'

'Cappuccino. Samantha?'

'Glass of red wine for me.'

'Two of those.'

'Coming right up.'

'What would your wife say?'

'I think she would have thought it was a bit . . . slow and just a shade too artistical.'

'If she could see us.'

'She just might lift an eyebrow.'

'I balled my brother one time,' Samantha said. 'When I was fourteen and he was thirteen. First time for both of us.'

'Some things I do not believe.' The voice came from above the table, like an announcement. But Adam knew whose it was immediately. 'Nobody told me you were in California.'

Adam said, 'The last thing I heard you say in this town was that you were never coming here again as long as you lived. Samantha, this is Mike Clode. Samantha's a student in the fiction class that I was teaching to suck eggs this morning.'

'Hullo, Samantha. I've seen a lot about you. When do I get to read it? The new script. Bruno says it's better than the book.'

'He wasn't going to talk to you before he talked to me.'

'Yes, he was. Much it matters. Because you'll never guess why I'm here.'

'OK.'

'Carlo. Pavlides. The one and only.'

'That totally prize shit, if I quote you correctly, and I do. You cancelled his deal when you were head of production and then he – '

'We were laughing about all that the other night. Because you remember that *Eliza* project?'

'*Eliza* as in *Lynch,* could that be? Period piece set in Paraguay that I remember you saying that no one in their sane senses would ever want to make. No, I don't. Why? You could sit down, Mike, and spoil our evening. Samantha's dying to listen to things she has no interest in.'

'They're interesting,' Samantha said. 'Everything has to be. Isn't that part of what you told us today?'

'Told who? And why?'

'Samantha's in my class at U.C.L.A. She's learning to be a writer.'

'It's come back to life,' Mike said. '*Eliza*. In a big way. I've got the new script to read when I get back to the Peninsula. You're *teaching* now?'

'Jill must be thrilled to have you on it. They fired Norman Segal, presumably.'

33

'Jill's not doing it. She could never do it. Carlo's finding her something else. Don't let people know, will you, that you're teaching? Only sadsters teach.'

The waiter came with the pizza and the calzone and the wine on a high tray.

Adam said, 'Where does that leave *Life and Loves*? Don't tell me: in the cab on the way to the airport.'

Mike said, 'Very good seeing you in the flesh, Samantha.'

Adam said, 'What does that mean? You truly are a prime louse.'

Samantha said, 'Don't worry about it.'

Mike said, 'Adam, can I see you outside for a moment?'

'Oh, are we settling this in the alley? I'll deck you, you bastard. Provided you're out of shape and I get to nail you before you're ready.'

'I need one private minute, Samantha, and he'll be back.'

'Take two,' she said. 'And a courtesy mint on the way out, why don't you?'

'Love your work,' Mike said.

At first half-turned, in apology, towards Samantha, Adam followed Mike past where the hostess was standing at her lectern and out on to the deck overlooking the dark flame trees on Ventura Boulevard.

'One question: does Barbara know about this?'

'You and Eliza Lynch? She will. Soon as I get back to the hotel the word'll be out.'

'Because you must be mad to be seen in public having dinner with that girl.'

Adam said, 'She's a student. We went to see a movie. Put it in the papers. Tell my wife. Make my day. *Mad?* Mad is talking to you as if you were a friend of mine.'

'One of hers did you see?'

'What are you? Dreaming? She's in my writing class. She isn't even in the movies.'

'No? Then how come I saw her in one last night? "Big Sam Does It Again, and Again", with two dicks and a Harriet.'

34

'Snappy title. You're kidding, as well as elephantine. Where's it on?'

'The porno channel. I just happened to trigger it while researching a way to get to sleep. And there she was. Samantha Sabatini, busy, busy, at both ends. Don't imagine I'm moralising – '

'It would require a stretch,' Adam said.

' – but like it or not, there's a huge audience out there that we have to . . . relate to. Use it or lose it; applies to people too. You didn't know you were having dinner with a porno star? I don't know whether I think more of you or less of you. Ask her about it, widen your horizons and stuff. Literally, if you want to, which I bet you won't. The last faithful husband in the world, if that's what you are, breaking bread with a porno star. There's a comedy premise for you. You'll find her on your hotel menu when you get back. And no one will ever know. You don't believe me? Ask her what it stands for.'

'I don't see the connection. What would she know about the B.B.C.?'

'Forget the "the". Nothing British about it. Take it from there.'

Adam said, 'Goodnight, Mike. Give my best to Paraguay. And Carlo. Love the guy.'

'Wait a minute. Because where are you staying?'

'Westwood Marquee.'

'What cheapskate put you in there?'

'*Buenas noches, compañero.*'

Mike said, 'What the hell do you want to live in France for?'

'You're thinking of *adios*.'

'Elephantine?'

'In a nice way,' Adam said.

Mike said, 'It stands for big black cock. Things you need to know, Adam, if you want to stay in the game.'

When Adam went back into the restaurant, Samantha was handing a mobile phone back to the silk-suited man at the next table. 'Thank you for the use of that. Saved my life!'

'Any time,' the man said. 'Did you close your deal?'

35

'I did as a matter of fact.'

'You're still here,' Adam said.

'Afraid I wouldn't be? Or afraid I would? Come on! He told you, didn't he? The way he looked at me, your friend, I knew he would.'

'Mike? He's been telling me for years.'

'Deception's something you're no good at. Believe me. I'm an expert. He took you outside to tell you you were eating with a porn star. Don't worry about it. It does not come as a shock to me. I have to pay for my courses, you know. The people I work with, it just may come as a surprise to you, some of them, they're very nice. Very . . . supportive. They also wash a lot. And shave, like crazy. Why are you smiling?'

'Probably because I'm getting old. Er.'

'Wondering if I do, are you, possibly? Shave. Sure I do. For me, it's strictly a means to an end.'

'Place none of us wants to get to,' Adam said. 'As a matter of fact, my brother married a Playmate. Two decades ago; three! Time flies; I hate the way it does that. Very nice girl. It didn't last.'

Samantha said, 'Remind me what does. Listen, this has been . . . yeah, but I gotta go.' She glanced at the man in the silk suit who was standing up and looking at her. 'You know what they say about all play and no work.'

Adam tilted his chair back as the waiter came by. 'Check here, please, could we?' Samantha was looking at herself in her mirror. 'Where are you headed?' Adam said. 'I'll run you. I've got all night.'

'Makes two of us,' she said. 'Chateau Marmont. You're not smiling. You can though. Because you're quite right. Except I happen to like the guy. Comes in from St Louis. Somebody has to.'

'Do you know his name?'

'I know his name. Why wouldn't I?'

On the escalator down to the parking area, Adam said, 'What the hell do you want to be a writer for?'

'How about same reason you want to be a porn star?'

'Getting to be a little late for that.'

'There you go! Boats against the current, isn't that what the guy said we all were? And, like he didn't say, no exceptions. They do do gigs with mature people, you know, if you're interested. Amateur. They also do sometimes do pro-am stuff too.'

They stood together waiting for the upgraded Ford which Adam had rented. 'How much do I tip the guy? Used to be a quarter.'

'Nobody does less than a dollar these days,' Samantha said. 'Clifford's quite a character.'

'Good teacher?'

'That too.'

'He seems very . . . versatile,' Adam said.

'Versatile should cover it. You're cool about it, are you?'

'Chateau Marmont. West Hollywood, on Sunset, right?'

'Was, last time I was there.'

'Any reason you know why I shouldn't be? Cool? Samantha.'

'No. No.'

Adam took Samantha to the Chateau Marmont and then drove back past the black hookers and along the Strip and on down to Westwood. He looked at the menu of in-house entertainment and saw that Adult Movies cost six dollars. There was no way of telling whether Samantha would be taking part in any of them. And if she were, would he want to see it? He rarely saw anyone he knew taking part in anything on the stage or the screen, especially if it had anything to do with sex, without wishing that he or she was a stranger. He watched the news about killings in Bosnia, saw an owlish ex-Foreign Secretary announce that nobody in the Balkans had any idea how to behave and then turned off the TV, and went back to reading the first volume of Shelby Foote's history of the Civil War until he could tell himself it was time to go to sleep.

When the telephone rang, he had no idea, for a moment, where he was. He turned on the light and frowned at his watch. 'Dear God . . . hullo.'

'Adam?'

Adam said, 'Who shall I say is calling?'

'Come on, old son, get it together.'

'What do you want?'

'I was thinking of breakfast.'

'It's four in the bloody morning. Isn't it?'

'Are you free? Because come to the Peninsula first thing. Or I can come to you. Which?'

'As the Spartans said, on a very similar occasion: neither.'

Mike said, 'One guess why I need to see you. One.'

'I can't imagine,' Adam said. 'And I don't intend to, unless I'm commissioned. Yes, I can though: you've just finished reading the new script of *Eliza Lynch* and it's crude garbage. In which case don't change a thing or Carlo won't like it.'

'It needs a lotta lotta work. Against the clock. Carlo already has a pay or play deal with Julia. Give me three weeks.'

'And you'll give me the world?'

'I don't know about the world.'

'Do you know about fifty grand a week?'

'Deal.'

Adam said, 'You'd better speak to Carlo.'

'I already have.'

'Damn. I should've told you to talk to Shapiro. Except I don't really want to do it.'

'Those are the things we always get to do, if we're lucky. Are they real did you discover?'

'Are what real?'

'Samantha's jugs. Your secret is safe with me, old son. Barbara need never know. Just do everything I ask you for the rest of your life. Like I'll see you downstairs at your place; eight-thirty, can you do?'

'Your tab.'

Adam sat there in the light and sighed and smiled. Then he reached for the telephone.

'The Peninsula Hotel, good morning.'

'Michael Clode, please.'

'Mr Clode is not taking any calls right now.'

'It's his mother, tell him.'

'One moment.'

Mike said, 'Yes? Hullo?'

'Mike, it's me.'

'For Christ's sake, they said it was my mother.'

'And isn't it?'

'Do you know what time it is?'

'I want to get something straight.'

'Straight? Do you know what town you're in?'

'I'm not saying I'm doing it, but I am saying I'm not doing it in L.A.'

'For this you have to impersonate my mother? I already told Carlo you can't write in this town. He says nobody can. So . . . Now let me get some sleep.'

Adam put the telephone down and turned out the light. It was already light when the telephone rang again.

'Don't tell me,' Adam said, 'I'll tell you: you like the script after all and you hadn't spoken to Carlo and there's no need to have breakfast.'

'Dad?'

'Sorry, darling. I thought you were Mike Clode.'

'Not today. Can we . . . I was going to say "have breakfast". But – '

'Are you OK? You sound – '

'That's the way I sound. But I would like a chitchat with you before . . . you know . . . your panel thing tonight. '

'Of course. Look, I can cancel – '

'Mike Clode? You can't cancel a thing like that.'

'Are you your mother's daughter by any chance? I'll be free at . . . ten-thirty. Shall I come to you? Are you sure you're all right?'

'Don't panic. I should keep till then.'

Mike came into the breakfast room in sunglasses. He was wearing a white safari suit over a black shirt. There was a double gold chain around his neck. He had Adam move to a bigger table because he had pages he wanted to show him at the same time as eating waffles with a side order of extra well-done bacon.

'The flags I put in there are just for-instance pages, because the whole thing needs major surgery, and then some. Starting on page one. How did it go with Samantha?'

'It didn't,' Adam said, 'and you know it. You can't start on the boat. Costs a fortune and does no work at all. Start at the opera and then . . . unless I'm wrong, we wind up with the same opera played over the scene in the jungle with Eliza and her furniture and stuff . . .'

'Adam, as your agent I forbid you to say another word. Have you at least got her number I could have? Samantha. For casting purposes.'

viii

There were already more than a hundred students and faculty in the Samuel and Esther B. Mauser auditorium when Adam arrived. Clifford Ayres, who was going to be the moderator, took Adam into a side room, where there was coffee and stuff, and introduced him to the other panellists: Theodor Rawicz, from the screen-writing programme, and Julie Polunin, who taught in the journalism school.

Rawicz, who wore a big beard and a sleeveless Peruvian jacket over black brush-cotton pants, had had a shared credit on *Three Strikes,* which Adam was able to say that he had seen and enjoyed, a lot. He did not disclose that he had watched only a part of it, without plugging in the head-set, on the flight over.

'I'll bet you did the hedgehog gag.'

'Jointly, with my partner, actually, Yolande Jimenez, who wishes she could be here to meet you. Aside from anything else, she read you recently on Spinoza and Judaism and she was like on the table, cheering.'

'I went out on a limb,' Adam said.

'Is what she liked. Like he did. So few people today dare to buck the tide.'

'Not too dangerous when you're nowhere near the sea.'

Julie's glossy black hair was in a pony-tail. She was fresh-faced, had unpainted fingernails, wore businesslike glasses, steep heels and a pinstriped pants suit with a sagging silver chain doubled around her waist.

By the time they went through the side door that took them up to the podium, there were people standing at the back of the hall, Mitchell Ambrose among them.

Clifford did the introductions and invited each of the panellists to make a statement about why and how he or she did the things they did in the writing field. Julie Polunin slid her fingers up and down one of the long yellow pencils on the trestle table and wondered whether journalism was now the substitute for ideology and thus, in some respects, a better source of new political initiatives than the old party-political machinery. 'They used to call poets the unacknowledged legislators of the world, now maybe – for better or for worse, who knows? – it's columnists and anchor-persons.' She talked about the challenge of electronic communication, the decline of a common vocabulary, the contrast between hermetic communities, with their esoteric languages, and international conglomerates in media and in political administration who used a truncated, metaphor-free code a little like that of the military. This meant – think of 1984, which they were now well past – that without anything being expressly forbidden, as it once was by Church or State, there were more and more things, especially about moral issues, in the widest sense, that simply could not be said, would not be said, because they had fallen off the bandwagon – 'some might say bland wagon' – of language. 'Way things are going, the world gets bigger and smaller at the same time; smarter and more stupid.'

Adam wrote something on the legal pad in front of him. Julie leaned towards him for a look at what he had written: 'Wittgenstein and lions'. She was wearing very pale pink lipstick.

Rawicz told the people about a movie, 'written by the gentleman here present in Wilson's House of Suede and Leather's number one outfit', called *The Woman in Question*, which – he hoped its author wouldn't mind him saying, much

– was probably ancient history to most of the people in the room, but had proved to him, when he was planning to be the next John Berryman but one, that screenwriting could be dangerous as well as rewarding. He wrote movies and TV because he liked the collaborative clamour. He liked the primer of other people's presence. He liked the daily orgy of confrontation, capping and clapping, cheering and jeering. You screwed and you got screwed, and what was wrong with that every day? He liked the rewards, but he did like to stick it to people at the same time.

'What else can hedgehogs do?' Adam said, smiling, and the room smiled with him. He could then look serious and tell them that his problem with journalism and with screenwriting was that you had to please people. His idea of being a writer was still that of someone who, finally, pleased only himself, but – he raised the flat of his hand to the murmur from the audience – that self had to be, oh yes, a critical one. You had to be the kind of carpenter who never told himself that a surface was smooth when he felt even the slightest snag when he ran his hand over it. He smiled at Julie Polunin and talked a little bit about Baruch slash Benedict Spinoza and how, finally, the artist, the writer, had to be someone who was willing to stand entirely alone, not caring what editors wanted, not caring what people liked, although in both cases he was allowed to hope that at least some of them would think he was 'let's start with unforgettable – if it's good enough for Nat King Cole, it's good enough for me'.

'Might have known the first mention of black people from this particular panel would be condescending.'

Clifford Ayres said, 'Questions later, OK?'

'I don't think so, Mr Ayres, because later is always too late and now is pretty damn late too as a matter of fact.'

'That's right,' came from some black students, several of them girls, standing with Mitchell Ambrose at the back.

'Let's have Mr Morris finish his statement and then we can have all the questions anyone likes to ask.'

Heads turned. Mitchell Ambrose was walking down the aisle

now. 'Very impressive to talk about Spinoza, like you're flashing the name of the main man here and everybody has to be on their best behaviour.'

Adam said, 'Is this his best?'

'What did you say? You said something. I assume it was about me. I'm entitled to ask what it was.'

Adam said, 'I was wondering if the way you're behaving now represents the best behaviour you're capable of.'

'You think you're a snotty Limey who can come out here and patronise people, am I right?'

'Pretty well,' Adam said. 'No . . .'

'Pretty well, you said.'

'I was trying to hit a light note. Let me try again. I don't actually – '

'Actually, actually. I don't think you're what you pretend to be, one bit.'

'That's a relief.'

'You think you're some kind of a Baruch Spinoza come again – '

'Mitchell . . .'

'Here comes Step'n'Fetchit to Hymie's rescue. I wondered how soon this would happen. Come on, Cliff. Sit down, OK? Because Mr Rawicz here, he just told us how he liked the daily orgy, I think he said it was "the corporate wallow in search of the lowest common denominator" – '

'That's nice work in there, Mitch.'

'Maybe I should join your – what do you call it – syndicate? I bet you do. Any persons of colour in your group, may I ask, knowing very well what the answer is?'

'Yolande Jimenez – '

'I'm talking *black* here, not – '

'You've had your fun, Mitchell. Now suppose you – '

'I have so far had so little fun I don't even want to talk about it. Who said anything funny so far? These people here, I don't deny it, they've made niches for themselves all right; they have raised themselves above the common herd.'

'Mitchell, come on, you're monopolising things here. Other people have stuff they want to say.'

'How about we waited, they can wait? Mr Morris yesterday, no, the day before, he delivered a very moving eulogy on a professor called Bill Bourne. And I'm not surprised he did. Because if you want to talk about – what did you call it? – bad behaviour, if you want to talk about that, let's talk about how your friend Bill abused a visiting lecturer – '

'Mitchell, I'm going to have to ask you – '

'Go away, Clifford, you think you're Othello, tupping his white ewe, if I have Doctor Rachel's name right, but in my book you're Harriet B. Stowe's own best nigger.'

It seemed to Adam that the audience had receded; its reactions were so muted that it might have been watching the loud scene on the podium through a glass panel. Mitchell Ambrose was standing to the right of the stage now, with his escort on the steps leading to it.

'When Professor Jeremiah Lee Lanning came to this campus, he was heckled and abused by the dear departed – '

'He was neither, Mitchell,' Julie Polunin said. 'He was challenged, after Lanning – '

'*Professor* Lanning – '

' – had said a lot of things which were manifestly untrue – '

'That's your opinion.'

'True and false are not opinions. He said things that anyone who knows anything has to recognise as absurd, or forfeit all – '

'Don't lecture me, Julie; I'm still a tenured professor, even if some people – and I will name names, if I have to – would like to see me out in the wilderness. Bill Bourne may not be one of the Chosen, but – '

Adam leaned towards Clifford. 'Is this where I take offence, invite him into the alley, lose two front teeth and get my nose broken? Am I covered?'

Clifford said, 'Sit tight. He does this.'

' – he deliberately demeaned a visitor to this campus who has been in the forefront of the struggle of black people to shake themselves free of the patronising, oh yes, and repressive, yes again, domination of the Jews – no, no, I'm not ashamed to say it, which is more embarrassing for you than it is for me, believe me – of the Jews and the media they control. You don't like me saying "the Jews"? How often do you people talk about *Schwartzes*? All the time. All the time.'

Adam wrote 'Are you Jewish?' on the legal pad and showed it to Julie Polunin.

She wrote something and swivelled it to him: 'Only some of the time.'

'How many jokes have you told which make black people look stupid or crude or anything else that's supposed to be different from all the intelligent, liberal-minded Hymies who think of nothing but money and imagine that Israel is a good cause, if not the only one? Deny you know any jokes that make black people look like . . . how about *schmucks*?'

'I can't,' Adam said. 'Deny it.'

'How about you tell us one? Just the one. From your, I'll bet, extensive repertoire.'

'Promise you'll laugh? Because I do have one – '

'It's funny, sure I will.'

'Second thoughts, I'm not sure this is such a good idea.'

'Tell it.'

Adam said, 'How to commit suicide without really trying. Hymie – as you might say, Professor Ambrose – and let's call him Darnell die at almost the same moment.' Adam looked at the audience. 'Do you all know this one?' Heads shook. 'OK, and they both arrive at heaven's gate. St Peter explains that there's no longer any question of restricted entry; everybody gets a welcome gift and in they all go, but the black guy arrived first, so if Hymie wouldn't mind giving him some privacy . . . St Peter then asks Darnell what he'd like as his gift and he says, "I'd like all the money in the world." "No problem," St Peter says, "walk on up to that little booth and the angel will have it all ready for you." Now it's Hymie's turn. What would he like? And – wouldn't you know it? – Hymie says, "All the money in the world." St Peter says he's really sorry but the black guy – I'm sorry but that's what he called him – the black guy walking up there just asked for that, so what else would Hymie like? Hymie thinks for a split second and then he says, "Twenty bucks' worth of junk jewellery, and ten minutes with the black guy." In the silence, Adam felt Julie Polunin's hand on his fly.

'And that's the joke?'

'That's the flat joke,' Adam said. 'And I'm not as stupid as you have some right to think. I knew right from the off that no one here was going to laugh. Not that I didn't when I heard it. Not, I bet, that some of you did not. So why would I walk into the valley of death? It's racist, it's contemptuous of black people's intelligence, it's a whole slew of things like that. But now try this, and try being honest while you do: imagine now that tenured Professor Mitchell Ambrose just told you that story. Imagine what some sad little self-pitying Hymie would think when he heard it from Professor Ambrose's lips? He would think . . . he would think, and with some reason, that it was an anti-Semitic joke, albeit a funny one. And that's where Freud missed some of the point about jokes; they don't return the repressed, they flip it like a pancake and it's edible on both sides, when it is. And now I wish I'd never opened my big mouth.'

'Ten minutes with the black guy,' Theodor Rawicz said. 'Not a bad title.'

'Like that's what Clifford had with his daughter.'

Clifford Ayres stood tall. 'That's your third strike, Mitchell. Now get out of here. I'm warning you.'

Mitchell Ambrose said, 'You and who else?'

Adam said, 'Clifford – '

Clifford Ayres said, 'I don't think so. At all. You did what you came here to do, Mitchell, now please exhibit the courtesy for which you're so famous and walk, with dignity, out of this hall, would you do that?'

Mitchell Ambrose said, 'And I hope a lot of people will have the decency to do it with me.'

The audience applauded as Ambrose and his followers applauded them.

Clifford waited till the doors closed and the room was quiet and then he asked for questions. Some were asked, but they lacked spontaneity. The meeting lasted another twenty minutes, but Clifford himself had to ask the panel a last question, about their work in progress, to bulk out the time. After Clifford had thanked the guests and the audience, there was again applause. Some people stood up to clap their hands high, but not a few of them were on their way out at the same time.

Adam said, 'Did I screw up?'

'Not for me,' Julie Polunin said, 'not yet anyway.'

Adam walked over to where Clifford was talking to an older black woman. 'Should I apologise?'

Clifford said, 'Possibly.'

'For – ?'

'Clifford's kidding,' Theodor Rawicz said. 'As it happens, his middle name is Darnell, but how could you know that?'

Clifford said, 'But I certainly should. Apologise. On behalf of . . . brother Ambrose.'

'He has a case.'

'And there's no known cure. So let's leave it that way.'

Adam said, 'I'm having a good time with the writing group.'

'They like you,' Clifford said, 'a lot of them.'

Julie Polunin followed Adam out into the thin purple of the evening. He stood between the Corinthian pillars of the Samuel and Esther B. Mauser building and sighed.

'Happens all the time around here.'

'What's that?'

'That.'

'I blew it,' Adam said.

'Sometimes you blow it; sometimes people blow you. I loved you in there. Any reason why I shouldn't?'

Adam said, 'My daughter's waiting for me.'

'How about I give you my number?'

'You've been very . . . tactful, haven't you?'

'Have I?' Adam said. 'Not consciously. About what? And since when?'

'Since you got here,' Rachel said. 'Because here's the problem; part of it. You don't want to hear this, but here it is: I don't know for sure who the father is.'

'So let's get to it,' Adam said. 'How long have you . . . known you were pregnant? And how sure are you?'

'I've only missed one period. But I have absolutely no doubt. It's not that terrible, daddy. I'm twenty-three. Nearly twenty-four.'

'Who said anything was terrible? But if we're going to be grown up, I have to ask a grown-up question: how many candidates are there exactly?'

'What do you think I am already?'

'California does funny things to people.'

'Now you know why I didn't want Mummy to come. Bill and Clifford. And either way . . . You remember the Caudine Forks? Here we are again. I'm not apologising by the way.'

'To whom? To me? I'll say not. It's none of my business and also . . . none of my pleasure. If you want my help, you have it; if you want my advice, you don't. I love you and whatever you do or don't do . . . that's your life. If you need help picking up the pieces, here I am.'

'I needed you to be here to know what to do. Not to tell me.'

'One thing I can tell you. News recently in. Whoever's it is, it isn't Bill's. He was sterile. Joann told me the other day, as it happened.'

Rachel said, 'All right. I know. He told me. That's why we didn't . . . use anything, which also . . .'

'Do I understand any part of this? I hope not.'

'You know; I know; Clifford does not know. About Bill. That's my problem. And also my solution. And don't think I'm not ashamed and scared and . . . very glad you're here.'

'If being completely useless is any help to you, so am I. Clifford – '

'Exactly. If he knows it's his, he'll think I'm getting rid of it because . . . because!'

'And what would he do if he did? Know.'

'Say he understood. I imagine. He's a great guy. Say I should do whatever I want to do. It's not exactly something we ever planned to have happen, either of us; any of us.'

'Then why not tell him?'

'Because I don't want him to have to be understanding. Understanding is a terrible thing for Clifford to have to be. He'd say nothing had to change, and everything would.'

'Then tell him it's Bill's and get rid of it. And . . . then you're free to do whatever you want to do. Clifford never has to know. He has never to know.'

'And I always will,' Rachel said.

'You told me you were a big girl.'

'You want me to get rid of it, don't you?'

'I want you to do what you want to do. And I don't want it to have anything to do with me. But it does, of course, have to do with me.'

'I lie to Clifford, I have to break up with him. And I break up with him, he'll know I lied. How many catches out of twenty-two is that?'

'Then you don't make a decision either way. Yet. You . . . let him be the one. You ask him to say what would be best, for both of you. If he's the guy he seems to be, that means he'll say what he thinks is best for you. That way he's the hero and . . . you're home free. What's wrong with that?'

'Mummy mustn't ever know.'

'Mummy – '

'I don't want to know about that. Even if that's not what you were going to say. I just don't want her to know. Period. Ever.'

'Then I won't tell her. But if *you* ever do – you know what it will do to us. All of us.'

'I will never do that.'

'Because if she ever knows that you and I had a secret we – no, I – didn't tell her . . .'

'I will never do anything to hurt you. I swear to God. You won't let it come between us, will you, dad? Promise.'

'I'll make the promise, a hundred times over, but you're the one who has to keep it.'

'I love you so much.'

When Adam got back to the hotel, there was a message from Mike Clode and another from his agent (Shapiro had closed the deal on *Eliza*) and a boxed bottle of single-malt whisky from Carlo Pavlides. Adam got into the elevator with a woman who did not quite look at him. Eyes on herself in the mirror, she moved her mouth in a little sideways motion, like a stranger who had guessed what she was thinking.

He was cleaning his teeth when the telephone rang.

'Hullo.'

'Adam? Mike. Are you alone?'

Adam said, 'God, yes.'

II

After Adam had agreed to work on *Eliza*, Carlo Pavlides procured him an upgrade to first class when he flew back to Paris. He would then have no excuse not to start work immediately. Carlo also provided a stretch to take him to LAX. Its bearded, two-hundred-pound driver, in a sleeveless blue parka, threaded his way through quiet side streets. After he had gone straight across several red lights, Adam told him that he was not in too much of a hurry.

'Don't worry, the way I go, no cops are around to catch me when I shoot a light.'

'Why not just stop when they're red?'

'This used to be a free country, mister. I regard stop-lights as an infringement of my liberties. Were you ever in the service? Because I was. Including two tours in Vietnam.'

In the first-class lounge, Adam found a fresh copy of the London *Sunday Times*. He was reading the television reviews when he became aware of the entrance (and heard the sour, enduringly youthful voice) of the still handsome, still famous, English actor who had starred in *The Woman In Question*. He had been in other successes, before and after, including two with American directors, but he had never quite become the darling of Hollywood which, in his own estimation, he deserved to be. He continued to be solicited, frequently, by *auteurs* who were highly rated in *Les Cahiers du Cinéma*; he lived in a fine old *gentilhommière* behind the *Côte d'Azur*, was regularly honoured at festivals (he had been president of the jury at Cannes the previous year); and had recently received a knighthood from the Queen, despite his foreign residence. The copious honey poured over him never sufficed to abate his grievances. In the articulate whisper of one who expected to be overheard, he passed the time before boarding by delivering a soliloquy which itemised his disdain for lady executives and unduly famous actors. Of his male co-star in *The Woman In Question*, now mortally ill, he let it be known that 'his taste is, and always was, between his toes'.

Once in the plane, Adam settled in the complicated comfort of his first-class seat, ignored the in-flight entertainment, and opened the fat copy of Kenneth Burke's *A Grammar of Motives* which he had bought, second-hand, on Hollywood Boulevard. Its allusive ingenuities, and the author's assumption that the reader would be alert to them, retrieved the 1930s milieu of which Adam imagined that he would have liked to be a member.

He seemed only just to have fallen asleep when the captain announced that he hoped that they had had a good night's rest and that they would be landing in Paris pretty well on time. He soon heard the piercing whisper of the great actor wondering why 'a glorified deck chair came to be deemed first-class'.

There was no fast train to the South-West until early afternoon. Adam had several hours in which to loiter on the Left Bank. He bought a copy of Piotr Rawicz's *Le Sang du Ciel* from a *bouquiniste* on the *quai*, before going for a *choucroute* (Barbara never ate it) at the Brasserie Lipp. He had to eat with his elbows tight to his sides, to avoid his neighbour's, crossed to the *Flore* for a coffee, spent almost an hour in La Hune, where the books seemed so much more grown up than anything on sale in London, and then walked to the Boul'Mich and up to the *papeterie* Joseph Gibert, which stocked the spiral-bound, faintly squared *cahiers* that he favoured as notebooks. He still had time for a visit to the print shop facing Notre-Dame where he and Barbara had bought their Derain drawing (a sanguine nude), before he headed for the Gare d'Austerlitz.

He refrained from taking a taxi to avoid arriving at the station too soon. How, he wondered, had he come to know that Fred Astaire's family name was Austerlitz? As he trudged past the heavy brown door of the Tour d'Argent, he recalled how he had taken Barbara there, in the days when they could scarcely afford it, and with what condescension the waiter had presented them with a ticket with the specific number on it of the overcooked duck they had consumed. He had used the ticket for some time as a bookmark, but became disgusted by the precision of its numerology.

After five hours in the Capitole, he was relieved to get out into the calm of the Périgordine evening and find the Mercedes still parked where he had left it in the station yard at Gourdon. A week's accumulation of yellow and red flyers, stuck under the wide windscreen wiper, announced that he had missed a *Fête Champêtre à l'Ancienne*, two organ concerts, a sale of surplus bedding, a circus and a *Méchoui* animated by Jean-Michel Benjelloun *en personne*.

The sky was turning purple as Adam drove up the valley that cut north, along a narrow, straight road, under the lee of a burnt out château, towards Bouzic. He drove faster than he would have, had Barbara been in the car. The absence of oncoming headlights promised that he had the road to himself. He saw the young deer only as it made its leap, a yard ahead of him, up out of the field below the car. It skittered, off balance, in the roadway, hoofs gaining no purchase on the tarmac. One frightened eye was close to Adam as the headlight flared on it. The offside bumper thumped the soft creature in the flank and then it was gone behind the car.

'Shit.'

Adam stopped the car, pressed on the emergency lights, and walked back into the rouged darkness. Unable to see any shape in the black roadway, he stood listening to the silence. What noise might a wounded deer make? What should he do if he found it huddled, but still alive? Headlights, half a mile away, winked between the tree trunks. The single oncoming car seemed like a posse on the way to the scene. Adam ran back to the Mercedes, jumped in and drove on. Only as the other car came past did he think to switch off the blinking emergency lights.

When he had driven through Bouzic, he stopped under a street-lamp at the far end of the village and checked the bumper for fur or blood. He found only that a chip of transparent plastic had been knocked out of the housing of the offside headlight, which was still working.

He turned up the drive towards *Écoute s'il Pleut*, past the raw little holiday house which a Dutchman had built the previous year (his unhitched caravan remained propped among the pine trees), and parked in the gravel in front of the open doors of the big barn where Barbara had garaged her grey Toyota Yaris. As he approached *Écoute s'il Pleut* from the side, Adam could see no welcoming light.

'*Il y a quelqu'un?*'

'. . . of course,' Barbara was saying. 'That would be fine. Of course I'd like you to. Nothing better! Stay as long as you want. Of course he will.' Adam stood in the corridor listening to his wife's voice as though she were a stranger, or he was. 'I'll tell him as soon as he comes in.'

'Tell him what?' Adam said.

'Oh my goodness, he *has* come in. And given me the shock of my life. Probably. I'd better go and . . . He'll call you later. Oh. In the morning then. No, you're quite right. The afternoon then. Lots of love . . . to everyone.'

'I thought for a moment you were talking to your lover.'

'No such luck, to tell you the truth.'

'*Veritas* without the *vino,* never much of a party really.'

'That was Tom, but you never guessed. How was it?'

'It was. The imperfect tense says it all, some of it. How about you?'

'They want to come to Tregunter Road for Christmas.'

'Meaning he . . . feels it's about time they did and . . . Juliana isn't making any audible objection. Or does she plan to spend *Heilige Nacht* in her not so native land?'

'She and Tom and Alexi; they're all planning to come.'

'And we should be pleased.'

'I am. Are you not?'

'Not as pleased as I am to see you.'

'Are you hungry?'

He came and kissed her. 'Can you not tell?'

Barbara said, 'Food-wise, I meant. Something's happened.'

'Has it? What?'

'To you.'

'All right, let's get it over with: I got saddled at the last moment with this dollar-fattened rewrite. Mike Clode strikes again. Quite fun actually, which is even more depressing. The happy hooker with the long face, that's me. Which reminds me . . .'

'Of what? Are you wondering if I'm old enough to be told? Or too old, perhaps?'

'I also had a steamy pizza with a porn star cum hooker. There: it's come out.'

'Can happen. How so?'

'She was in my class.'

'Yes? And were you in hers?'

'Writing class, as if you didn't know. Samantha Sabatini. Like Häagen-Dazs.'

'Not all that.'

'In the sense that it's a completely confected brand name. Sounds sexier than Terri Shatz.'

'I don't know though. That reminds me: do you know a man called Lars Waring?'

'Should I? Doesn't come from Veii, does he?'

'Didn't say so. He called. Bit of a smoothy. He sounded like . . . a skimmed version of the *crème de la crème*.'

'I know someone called *Lord* Waring. In the sense that, yaws ago now, Derek and I had lunch with the smooth old fart just after they'd swindled us over that TV franchise thing. Thank God they did. Otherwise I'd now be a TV drama executive finding plausible reasons not to commission any worthwhile drama. But he was called Monty. What did the Lars version want?'

'A word. It can keep till we're back in London, but he thinks you're an important . . . I think he said "intellectual" . . . who might be interested in a project he has in mind. Sorry, not important; "distinguished". There's some cold ham.'

'I prefer important. Distinguished implies hair loss. And a greying chest.'

'How was hers?'

'What?'

'Chest. La Sabatini's.'

'A treasure she kept discreetly unrevealed. Mike Clode saw it in . . . shall we say another context? And other parts. All delectable, he took care to tell me. On the adult channel in his suite. I saw only one of her unbuttoned short stories. Any eggs?'

'All about her abused childhood, I bet. Scrambled?'

'Extremely. Trailer parks and hook-ups and porno shoots. They all shave, you know. Down there, as they used to say. Males and females. I'll do the eggs.'

'Mary Quant did forecast, in the 1960s, that pubic coiffing would be the next great fashion breakthrough. There's something you're not telling me. Is that going to be enough for you, food-wise?'

'I had a tepid *panini* before I got on the train – or is that *panino* when singular, as this one certainly was? So . . . how's the weather been?'

'About Rachel presumably.'

Adam said, 'OK: Bill wasn't her only lover. Is the thing that came as a small surprise to me. But then, once I knew, I wasn't all *that* surprised. Are you?'

'He can't have been unduly . . . functional in the ready-when-you-are department in recent weeks.'

'Lars Waring . . . what the hell can he . . . ? You can still sometimes say things I don't expect, can't you?'

'I can try,' she said.

'He's black.'

'Didn't sound it to me.'

'Clifford. Ayres. Rachel's . . . supplementary friend. Young, handsome, smart, but not yet tenured; black and pantherine. Nothing to do with Elijah Muhammad, as far as I know. Plenty of him to go round too. Six foot four.'

'And you don't mind a bit. You're telling yourself.'

'I'd be happier if he were tenured.'

'No you wouldn't though. She's a lot bolder than I ever was, your daughter.'

'I don't know; I can imagine you, given the chance . . . can't you? Do you think there really are men who can go on all night?'

'Something in you wants me to think I've missed something, doesn't it? In the bumpsadaisy department.'

'Or fears you have. You don't think they've got money problems, do you? Tom and Juliana. Property's still booming, isn't it, in Spain? Is her grandfather still alive, do you suppose? Juliana's? The Nazi one.'

'You can always ask her while you're carving the turkey. All night equals cystitis as far as I'm concerned. Now where are you going?'

Adam called from by the front door. 'I forgot! I didn't forget: I bought you a present.'

'You should have, you should have!'

'Two in fact. One. Two. And three! Straight from Rodeo Drive. The cheap end, of course. If the cap doesn't fit, don't wear it.'

'It fits. Do I look like a babe at all?'

'You do to me. Great shirt too. This might go with it. Came after Mike and Carlo laid all that moolah on me to do *Eliza Lynch*. Don't thank me, blame them.'

Barbara undid the gift wrapping. 'That is some rich bitch's robe.'

'But on you it looks good. So much for Christmas. Until Christmas.'

Barbara said, 'In fact, it's so nice it's very close to being one step short of an apology. Are you sure nothing else happened at all?'

'Very little,' he said. 'In the X-rated sense. I had no idea Samantha was a hooker when we went to the pizza parlour. But then I did chauffeur her to her next business meeting. She brought out the pimp in me, or was it the cabbie? I was a little disappointed she didn't slip me five bucks she'd tucked in her garter. Comes of her not being called Frenchie.'

'Is he dangerous, do you suppose? Clifford, is that his name?'

'Rachel says "supportive". And I believe it. Good guy.'

'But you're not that happy about it.'

'It all reminds me that she isn't . . . mine any more. In spades. Yes,

I can see Dr Freud smirking into his notebook. She's going to send me the book she's done from her thesis to show to Sheridan Reece. So . . .'

'Are there any other messages at all? Is what you're wondering. There are; is: Jason Singer. Connie Simpson wants you to be one of the stars at their sales conference, beginning of November. They're having a three-day huddle in some once stately home and you're one of the trio of top authors who're supposed to go and electrify the reps as they prepare to go over the top.'

'So tell me about your Dutchman. What's his name?'

'Rejn.'

'Has he come again?'

'Spelt R,e,j,n. You really do half wish you'd married a slut, don't you?'

'Really? No. But then again . . . doesn't everyone? If only . . . that much. Until they do. Blessings are never the things you count, are they?'

ii

Two days later, when Barbara had gone into Caillac to collect some cleaning and to see if she could find a more refined pepper mill, Adam telephoned Rachel.

'How goes it, darling?'

'It's gone,' she said. 'No trouble at all. A touch of *angst* but a whole lot more totally selfish relief.'

'And how about . . . ? No problems there?'

'None that he parades. Thanks for everything you did. And didn't.'

'You haven't sent it yet, have you? The Catullus.'

'Still checking the notes and stuff. Again.'

'Only we're going back to London next week so you'd best hold off and mail it to Tregunter Road. I'll call Sheridan when it arrives and – '

'Read it first. Twice. In case of grammatical horrors. Or

anything else that provokes the Morris ouch. Or might prompt the Sheridan wince! Where would I be without you, dad?'

'Pretty well where you are now, wouldn't you?'

Rachel said, 'You didn't tell her, did you? Mum.'

'I promised I wouldn't; but I still didn't. Are you coming back for Christmas at all? No, that's not the plaintive treble of the Treasury Bench; but Tom and Juliana and Alexis say they're coming and . . .'

'You'll have a house full.'

Adam said, 'Full, but not complete, unless you're there. If Clifford . . .'

'I need to sort out exactly what I'm going to do. How is Tom? Still in Cordoba?'

'Still; as far as that's compatible with perpetual motion. Being your uncle Derek's right hand involves getting plenty of exercise.'

'And buckaroos, I imagine.'

'I imagine. It's a living. How's Clifford about everything?'

'He's Clifford, and that's fine with me, till I – '

'You can say "None of your business" better than anyone I know, Raitch.'

'That's you, not me, saying that. Love you, dad.'

Adam returned, with sighing relief, to his work on the script of *Eliza Lynch*. He took prolonged care over what Hollywood's money had commissioned and haltered pride had promised to deliver. He found perverse pleasure in engaging his imagination in touches which Mike and Carlo Pavlides would never notice or might later delete as unduly subtle. He finished the script, which Barbara slightly distressed him by saying she liked, a lot, only three days before they were to close the shutters on *Écoute s'il Pleut* and return to London.

The walnuts from the big tree next to the cottage had fallen in a week of early October rain and had to be collected before they left. As a result, Adam and Barbara closed and zipped their bags with browned fingers, their bodies stippled with tiny bites from the invisible, invasive insects which, Norbert Malaurie had told them, the peasants called *vendangeons*.

'They're about the only reason I'm glad to leave,' Adam said, when Barbara had finished locking up and joined him in the Mercedes. He had disconnected the battery in the Toyota, which stayed in the barn. 'Every time we have to drive north, I die a little. Do you think the day will ever come when people look back on John Major's administration as a Golden Age? Can these really be the days?'

'What would you think if Rachel had a baby with him?'

'Clifford? Can we keep this between ourselves? I fear I should hope it was a girl.'

'You still think girls are beautiful and males are trouble.'

'Try to conceive that I was thinking only of the child I don't in truth believe she'll have, and its prospects in life. Girls *are* beautiful; can be, at least, whereas males . . .'

'Always look Jewish.'

'Would be one way of putting it. A well-worn way, you were about to say, but I'll save you the trouble. I don't think she'll be doing pregnancy any time soon. She seems very serious about an academic career.'

'Nature rarely gives a damn about what females are very serious about.'

iii

The printout of Rachel's book on Catullus arrived at Tregunter Road on Guy Fawkes Day. Although Adam conned it with a red Le Pen (acquired in L.A.) in hand, the text excited more smiles than marginalia. He suspected that Rachel's few solecisms might have been planted to allow him the satisfaction of weeding them out. However, when a quotation from a Byron version of one of the poems struck him as implausible, he checked it and found that Rachel had got it right. He smiled, and sniffed, and brushed the back of his hand across his eyes. Then he called Sheridan Reece's number in Cambridge.

'Patricia Reece.'

'Oh, Patricia, hullo. This is Adam Morris. How are you?'

'Oh yes. How are you?'

'I'm fine, very well. It was very nice seeing you when I was up . . . doing Alan Parks's silly programme on the radio. And of course I was very sorry when . . . you know, they didn't . . . elect Sheridan Master of the College.'

Patricia Reece said, 'He isn't here at the moment.'

'Ah! Any idea when he'll be back at all?'

'They've taken him fishing. Simon Beazley and Guy. They'll probably be a while. They'll bring him back when it's dark.'

'Right. I'll . . . try him then. He must miss teaching.'

'He says not. Actually he always hated it apparently.'

'He hid it well.'

'Yes. That and other things, it seems. Now they tend to come out. In something of a rush at times.'

Adam said, 'Here's the thing, Patricia. My daughter Rachel, who was a pupil of his whom he showed every sign of enjoying teaching, she's written a book and she'd be immensely grateful if Sheridan could take a look at it. And so, of course, would I. Much it matters. Might I send it to him, do you think?'

'Can you not come up to Cambridge and present him with the book yourself? He might like that.'

'And I'd like to do it,' Adam said. 'But . . . not this week. Nor next unfortunately, because . . . How about the week after? Which day would suit him? How about the 22nd? Could I come and have tea?'

'One day is as good as another,' Patricia Reece said.

'Let's make it the 22nd then. I'll look forward to it. Please give Sheridan my best. How is he?'

'He's still Sheridan. A good deal of the time.'

Adam put down the telephone and looked at it as if it were a puzzle. Then he picked it up again and left a message for Lars Waring to confirm their date to have coffee at the Brasserie on the Fulham Road the following Saturday morning. When the time came, Adam considered at silly length what book he should prefer to be discovered reading if he happened to arrive before his host.

He decided on the proof copy, which Connie Simpson had – as Californian agents always said about screenplays – slipped him, of Samuel Marcus Cohen's imminent volume, *The Necessity of Chance*, a compendium of 'essays and assays'.

Having no notion of Lars Waring's appearance, Adam scanned the loud café, hoping that, if he was already there, he would recognise him. After a moment, a single hand was raised, turned slightly sideways, as if voting for itself. Lars did not stand up; but, by straightening himself in his seat, appeared to do so. In his late thirties, he wore a bottle-green fly-fronted jacket, fawn trousers, grey silk shirt, no tie. He had longish, slightly curly brown hair, even features, grey eyes. With his pale lips shaped in a decided but unamused smile, he sat among and yet apart from his animated neighbours, like an insert in a team photograph. As Adam approached, Waring lowered his right hand. It both indicated the empty chair at the table and was available to be shaken.

'So,' Adam said, 'you've raised your standard.'

'I'm sorry?'

'Like Charles the First at Oxford. But we can let it pass. How's it going, whatever it is?'

'You were one of the first names on my list. Coffee at all?'

'Cappuccino, please; strong one.'

'Croissant?'

'Now you mention it. List of what?'

'People I'd ideally like to have associated with *Options*. At the editorial end of the ship. It's a tentative title, but I like it.'

'For what exactly?'

'The magazine of ideas I want you to help me launch, and keep afloat. You've got a lot of the edge I'm looking for.'

'I can be serrated when suitably primed, and seconded.'

'You're someone who, from what I've read and heard, can make being reasonable sound interesting.'

'In Hollywood this is what they call blowing smoke up my ass. Not easy to take offence at that. Remind me of what you've . . . written yourself.'

'Nothing you need have been aware of. I've been doing the

"Threadneedle" column in *The Economic Review* for the last four years.'

'And made quite an anonymous name for yourself.'

'In some circles,' Lars Waring said. 'But it's now high time for a change. So I'm sounding out a select few people. I reckon there's a hole in the top end of the market, for a journal of opinion.'

'There are already one or two. Of which Innes Maclean has edited at least eight.'

'I like Innes, but I don't intend us to be too artsy. Radical, but . . . free-ranging. I want to be a positive influence on the incoming government.'

'You're a socialist.'

'I don't see it as necessarily socialist.'

'You think Major can win again, again?'

'I'm sure he won't,' Lars said. 'But ideology seems now to be the least of our political priorities. Tony agrees.'

'Well, that makes two of you,' Adam said.

'The wall's down. Game over, as far as the classic Left/Right stand-off is concerned.'

'The Open Society has lost its best enemy, is that your point? And now it has to become its own.'

Lars said, 'I wasn't going to put it that way.'

'I'm here to help,' Adam said. 'Shall I have to come into the office or anything nine-till-fiveish like that?'

'First things first.'

'Absolutely. And what are they?'

'The right people and . . .'

'The cash that goes with them. Comes and goes with them. You're not going to review books, I suspect; least of all novels.'

'Not as such. The odd one. That deserves serious attention.'

'Enough to get the comps flowing in. I used to live on selling review copies. Tax-free income for struggling novelists. The double yellow lines killed that: couldn't park in Fleet Street, outside the bookshop in the alley by the Cheshire Cheese.'

'How old are you?'

'Quite right. Silly of me to draw attention to it. I can even remember *ITMA*. Are you related to Monty Waring at all?'

'Only in the sense that he's my father. I'm very optimistic about the future. *ITMA*?'

'Forget it. Which you can't because you can't remember it. Hence sociology and attendant ills.'

'Do you know Gavin Pope?'

'We say hullo! and cordial things of that nature. As it happens, I'm scheduled to go down to Arundel with him next week. We have a publisher in common. And we're off to electrify the Suliots. Why?'

'I'm looking to put together an editorial committee with a rainbow complexion – '

'Yes? Who do you have in mind for indigo and violet? Tough spots to fill. Are you thinking of weekly?'

'Ideally, monthly. Plump enough to be manifestly distinct from the traditional flimsies. Ninety pages, heading for a hundred plus. Who are the Suliots?'

'Some dodgy Greeks Byron tried to teach fair play to, a bit like our gallant troupe of foreign secretaries in Bosnia, only more gallantly. Forgive the base question, but where's the big money coming from? Have you got some angry angel prepared to ante up in return for some space to wing it in? Or have you got the C.I.A. involved? I've no objection to buckshee bucks, have you?'

'That's one of the things that we have to deal with.'

'You're putting in a chunk yourself presumably?'

'I don't make the sort of money you do,' Lars said.

'Nor do I all that often,' Adam said. 'Your father isn't short, is he? He can always cut you a slice of the Bahamas or somewhere, can't he?'

Lars said, 'Truth is, I'm aiming to mount this independently. I'm going to be forty next birthday. I'm a little tired of being papa's third-brightest boy. My brother Odo's a fellow of All Souls.'

'Odo! Bound to be. And who else's wake are you in?'

'Galen's a consultant neurologist. But that's not really relevant.'

'Is it not? So . . . What do you want from me exactly apart from the number you first thought of, which I may well not have on me? In the writing department. How about a regular column?'

'Certainly a possibility. If you can spring to it.'

Adam pressed some crumbs together from his croissant. 'And now do you want to talk about my brother?'

'I didn't know you had a brother.'

'Derek Morris.'

'Is your brother?'

'You've guessed.'

'You just told me. I've written about him in "Threadneedle". Several times. He travels light and he travels fast. Very shrewd character. Property plus plus. Am I right? Morris isn't all that rare a name.'

'We just may change it to Levinsky.'

'Why would you do that?'

Adam said, 'We both had lunch with your father a few years ago. Didn't go particularly well. He never told you?'

'My father and I are Christmas, weddings and funerals people largely. Do you think he'd write for us?'

Adam said, 'Are you a poker player at all?'

'I only ever play rackets these days. I used to be quite useful. Why?'

'I'll ask Derek to get in touch with you, if you want,' Adam said. 'And if he does . . . you never know. Thanks for the coffee.'

'This isn't about money, yet.'

Adam said, 'It better be soon. If you want to attract the kind of writers who tell everyone they don't care about it. Amazing how expensive your top altruists tend to be.'

'This country's on the verge of a new era. The next government is going to have to break the mould.'

'Break the mould,' Adam said, 'and more often than not, all you get is a funny-shaped jelly.'

'We need a new social alignment. Possibly a new constitution. I don't rule out a republic. Business and government. The Crown just may no longer be the reconciling force it has supposedly been since . . . oh . . . Victoria's Diamond Jubilee. Majesty dwindles to utility and then to obsolescence.'

'How many words by when?'

'I want *Options* to supply a forum for intellectuals who are actually *for* something. I want us to supply the chip – '

' – on authority's shoulder? I can always lend you one of mine.'

'In the computer sense: a small, but vital, component that generates ideas the next government can chew on. Basically, an independent think tank with a constructive, uncommitted agenda.'

Adam said, 'If you want politicians to pay attention, you have to stick it to them.'

'Precisely why I want you on board. Money is by no means of the essence.'

'Right. So how much do you need?'

'I'm asking the core team for a token amount. Say two thousand each, with an option to ask for the same again. I've got a draft prospectus that I can send you, sets everything out. I look to break even in three to five years.'

'I favour no fancy artwork,' Adam said. 'Do you remember the old *L'Express* Mendes-France used to write for, and Sartre, and Mauriac? You don't. How about *ITMA*? It ought to be like that, *L'Express* I mean. Grainy and full of stuff. No pics.'

'Layout we can come to.'

'Vital question,' Adam said, 'who're you going to get as editor? We're going to need someone charismatic. A man – possibly a woman – people really want to write for. Only way a mag ever works. How about . . . wild shot: Alan Parks?'

Lars said, 'You're being funny.'

'Was I laughing? Have you got a candidate in mind?' Adam looked up. Lars's grey eyes seemed to hold no highlight in them. The blink, when it came, was very slow. 'Ah! I see. Right. Got it! No need to drag you to the editorial chair, is that the size of it?'

'I want you as closely involved in decision making as you feel inclined.'

'Fine. Well . . . look . . . send me the bumf and . . . on we go.'

Lars said, 'This is going to be very exciting. I can feel it.'

'Are you married at all?'

'Of course. To Davina Gedge. She runs the Carrington Art Gallery. Why?'

'I was being civil. Children?'

'Three. John, James, and Luke. Only two of them are mine.'

'Should I guess? James.'

'What?'

'Isn't yours.'

'It's Luke actually. I want to get a dummy together as soon as we possibly can. And do talk to Gavin, won't you? Key element possibly.'

iv

Connie Simpson arranged for one car to collect first Adam, then Alan Parks, then Gavin Pope, and take them to Arundel for the Plantagenet Publishing Group's sales conference. Adam put on dark brown corduroy trousers, an open-necked maroon shirt, a sleeveless grey woollen waistcoat and his antelope-skin Gucci jacket. While waiting, on cue, for the car, he asked Barbara whether, if called upon to entertain the company, he could dare to tell Bill Bourne's now thirty-year-old joke about the Martian who arrives on earth, goes into a petrol station, walks up to one of the pumps, and says, "Take me to your leader." There's no reply, so the Martian telepathises his control and asks what he should do. "Ask him, louder." "I've done that," he reports. "And?" "He just stands there with his penis in his ear and won't say a word."'

'Strong case for playing it by nose,' Barbara said.

'Alternatively, I'll just snow them with some chat about the imaginative process and how big an unearned advance it continues to deserve. Not many laughs there. I don't have to wear a tie, do I?'

'You're creative,' Barbara said. 'You have not to.'

'Don't wait up, OK?'

It was already lighting-up time when the black Jaguar arrived at Tregunter Road; dusk by the time the driver, whose declared name was Nuni, reached Broadcasting House; and darker again before they could leave it: Alan Parks was in with the controller, discussing things that couldn't wait. Adam sat, with calm impatience, reading Samuel Marcus Cohen's reappraisal of Carl Schmitt, a Nazi philosopher of whom Adam had never previously heard. Schmitt's case for the necessity of antagonism, as venomous as it was humourless, if a pointless bourgeois world was to be avoided, at once chimed and clashed with Samuel Marcus's own critique of contemporary western flaccidity, in which 'tolerance supplied a vicarious pharmakon for an ideology incapable of speaking its name'.

Alan Parks came out, back first through the heavy doors. A big leather coat burdened his hunched shoulders. He sported a broad-brimmed felt hat that he might have borrowed from Wyndham Lewis, with the brim turned down all round. He bent down, one hand half-saluting Adam and then took the place next to the turbaned driver.

'So what's your new book about, Alan?'

'Books,' Alan put one arm over the back of his seat to be able to swivel enough almost to look Adam in the face. 'I'm a pluralist. Bivalve anyway. I come in twos, though not as often as when in my prime. First one's called *Thatcherism colon a Dialectical Prosopography*. How about that for a title to stop people in their sad diurnal tracks?'

'Every colon tells a story,' Adam said. 'Bit fancy, isn't it?'

'And why not? Give the Great British Public the idea that they need a lot of brains to eat soft-centred chocolates with and they'll munch their way through more boxes than you can imagine. Once you get into it and pull the covers up, it's basically a re-heat job: beefed up transcripts of radio and TV interviews. Nothing succeeds like giving people the same kind of originality they've seen before.'

'Traffic is very, very thick tonight, I'm afraid, gentlemen.'

'The other one's a truffle marginally more challenging. *Thank Christ*. Is the title.'

'No colon?'

'According to some sources, Our Lord, if not yours, Adam, didn't need one. His divine nature ensured that He totally absorbed everything He ate, including the kosher sarnies at that wedding in Cana of Galilee where He turned the water into wine. Bloke at the end of the table would've preferred water apparently. Are you a Christian at all?'

'I am a Sikh, sir.'

'And ye shall find Lincoln's Inn Fields, is that where we aren't – ?'

'If the police will allow us through. There seems to be some kind of a commotion somewhere.'

Adam said, 'Is it really about Jesus, your other one?'

'The other one's the other one. This is *the* one. To put it simply and without a trace of affectation, it's an eclectic chrestomathy with a dexterous admixture of iconoclasm.'

'Sounds like something from the school of Samuel Marcus.'

'Not for lack of trying. I do wax briefly parodic, as is my wont, and my will. Text consists of interviews with various people I've managed to bump and bore over the last two thousand years. For and against Christianity. I reckoned it was time to change gear and put my thinking crap on. So I contrived to snatch an intimate word or three with people such as . . . I kick off with Pontius Pilate, who's still asking what the truth is and swears he isn't jesting. Then there's Judas Iscariot – speaks very well of you, by the way – and Julian the apostrophe and on into Saint Augustine – a bit of a dill in my view, but he had some cracking chestnuts about his pre-chastity, *amans amare* days. Then I took the ferry to Algeciras and had a matutinal *churro* or two with Torquemada. You'll never guess who some of his best friends were. Do you menstruate at all, Adam?'

'Not recently, that I've noticed.'

'Torquie still thinks Jews do. Punishment for what they did to sonny J. Then over the Pyrenees, I make a molehill out of a

Montaigne, and then on to his *frère-ennemi* Blaise Pascal, who was kind enough to give me the time of day, seeing as he was the first guy to have it on him. Invented the portable watch, did you know that? Helped him make sure to get his metaphysical bets on in time. By the way, a man from Lecce invented the digital clock, if you ever get a quezzy on that. I go on down the line to Martin Luther Luther, Henry the Eighth, Baruch *atoi* Spinoza, Voltaire, Calvin – who knew all the answers before he heard the questions – Cardinal Manning – *somewhat* maligned, I conclude, by that superficial smartass Lytton and on down to Grime Greene, Weeviling Waugh, Pius twelve, who told me a few off-colour jokes about friend Benito and had his people read out a list of the eight hundred and thirty-three thousand four hundred and seventy-one perfidious Hebes he personally saved from what, until week before last, the Catholic Church considered they richly deserved.'

'No women?'

'Hang about. The Virgin Mary declined to be interviewed. She'd recently been let down by Oprah, got bumped off the programme by Gore and Toni, so she was understandably wary, went off to do a gig with some slum kids in São Paolo ahead of the Holy Polack's visit to those parts. Wojtyla's a Mariolater worth putting in an appearance for. Prior to that, or prioress if you want to be like that, I do have Simone Weil in there, knocking on the Church's door and refusing to be let in when they open it. Teresa of Avila revealed that she'd been quite a goer in her younger days; then she saw the light and never went out again. Joan of Arc was burning to give me a few words. Sadly Muriel Spark didn't kindle to me. It's quite a solemn little tome, truth to be told.'

They had to wait in the Strand while three police cars threaded their loud way towards Waterloo Bridge. After they arrived at Lincoln's Inn, it was twenty-five minutes before Gavin Pope appeared. He then stood on the steps of his Chambers, talking to a tight-mouthed, hot-cheeked young man, in black coat and striped trousers, before coming, unhurriedly, towards the car (two paces from it, there was one more thing he had to mention to his junior). Gavin was wearing calfskin half-boots, a green and brown tweed suit and waistcoat, faintly striped pink shirt with a brown woollen tie. He carried a tartan-lined Burberry raincoat. Nuni got out and opened the car door for him.

'Hope I haven't kept you.'

'You have though, and not in the style to which we're accustomed, is it, Adam?'

'I had the next P.M. on the line. Not for publication, he was fishing.'

'Fishing line, was it?'

'You must be Alan Parks.'

'And never for want of trying. What's Tony asking you to do?'

'Know him, do you?'

'We've rallied from time to time. He's not bad at the net, or the gross either, when occasion arises. I knew him when he ran a bar.'

'He's taking independent soundings on education policy. The great model used to be the Classics. The next one, he agreed with me, could well be the Law. Involving reason and persuasion as the intellectual underpinning of a new social grammar.'

'Not many laughs there,' Alan said. 'And how does your ex-best friend, the current P.M., view your flirtation with the Messiah-to-be?'

'I was never an out and out party man, John knows that. I've always been basically a conservative with a small "c".'

'That's between you and the ladies; and has been quite often, I gather.'

Gavin said, 'Are you going to try this hard all the way to Arundel? And are we ever going to get there, Nuni? How are you?'

'I am very well, sir, thank you. They're telling me that Westminster and Vauxhall bridges are closed. We shall have to go west to come east, gentlemen, I'm afraid.'

'Judging from previous performances, if anyone can get us there, Nuni, you can. There's also talk of fog about. Closed why?'

'Precautionary measure. There has been an I.R.A. bomb warning. They've just closed Chelsea Bridge as well. I can try Wandsworth.'

'Do whatever you have to to get us there,' Gavin said, 'but please don't keep us informed. How are you, Adam? Taken a vow of silence, have you?'

'I was biding my time.'

'Rarely a good move, *expertissimo crede*.'

'You were a colleague of Bill Bourne's at one time, weren't you?'

'That was in another life,' Gavin said.

'The wench didn't die; he did. Did you know?'

'Black lady, wasn't she?'

'Joann. I met her at the wake.'

'Impressively prehensile, if I remember her anatomy aright. She liked to perform with her specs on. Quite inspiriting, I found. But that was long ago, and not all that far away from here as a matter of fact. On a brightly polished floor.'

'So what's it all about, Gavin? You appear to be the one who's made good even better.'

'Paths of Glory, Alan, Paths of Glory; you know where they lead.'

'But to the gravy, it would seem, in your case.'

Adam said, 'Do you read the "Threadneedle" column at all, Gavin, in *The Economic Review*?'

'My reading, at this season of the year, is largely confined to briefs, and very long most of them are.'

'Monty Waring's son writes it.'

'Odo?'

'No, no – '

'Marcus? Gabriel?'

'Lars. Big family.'

'Every time Monty Waring shagged another woman, he came back and made his wife pregnant by way of aggressive apology. Hence no shortage of progeny. If that reminds you of somebody else, kindly be good enough not to say so.'

72

Adam said, 'You know something, Gavin? You sound as though you've been to Eton since we last met.'

'I have. Several times. To dine with Bobby Ramsey.'

'Your accent's had an upgrade.'

'I no longer speak *blotto voce*, you mean. Good of you to mention it.'

'They're not going to make you a judge, are they?'

'Couldn't possibly afford to let them do that yet awhile.'

'We're never going to get to Arundel for dinner, are we?'

'We can always stop at a hostelry, dine on whatever isn't the wild goose we seem to be chasing. Fog's getting thicker. What do they want us all to trek down to Arundel for?'

'Electrify the Suliots, I assume.'

'George Gordon, the Lord Byron, that was, wasn't it? Citing one George Primrose, possibly an antique kinsman of mine; who went to Holland to teach the Dutch English.'

'Who were fond of it to distraction.'

'Seems to put that one to bed. What precisely led you to drag it in in the first place?'

'Lars Waring's very keen to have you on the editorial board for this new mag he's starting. *Options*. Not the first title I'd've chosen.'

'Recruiting sergeant, are you?'

'Corporal. I have no shillings to distribute or receive. Lars'd never heard of the Suliots, when I ran them past him, but he obviously needs people in the galley who have.'

'And why are you devilling for him exactly?'

'Innate servility, wouldn't you say? In the face of Etonians with Latinate forenames. Even if they were commoners.'

'You've not yet lost this aptitude for sounding aggrieved, have you? Still the Jewish pebble, is it, in your shoe gives you your pseudo-Byronic scowl?'

'A smooth one, Gavin. Straight from the brook Kedron. Identical with the one that smacked Goliath in the forehead. Nothing like them for rainy days.'

'Sarcasm is sufferance on its day off. Why does that occur to me?'

73

'My main motive has to be the one about never knowingly refusing access to a printing press. Who was it advised that?'

Alan said, 'Paul Goodman. The fuck or get fucked man. Preferably both in his case. Of whom a Greenwich Village friend of mine, back in the nineteen sixties, once said that he was so immeasurably promiscuous that it was unwise to leave him alone with a dish of chopped liver.'

'This looks like Esher, Nuni. Is it? And should it be?'

'It is Esher, sir. I was hoping to circumvent the fog.'

'As long as we don't end up on Bodmin Moor. I should hate to miss the prawn cocktail.'

Alan said, 'So what's your book about, Gavin? Late starting?'

'In short, but at some length, the disaster of 1940. From which we are still reeling.'

Adam said, 'Dunkirk? Fall of France?'

'W.S. Churchill, basically. Late starting may well have some-thing to do with it. No Churchill, no false romantics, no fighting on the beaches, no endless rodomontade from the unending Glory Days industry. And above all no grovelling to the Yanks. Who were no better allies than the Russians, who at least were too busy to do us out of the empire, which was F.D.R.'s fondest wish. No W.S.C. in May 1940 and Halifax would've been P.M. and he'd've made a civilised deal with the Germans. Hitler never hated the British as he did the French. In fact he was rather in awe of us, as we then were, or as he imagined we were. We'd also have been left with enough treasure, troops and vigilance, to deter the Japs from marching into the F.M.S., which would have avoided *the* biggest humiliation of all, and hence the one least mentioned: our eviction from the Orient in general and India in particular, not to mention Singapore which no one ever, ever does. Winston was Lord North with a fancy prose style: lost us everything while seeming to save the day. Always was good at putting on a show with other people's treasure. Remember Gallipoli, Alan?'

'Nothing wrong with the idea, to tell the truth. It wasn't Winston's fault the military landed on the wrong beach, the one with the hundred-foot cliffs.'

74

'I'm really concerned with the proliferation of cant, which was his special subject.'

Nuni was going more slowly than before. They were wrapped in a soft muffler of fog. It was nearly a quarter to nine.

Gavin said, 'You've gone loudly silent, Adam. Instead of re-affixing your yellow star, try thinking out of the box. At least open the lid and have a look around. No righteous Winstonian rhetoric, no total war. Instead, a resumption of diplomatic horse-trading and very possibly no Holocaust in the mass murderous form that secrecy and paranoia allowed it to take. Suppose that to be the case. Now what do you think? Because what did Churchill's war do? Built the wall, and put our backs to it; bankrupted Britain, let every swarthy genie you can imagine out of his misshapen bottle, and left us with a lot less than the number we first thought of, including of your people. No wonder Master Winston wrote the history of it before anyone else got the chance. Is Chichester really a good idea?'

'I am doing my best, sir, to get you there.'

'Hitler would still have attacked Russia.'

'Without obliging us to pay homage to the Left forever after. Stafford Cripps need never have happened. Still less the man of Harlech.'

'We should just have stood and watched, should we?'

'Didn't we, you and I, when Saddam attacked Iran? And licked our lips, discreetly? The Iraqis and the Iranians slaughtered millions of each other wholesale for years. How many nights did you lie awake thinking of the little boys with plastic keys to paradise that the Ayatollah sent out to trip across the Iraqi minefields in their brave bare tootsies? Suffer the little children indeed. Hitler and Stalin would almost certainly have slugged it out, if we'd managed things properly, and we could've played the enviable role of the Walrus to F.D.R.'s carpenter. None of it's pretty; quite a lot of it's painfully true.'

They sat there in the slow, fog–muffled car.

'Binsted 5. That's a good sign, sir!'

'It would've been a better one an hour or so ago.'

'The guy's doing his best,' Adam said.

'That is indeed the bad news. But we must on no account say so. Why do you say "guy"? When did that start?'

Alan said, 'What's it called then, Gavin, your book?'

'*Winston, The Mistaken Hero.*'

'You risk being crucified.'

'Only to rise again,' Adam said, 'as a thirteen-part TV series.'

'May well happen, but not of the essence. The what-if aspect is of less interest to me than the truth, which is that the history industry has for decades peddled an illusory notion of Britain's finest hour, generating a million pages a year, it seems, of reheated waffle.'

'You'd never have dared if the beady-eyed seductress was still P.M., would you?'

'Would *la bella* Margarita entirely disagree? No 1940, no 1945; no Welfare State to hobble the economy, no post-war illusions about Master Stalin, whether he'd won or whether he hadn't. Madam might never say so out loud, but she'd see the point. The N.H.S. is all very well as a revised version of salvation this side of the grave, the latter-day Church of England when you think about it, full of white-coated vicars, but morality isn't much of a substitute for being a world power.'

Adam said, 'Naughty boyism, Gavin. Alan Taylor-made rather, aren't you? You're only doing it because it teases.'

'No necessarily bad reason. Seduction has been known to begin with a tickle. Churchill probably hated the Tory party more than he did the Germans. That didn't improve his judgement. If they'd given him a big kiss a little earlier in the proceedings, who knows what he mightn't have said or done, or not? Look at the way he backed that arch clown Edward the Eighth, just because Baldwin didn't. Never underestimate the opportunism of the principled.'

Alan said, 'The present P.M.'s not exactly all that keen on certain parts of his own party, is he?'

'No? John's got more sympathy for the Eurosceptics than might be good for the pound. You don't call people bastards without a measure of envy.'

'Then why does he keep threatening to resign?'

'Obvious: because he knows they can't afford to have him do it.'

Alan said, 'What would happen if he looked as if he seriously meant it?'

'Oh look here,' Gavin said, 'two senior members of the Tory party would take him quietly by the elbows into a small soundproof room and tell him, "Don't be so bloody silly; where else are you going to find a job with a car and a driver?"'

Adam closed his eyes and slid lower in his seat.

'We are not far from Fontwell Park at this point, gentlemen.'

Gavin said, 'Don't bother to pull in, Nuni, will you? I suspect we shall have missed the last race.'

Alan said, 'Tell me something, Gavin. You're a member of Gents, aren't you?'

'Last remaining place in London you can still get a decent mixed grill. Why?'

'Is it true you wouldn't have Michael as a member? Even though he was in the cabinet?'

'No great secret, is it?'

'Andrew D. wouldn't have him, is that true?'

'I don't think Andrew had a lot to do with it. He owns the lease, but that's as far as it goes. He isn't on the scrutiny committee. I am, as it happens.'

'Then why wouldn't you? Have Michael?'

'Why do you suppose?'

'Because he had to buy his own furniture, was it?'

'Plenty of people have to do that. The eunuchoid Ken did. And very suburban it is too.'

'So what did the poor bugger do that meant he doesn't deserve a decent mixed grill when he wants one?'

'Oh look here,' Gavin said, 'he combed his hair in public, didn't he?'

They arrived at the conference centre after three and a half hours on the road. Neither Alan Parks nor Gavin Pope had thought to ask Adam the nature or the title of the book which he was about to have published. As they got out of the Jaguar and inhaled the smoky coldness of the evening air, Adam said, 'Don't you think we should tip the driver?'

'He gets paid,' Gavin said, 'but by all means do what you want, if that's what you want to do.'

As the other two walked up the wide, shallow sandstone stairs into the conference centre, Adam gave the driver three pounds. Then he wondered if it was enough.

The Plantagenet staff had almost finished their dinner, but a congealed version was served to the authors. Adam sat at a round table with a party of reps, editors and secretaries who were quick to tell him what difficult times these were for 'literary' fiction.

Connie Simpson had assured Adam that there would no speeches, but Alan Parks was easily coerced into interviewing Gavin Pope about his new book. Its provocations were paraded in the form of donnish quips which gave the reps and executives a chance to applaud their own alertness. Alan's last question was whether Gavin would now care to do him the honour of inter-viewing him. When Gavin suggested that Alan would do better to interview himself, the latter put on a masterly pastiche of current styles of intimidating toadyism and authorial mock-modesty.

Adam smiled and smiled and asked Connie, quietly, whether he might have a car to take him back to London, immediately. Connie took his hand and held it against her thigh. Alan's increasingly salty improvisations, which sandwiched not a few recognisable slices of chrestomathy, sailed the proceedings, on a following gale of laughter, towards the small hours. Only when one of the waiters fell back on the ruse of inadvertently turning off the top lights did Alan ask himself why he felt obliged to talk so much, took offence at the question and wondered whether the huff he was leaving in was possibly at the door yet.

'How did it go?'

'No,' Adam said, '*why* did it go? *I* go. God knows. Didn't leave bloody Arundel till after one. They wanted me to stay the night, but I was damned if I would. Go back to sleep.'

Barbara said, 'Did you decide to tell them Bill's "Take me to your leader" joke or not?'

'No. I just stood there with my penis in my ear and nobody even noticed. I was not, in the event, called upon to speak. Time was up before I was.'

'What the hell did they ask you to go for?'

'Is your finisher for ten. I did hobnob with a few reps and people at a table with used carnations on it. A lady of indeterminate sex was curious to know what Saul Nathan really did, or didn't do, with the black whore in chapter three. Could be a big selling point in Weston-super-Mare apparently. Never again. Make quite a good article that: all the things it isn't *that* terrible to think one may well never do again. Eat rhubarb, drink cider, sit through the Ring cycle, ride a camel, wear studs, wait for Godot, read Crow, go to Swansea or Luton or Wolverhampton . . . What else?'

'Do you really have to write it now? It's three-fifteen in the morning.'

'I'll just go and make a note and then . . .'

vi

'Patricia! I hope I'm not . . . too early. I seem to be holding these. They must be for you.'

'Very kind of you. There was no need.'

The Reeces lived in a large, gaunt house off the Madingley Road. Adam had the impression that nothing new had been brought into it in many years. Patricia led him along a passage with a threadbare runner. 'Sheridan was in the conservatory the last I saw him of him.'

Adam said, 'What've you done to yourself, Patricia?'

'Done to myself? Oh, I . . . had a silly fall. The sling's only a precaution. It's not broken, just bruised.'

'Pray, who is that you're canoodling with, Mistress Patricia?'

Patricia went into the conservatory. 'Adam Morris is here, Sheridan, to see you.'

'Adam Morris?'

Adam said, 'Hullo, Sheridan. Very good to see you.'

Sheridan Reece was sitting in a white wicker armchair, two uncased pillows behind him and a fawn cotton rug over his knees. He had nicked himself when shaving, it seemed; a dot of blood had dried, like a fat full stop, just below his left nostril. Two open books and a folded *Daily Telegraph* were on the floor by his tartan-slippered feet.

'How was your flight?'

'I elected to drive up actually, Sheridan.'

'You've written a book, it seems.'

'Several even. But more important, Rachel's written one.'

'Rachel When-from-the-Lord. Where does she come from?'

'Proust, could it be?'

'Very elaborate, aren't you, some of you?'

'Writers, is that? Can be. Personally, I try to keep it simple. But that can be quite complicated. I'm talking about my daughter.'

'Do we need any more books, do you think? Is there a case for a moratorium?'

'Life changes,' Adam said. 'Things change. Most of it's been said, I grant you, but some things haven't.'

'And must they be? *Must* they? Your latest, it's about what?'

'Novel? It's called *Into Africa*.'

'*Aliquid novi*. You're a man in need of breakfast.'

'A cup of tea would be nice though.'

Sheridan turned slightly in his chair. 'Miss! Deaf as a post. Say anything you like to her, doesn't hear a thing. I am *not* complaining. Written a book, has she?'

'Rachel, yes. Dedicated to you.'

'She's not here though, I note. A well-shaped young person in the pectoral department, do I have her to a nicety?'

'She's in California. Teaching. I'm the messenger.'

'When did they ever kill the messenger? I don't remember them killing the messenger. Do you remember them killing the messenger?'

'The Spartans did, didn't they? The Persian heralds who came asking for whatever it was. Bread and salt, can it have been? And they threw them into a well.'

'That chap in the barber's shop. The Athenians gave him a short back and sides. I wouldn't call heralds messengers quite. Not within the meaning of the act. What's a shibboleth, Morris? I keep remembering.'

'Some sort of . . . um . . . outmoded trademark belief, isn't it?'

'Ear of corn. The original meaning.'

Patricia came in with a tray of tea and biscuits.

Sheridan said, 'How long have you worked here?'

'Forty-two years, haven't I?' Patricia said.

'And you still haven't learned. Shibboleth. Have I said it correctly?'

Adam said, 'I don't think I can do any better.'

'Then I'm in the claret. What have you done to your arm, my dear?'

Patricia said, 'I hurt it.'

'Mysterious hurt. Whose was that?'

'Henry James, can it have been?'

'Castrated himself sliding down a fence according to some more or less reliable sources.'

'Henry James,' Adam said.

'Is there anything else you want, Sheridan?'

'Unwise question,' Sheridan said. 'To which you will not have the answer. Come hell, come Hiawatha.'

Patricia said, 'I'll leave you men to talk.'

Sheridan watched her go. '*Ter sunt conati imponere Pelio Ossam.* There's a shibboleth for you. Meaning what?'

81

Adam said, '"They tried three times to stack Ossa on Pelion."
At least it did last time I looked.'

'Georgics 1, 281. What Virgin don't tell us is that the fourth
time, they pulled it off, do 'e?'

'Vir*gil*.'

'The Olympians are all titans in disguise. All gods are impostors.
The marines are the only ones who know it, and they ain't
talking. You never served.'

'No, I've been lucky. I've dodged through the twentieth century
without coming under fire, except from you, of course, Sheridan.'

'The need to jest,' Sheridan Reece said, 'is the price of
cowardice.'

'Of not being sure whether you're a coward or not; would be
a more generous view.'

'Show it to me. Assuming you've brought it with you.'

Adam said, 'It's rather insecurely bound, I'm afraid, Sheridan.'

Sheridan Reece looked over the tops of his thin spectacles.
'You don't have to call me Master, you know.'

'I always think of you as one, however.'

'Not at this late junction. Clapham, is it? Or is it never too late?
Or is it always? Now abide these three, but I could never abide
them myself. Especially hope.'

Adam said, 'I'm just finding you Rachel's dedication. There we
are.'

'*Ad Magistrum egregium tam doctum quam severum*. To a – what?
– exceptional master as clever as he is severe. Aha! I have a rival,
it seems, in mastery.'

'No, no. She's referring to you, Sheridan.'

'You can tell the difference nonetheless. Can't you?'

'Between what and what would that be?'

'Indeed. Get a pin between them and you've pulled it off.
Pulling. Why are men said to pull? Females, feathered. When
their real ambition is, surely, to push?'

'She's rather hoping the Press might do the book. If you think
it's good enough, a word from you might pull the chocks away.'

Sheridan turned some pages of the manuscript, but hardly gave himself time to read anything. '*Odi et amo*. Hardly worth mentioning, I often think. The *Odi* lasts longer than the *amo*. One never has enough ammo, but you wouldn't know that, would you?'

'Fortunately not. I only ever fired blanks, or was steady under them.'

'Catullus had a brother.'

'Yes, he did.'

'Yes, he did,' Sheridan said, rather as if he had been contradicted. '*Odi et amo*. Could've been about him, couldn't it? I bet you never thought of that.'

Adam said, 'Funnily enough – '

'Shibboleth, you see?'

' – Rachel does hint at that. Perhaps she got it from you.'

'I haven't had anything to do with that sort of thing for longer than I can remember. When did you last have occasion to roger your comely lady? Do you recall?'

Adam said, 'Rachel says please to scribble anything you feel like scribbling on the text. It's not the only copy or anything. And she can deal with it.'

'They were supposed to drown me. Everyone knows that. Your brother. You put him up to it. Deny it. Still rise to the occasion, are you telling me?'

'Derek? I don't need to put him up, Sheridan. He's got a place of his own, and a mind. Up to what?'

'I'll look at it right away, if not before. Why do we remember what our fathers said and not what our mothers did?'

Adam said, 'No hurry.'

'While I'm still here. The S.C.R. ceiling.'

'Take your time.'

'Will you return? To collect it. If summoned. Before they get here preferably.'

'If you want me to,' Adam said. 'Who are "they" exactly?'

'You may be surprised to find me . . .' Sheridan suddenly spoke very loudly, '. . . still alive. He got his due reward, didn't he though?'

'Who was that, Sheridan?'

'There is that about it. More orphan than not. Your brother. I entirely understand, by the way. Why he would want the person he did want. In the magisterial department. Birds of a father frock to get her.'

'I'm not sure that I'm with you.'

'Blood runs stickier,' Sheridan said.

Adam looked at his wrist and stood up. 'Time I . . .'

Sheridan said, 'Do you know what I shall do as soon as your back is turned?'

'Read Rachel's manuscript with the attention it deserves, dare I hope?'

'I shall detach the small tab of blood which adheres to my upper lip and crack it, with some pleasure, between my front teeth.'

Adam said, '*Bon appetit.*'

'*Excepto quod simul esses, cetera laetus.* As Jew-veenal has it. How true that can be, especially when false! I am untouched, you know, Morris, unmoved, unaffected by the gent what they elected to elect. Master Steinberger, was it? Name of father if changed pretty well covers it. I will say this for them: French scholars produce the most readable fiction in the modern canon. *Chapeau* should cover that.'

Adam smiled in an impersonation of deference and touched Sheridan's shoulder when he failed to offer his hand. He walked audibly along the corridor and put his head around the kitchen door. Patricia was sitting at the unpolished table with a sewing box, repairing a seam on something shiny and pink. Her empty sling was a soft necklace.

'Thank you for my tea, Patricia.'

'One of his better days today.' She bit off the thread and stood up. 'Thanks to you.'

Adam said, 'What're you going to do?'

'Wash up the tea things.'

'He's still . . . Sheridan, but . . .'

'He hates the name,' she said, 'so he told me recently. Stage

84

Irish, he told me it was. Blamed me, of course. I'm his mother, as I'm sure you've always known.'

'It's not fair on you, Patricia.'

'What would be, do you suppose? You're here today; I'm here every day. I shall do nothing, until I have to. And then I will. If he hasn't killed me first. It's not likely to be with kindness, is it?'

'He honestly thinks my brother – '

'He thinks *everything*. I'm not sure how far honestly comes into it.'

'What Derek did he did only for Sheridan. You know that. And attached no importance to it beyond that.'

'Thank you for coming, Adam,' Patricia said. 'I thought you should see for yourself. And he enjoyed it. Leave at that, shall we? Please.'

Adam walked along the Madingley Road to his old college. The porter had allowed him, against the rules, to park his car beside the chapel. The shadow of a cross lay over the bonnet and fell on to the shining cobbles. Adam sat in the car trying to know what to think. He could not weep and he could not smile.

vii

'What would you do?' Adam said.

'Nothing you can do.'

'If I got to be like that.'

'No use even wondering,' Barbara said. 'Do you want a drink, as grown-ups are always saying?'

'I wish I did. I don't want anything. He obviously . . . hurt her. I realise now. She had a look on her face that was somehow . . . amused. Abused/amused; cousins, aren't they?'

'But they don't kiss much. Don't wish him not there. Anything's better than being alone.'

'I realised on the way home that he misquoted what he said was Juvenal. "*Excepto quod simul esses,*" he said, "*cetera laetus.*"'

'Remind me what he should have said. As if I ever knew.'

'What he *said* means "Apart from the fact that you're here, in other respects I'm happy." And it was Horace, in fact, who said "*Excepto quod* non *simul esses* . . ."' Apart from the fact that you're *not* here . . . perfectly happy. Freudian error or scholarly scandal? I wasn't sure if he meant me or her. I was really. Patricia's been everything he had any right to expect her to be.'

'When was that ever enough? Except when it was too much.'

'Never wonder why I love you,' Adam said, 'by the way.'

'Thank you. And now answer the phone.'

'Hullo.'

'Is that the "allo" man back in dear old Blighty, do I gather?'

'Very dear and very old. And I'm no rosebud, OK?' Adam somewhat covered the white receiver and said, 'Mike.'

'See you next Tuesday.' Barbara went out of the living room as if she had all kinds of better things to do.

'What did she say?'

'Give him my love. Roughly speaking.'

'I must say, maestro, you seem to have pulled it off.'

'Can happen apparently, if you do it often enough.'

'Never mind your barrack-room memories, she not only loves it, Julia, she *loves* it. She can't wait.'

'And rarely has to, I gather. What about the script?'

'Funny man. Is what I'm talking about. She wants us to get together. Nothing major. She's longing to see you. I told her you weren't all that much to look at, but still . . .'

Adam said, 'I'm not coming back to California.'

'How about Paris? She's coming over at Christmas. You've landed us the big one, Ad. Can't you break the habit of a lifetime and enjoy something? Carlo's talking to Shapiro about *Life and Loves* by the way. Back-to-back time.'

Adam said, 'Not easy to do what Carlo usually does to people in that position.'

'Two nights at the Plaza-Athenée, limo to meet you at the airport and available twenty-four hours a day, what's the catch? Bring Barbs. Yves St Laurent's just across the road. She can go and pick up a few bargains.'

Adam said, 'I bluffed the opera stuff a bit.'

'As in "Donizetti's *La Forza del Destino*".'

'A lesser-known work than Verdi's, some might dare to argue.'

'I never noticed, did I? But I can fix that, and/or publicise your boo-boo. Oprah is us, you know that. It's still an in principle brilliant idea of yours for the finale.'

'And soon to be yours, no doubt.'

'The jungle as auditorium. Eliza starring in her own production. Yours *and* mine, old son. *Tosca* with a happy ending.'

'Good old Rossini. Look, Mike, seriously, Christmas I have to be in London. Julia'll have to be before or after.'

'She'll love that. Next year in Paraguay, old son. Forget Jerusalem! You don't think you're an operator, do you? You are. And I'm glad. Take the good news with a good grace for a change, you old sourpuss.'

'Love it,' Adam said.

He went into his room and wrote Lars Waring a cheque for two thousand pounds. In his covering letter, he announced that he hoped to earn it back as soon as *Options* became a reality. He then remarked to himself, in his notebook, that he had small wish to be a regular journalist. Any work which involved soliciting the applause of editors and film directors was a form of what Etienne de la Boétie called '*servitude volontaire*'; but then again, he had to say, such solicitation was more addictive, and the applause more pleasing, than La Boétie can have known. Journalism was the scribbler's most available promiscuity: deadlines stood in for assignations, the despatch of proofs petty climaxes, and cash abated post-scriptural *tristesse*. Hence (he added next morning) you might meet rich and famous journalists, but you never met happy ones. Then he addressed himself to an article which he had promised to *Janiceps,* the inter-cultural magazine which Clifford Ayres edited, about Bill Bourne's *Petronius*.

The immediate effect was to distance Bill from the author of his book and to refrigerate the tone in which Adam spoke of it: '. . . even Professor Bourne seems to be tempted to portray Nero as a well-intentioned political innovator who wanted to make the arts, rather than war, central to Roman society. The emperor's problems with his mother and with his wife Poppaea, both of whom were done to death, the latter by his own action in jumping on her pregnant belly, are passed over as if they were the local difficulties which any busy autocrat might have to deal with. My guess,' Adam continued, after thought, 'is that Nero preferred the theatrical to the military only because he could more easily delude himself that he was a great performer than prove that he was a great general.'

The telephone was ringing as Adam finished his paragraph. He went back and changed 'only' to 'principally' (to chime with Nero's principate) and then picked up the phone.

'Hullo.'

'Sheridan Reece.' The tone was of someone who had received the call, not entirely to his pleasure, rather than of someone initiating it.

'Sheridan!' Adam said. 'How are you?'

'Yes. Indeed. In truth, I should like to see you.'

'Whenever you say.'

'You were perfectly right.'

'I'm glad to hear that. About what, was I?'

'She's done it. She always threatened to. And now she has. Not that I blame her. Perhaps it was your idea.'

'Who's done what exactly, and how should it be my idea?'

'Just as I suspected. Be that as it may, and it often is, tomorrow . . . I have a . . . window. Is that what I have?'

Adam said, 'People do have them these days. Tomorrow.' He leaned back and blew out an invisible candle. 'All right. Mid-afternoon. How did you find it?'

'It'll have to be before the meeting. The meeting's at five, on the button. And you know what pantomimes are like up here. Buttons all the way; rarely Dandini.'

'Directly after lunch then, if that suits.'

'*Convenit optime,*' Sheridan Reece said. 'Come to the lodge and they'll bring you across.'

'Oh, you're going to be in college?'

'Why would I be otherwise? *Sic simper tyrannis.*'

'Indeed. When one gets the chance. I'm just writing a piece about Bill Bourne's *Petronius*.'

'*Ex nihilo nihil fit*, but on no account inform the marines. Two-thirty. At the lodge. On the button. See you then. Good, good. Thank you for calling.'

Adam went back and read his article on Bill Bourne again from the beginning. Then he checked the Reeces' telephone number. Patricia answered in her impersonal way. '636431.'

'Patricia. Adam Morris. I expect you know, but Sheridan just called me.'

'Oh Adam, hullo. He isn't here.'

'Oh! He called me from college then, presumably. He wants me to come up and see him tomorrow, which I'm happy to do. I just wanted to check with you. He said something about "the lodge". Does he mean the main gate or . . . ?'

'Do you not know? But then why should you? He's gone into Herschel House. We had . . . an incident. I had a . . . fall and it meant my spending a night in hospital and it was decided he'd be . . . better looked after there. It's 8, Herschel Road if you remember where that is. They're agreeably liberal about visiting hours.'

Adam said, 'I'm so sorry, Patricia.'

'No need for that. You'll find he's considerably . . . *relieved* to be there.'

'Yes? And how are you?'

'Goodbye.'

viii

Herschel House was a three-storey fawn brick building with a high wall enclosing an ample garden. After Adam had pushed the buzzer, a porter in a grey cloth coat came out of the Strawberry Hill-style lodge and opened one of the gates. Adam said who he was and whom he had come to see. His accent and manner seemed enough to confirm his identity: he was allowed to go on up to the house. A man wearing a black coat and trousers, who looked very much like a college porter, was waiting at the door. He indicated that Adam should follow him down a polished corridor to a heavy door, on which he knocked, not too loudly.

'You may indeed.'

Sheridan Reece was sitting at a wide table. There were glass doors to the colourless garden behind him. He wore a burgundy-coloured silk dressing gown over grey flannels, stiff slippers. There were flowers on a side table with a lowered flap. A long case against the wall held three shelves of books; several of them, on the top shelf, lolled sideways, like stiff casualties. There was no fire in the fireplace, but the room had a pleasant, warm air.

'Mr Morris to see you, Master.'

'Very good, Partridge, very good. Egregious, some read. Good of you to come across, Morris. Patricia hasn't been unduly well, I'm afraid. A touch of Caesar's wife. They think it's best. So much to do at this time of year. *Bis dat qui cito dat*, but that's rather against the run of play. Your last was not as good as some, am I wrong? But then whose was?'

'You look rather comfortable here.'

'Enviable state, no one denies it. Waited a long time. Not everything comes to those who do that, by any means. What was his name? Jacko was it?'

'Jacko?'

'In what purported to be a novel about Jesus, was it? Or was it Christ's? *Consensu omnium capax*, only then he didn't make it. C.P. Snot.'

'Jago,' Adam said. 'Snow.'

'As you're here, shall I come directly to the point?'

'By all means.'

'We're not going to be able to take you, I'm afraid. I've talked to those in the appropriate quarters and that's the feeling. I thought I should tell you man to man. A blow it may be, but there it is. You people do have this exclusive attitude and won't, I trust, resent its reciprocation. *Habent sua fata libelli*; at this stage what sense in denying it?'

'Of course, Sheridan. Talking of . . . *libelli*. I wonder if I could trouble you . . .'

'Not a letter of the alphabet which I have any inclination to wish away.'

'. . . for Rachel's um manuscript,' Adam said.

'My dear fellow. Well, not Fellow perhaps, not yet, not ever in all likelihood. Nonetheless . . . You don't suspect me of dereliction, I trust? I have read, and read with . . . then again, so much to do these days. Exciting times – *mouvementés,* did you hazard? – for the college, exacting too. I never liked the Greeks. Nor did the Greeks, of course, in most instances, however gifted. You're wondering what I thought.'

'I am indeed . . .'

'Still Sheridan to you, am I? Marry the wrong woman and that's what you gets, when you gets it at all. You took it upon yourself, and there you have it. Clever girl, give you that. If money could talk, we should all understand it. Lions of a feather. Manuscript!' Sheridan Reece had opened the drawer in the table at which he was sitting and he now brought out Rachel's manuscript. Adam could see at once that a great many pages had been interpolated. Bright-eyed, Sheridan Reece pushed the thickened volume across to Adam.

'You've taken a lot of trouble, Sheridan.'

'I have done my job, you mean. Done my job, you mean. DONE MY JOB, YOU MEAN. DONE MY JOB, YOU MEAN. You people, you people. You DAMNED people, DAMNED PEOPLE.'

The door was opened, promptly but without haste, and the man in the black coat and striped trousers came in and walked up to where Sheridan was drumming the soles of his slippers on the parquet floor.

'You're quite right, Master. You're quite right: time for the meeting.'

'Changed the hour, have they, Briggs? Big agenda, have we?'

'Signs are, it could be a long one, Master.'

'Chopping and changing, are they?'

'They need your hand on the tiller, Master.'

'And the buttons. That they do. And they shall have it.' Sheridan Reece shuffled a few steps towards the door, with the nurse's arm as a prop and then he looked at Adam and frowned, chin down in pedantic concern. 'Oh my dear friend, my dear young friend . . . you're piping your eye. No time for lamentation now, nor much more cause! I've achieved everything I want, finally, almost. The purple I pined for. The masterpiece must wait. It must wait.'

Adam said, 'I was just noticing how much trouble you've taken, over Rachel's book. I know how grateful she will be. Thank you so much. Master.'

III

Barbara said, 'Do you want a piece of toast or anything with this?'

'I'd only want butter on it,' Adam said. 'I really do *not* want to go to Samuel Marcus Cohen's bloody launch party.'

'I know. So what time are you? Going.'

'I do wish you'd come.'

'So you can throw anxious looks across the room when I'm alone and palely loitering.'

'I've never seen you alone at a party, not for long. Samuel Marcus'd be all over you himself, if I know anything. Not that there's enough of him really. "Jacket and tie", the invitation says. Why do I *so* hate it when people say "invite"? And why was I on the verge of saying it? Oh look, I'm not going.'

'Stop kicking and screaming,' Barbara said. 'You know you will. So go.'

'Tell you what,' he said, 'I'll walk. By way of a penance. No, I will.'

'Until you see a taxi.'

'Has he really had all the women he writes about in his novels, do you suppose, Samuel Marcus? *Can* he have?'

'Have you?'

'Of course. And there you all are. What would you say if I suddenly came out and told you . . . ?'

'I'd say go to your bloody party before you make a big, big mistake.'

'All the same, there's always something you never know, isn't there, about the other person, no matter how long you live with someone?'

'And there had bloody well better be, probably, don't you

think so? Who was it who said somewhere, "It's a sorry fate to come to trust someone else completely"?'

'Especially when you can't trust yourself, he should have added. I can still see you walking down Brook Street that day and going into Claridge's. Does it have an "e"? I'm never sure.'

'Claridge's? Never goes out without one.'

'The Brooke in Brook Street. Or did it once babble? That's where this party is. He *is* trilingual, of course, Samuel Marcus. Must help having three tongues when it comes to chatting up the ladies.'

Barbara said, 'If you're really going to walk, I'd advise you to go. Now. And if I was ever going to meet a man, it wouldn't be in Claridge's.'

Adam walked, in the grey November afternoon light, through the Boltons and turned down the Brompton Road. It was beginning to drizzle as he reached South Kensington, but there were still some cabs on the rank. He walked on past the Islamic Centre and the Rembrandt Hotel (why did he never associate it with the painter, but always with rich, if not quite smart, foreigners?) and crossed Knightsbridge to go into Montpelier Square. A taxi driver, double-parked where he had just set down some passengers, turned on his light as Adam came abreast of him.

When the taxi had stopped where there was room against the kerb, a few yards short of the Savile Club, Adam could see that Brook Street did not have an 'e' in it.

'That's fine,' Adam said. 'Might I have a receipt though, please?'

'Want a blank one as well, guv?'

'No, no thanks; I'm not up to forgery. Yet.'

'Playing "Get thee behind me, Satan", are we? Adam Morris, can it be?'

'Delete that ageing hint of uncertainty, would you be so kind, Miss Hadleigh?'

'You can detect wrinkles in my voice, are you saying?'

'Ageing *me*, I meant. And you know it. It sounded as if you weren't sure whether I was still who I am. Whereas I – since I see you everywhere – am in no doubt who you are; or what you stand for: the National Anthem and nothing much else, I suspect.'

'That's a very full answer,' Joyce said. 'I'll settle for a kiss.'

One arm round the waist of her black coat, he kissed her on both cheeks. 'Have one, get one free. You're very handsomely booted. It's like embracing a very attractive secret policeman. The kind you rather hope will take you in and quiz you. Which is probably – '

Joyce said, 'I knew bloody well it was you. And you know it.'

'Have you too come to Samuel Marcus's sherry-type *klatsch* or is this one coincidence too many and you're actually on your way to a hot rendezvous? Or both. Nothing like hiding in the open. Life plots like a bad novelist, doesn't it?'

'No such luck in my experience.'

'Are you writing another breast-seller? With all your other activities, I don't know where you find the time to write novels. We'll omit "need".'

'Under my bed, don't I? The empty side. I'm also about to do a "Key Figures of Our Time" series of TV profiles for the Beeb. I truly don't know why I was asked to this thing. This new book of Cohen's looks gale-force intimidating. I had to look up words in the puffs even. Is there really someone called Gareth Crompton Krautheimer?'

'Wait till you try on Sammy's size fourteen footnotes! Because you're the good and the beautiful Joyce Hadleigh is why you were asked.'

'You flatter me.'

'Who doesn't? When you happen to be on the box and the air more often than the weather forecast. Plus you're *never* overcast. Samuel Marcus cares a thousand times more what you might say about his book, even if you never read it, than what I would, even if I said it. Who *are* the Key Figures of Our Time?'

'Oh God, don't look, don't look! Because here comes Innes Maclean. Let's go in before I have to be glad to do the cheek-to-cheek stuff with him. It's like cosying up to congealed porridge.'

'But it is congealed porridge you've been to Cambridge with.'

'That's true. Do I look as old as he does?'

'As Innes? No one does.'

ii

The Plantagenet launch party was in a large salon at the far end of the modest, dignified club. The modernised decor and lighting flushed it pink, as if it were slightly ashamed to serve a commercial function. Adam entered a room cleared of furniture, with enough prompt guests to supply chattering clusters into which a new-comer as confident of his centrality as Innes Maclean might choose to insert himself. Innes had, in his now lengthening day, edited so many magazines that clients and beneficiaries continued to defer to him, although he no longer had a chair from which to bestow as many favours as he had in his selective prime. Even when they were at Cambridge, where Innes had been quick to become the determinant of his contemporaries' literary merit, so making himself their immediate superior, Adam had not been among his clientele. Hunched and frowning, in a fawn and green tweed suit and waistcoat, Maclean now reminded Adam of some parochial Atlas, temporarily discharged from bearing the weight of the literary world on his sad shoulders, and more resentful than grateful for the respite.

Plantagenet's chief executive, Connie Simpson, had lived in England long enough for her American accent to seem more like a fashion accessory than a linguistic trait. In her black silk trouser suit, frilly white shirt, simple pearls, pearl and diamond earrings, uncomplicatedly upswept hair and steep heels, she had the unexaggerated allure of a woman who, having had all the qualities and successes of the temptress, now preferred, almost, to be businesslike. 'Adam! You're doing your Byron in a bad mood.'

'Comes of entering a room containing a hundred people more famous than I am. Well, seventeen. No, there's two-faced Innes: nineteen.'

She took his arm and fattened her lips just a little to kiss his cheek. 'Thank you so, so much for the work you did. On *Into Africa*. The new chapter five gave Bryce a hard-on. That doesn't happen every day, believe you me. Seriously: big, big difference.'

'Big, big *deference*,' Adam said. 'Not my favourite activity.'

'You must meet my brilliant new editor, Terry Slater. He's here somewhere, unless he's there; or both, because that's what he's like. Have you spoken to Jason recently?'

Adam said, 'He usually calls only when he wants to tell me what a fat deal he's made for some other writer. I'm surprised he's not here. Tamara is, I see. The face that lunched a thousand shits. So he's probably coming.'

'I love Tamara.'

'Tell me who doesn't. It's a shorter list.'

Connie said, 'Any film nibbles at all yet on *Into Africa*?'

'It's period, it's got locations, with snakes, and a main character who's a muddle-aged Jewish loser. Maybe someone'll make a stiff offer for the new chapter five.'

'Constance, *mon ange gardienne*! How do I thank you adequately for uncorking all this conspicuous sumptuosity?'

'How about you deliver the new novel, Sammy, before I compile our next catalogue?'

'How could I not?' Samuel Marcus said. 'As for you, *cher maître*, who better placed to answer the question that vexes me: why is film, if an art, so unevenly served by even its finest talents? No painter of quality ever painted pictures as bathetic as those which regularly figure in the filmographies of even our most noted *auteurs*. Take the latest by your vaunted friend *Señor* Jacob Leibowitz.'

'Make that "industry colleague". My article explained expressly why he wasn't my friend. He doesn't do friendship. He does masters and slaves. You've read Hegel. And what you haven't you can always make up.'

'Can we not detect, in such manifestations of sustained ineptitude as *The Siren's Song* the return of the repressed little-boyish desire to fail pitifully? What one effortful but not foolish wit, in full Hungarian flight, has called *la nostalgie de la boohoo*. The wish to be kissed better. Or smacked. Or, better still, both.'

'How many words do you want by when?'

Samuel Marcus said, 'No, no, we will not dissipate this particular evening in nugatory exchanges of facetiae.'

Connie Simpson said, 'Catch you later.'

'Why, pray, has our svelte mutual publisher chosen to leave us? Do you have intelligence?'

'I think you holed her with nugatory,' Adam said, 'and facetiae finished her off.'

'*Entr'hommes*, I have one paramount question to put to you. Israel. Have you yet had occasion to read my assembly of *obiter dicta et scripta* devoted to that vexed topos?'

'From what I gleaned, you've made a collage of quotations from a – shall we say? – congeries of serious names who aren't in favour of Jews being at home anywhere, armed it with an *apparatus criticus*, and signed it Q.E.D.'

'I was seeking, as no doubt you divined, to emulate Walter Benjamin in his unrealised wish to compose a consummate text which, while consisting of nothing but quotations, yet by their arrangement and juxtapositions transcends and glosses the compilation. There is, in short, a Borgesian pattern in my carpet.'

'As prognosticated in your *prolegomena*.'

'*Soyons sérieux*. Do you not agree that Israel has taken the place of the Wandering Jew which the pioneer Zionists hoped to render static? Theodor Herzl lacked the prescience to guess that the stigma that had been theological would metastasise into the political. You will have noticed perhaps the high place in my *tableau d'honneur* reserved for the abrasive views of the late Jacinthe Gerson Bernstein, despite our personal relations which were, to say the least, *maltagliate*.'

'Indeed. Was she your first or your second?'

'My first *wife*. My second marriage. The first was a matter – shall we say? – of an early *lapsus* and its parturient consequence. Who is now, I am belatedly proud to say, a tenured professor at Brandeis. *Aber jetzt*, Jacinthe had a mind and a passion. She provoked the primordial swerve which put me in electric touch with the quick of things. You take the Lucretian reference.'

'And run with it.'

'Her death has hit me harder than my frequent wish to be its author had led me to expect.'

Adam said, 'You thought of *killing* Jacinthe Gerson Bernstein? That verges on a triple slaying.'

'Montaigne claimed to hold nothing human alien to himself. So too do I. But that must – I venture to posit – include an *in*human dimension, a recognition of the appetite for blood which is frequently – not to say "regularly" – evident in the highest forms of genius, the *génie du Christianisme y compris*.'

'That's some cracker to pull this early in the party, Samuel Marcus.'

'You will recall Proust's letter to *Figaro* admitting – not to say advertising – his sympathy for a notorious matricide. It is a tribute to Jacey – or Jack as, alas, she came to be called by her militant lady friends – that I entertained the thought of killing her so ardently. Had I dared to realise her *achèvement*, it would have been a supreme, albeit murderous, act of – dare I say? – *hommage*. As it is, by her disappearance, she has draped a niche in my imagination in black. As the poet said, "To mourn is also to curse." Jesus's disciples, I am disposed to claim, *all* had their Judas moments. Iscariot was the projection of their corporate disappointment, and rage, that their Messiah might, after all, be no more than supremely *good*. They were literally a sorry lot. And the longer He took to come again, the more anxious Christians became that the Jew, who refused to believe on Jesus, was going to be vindicated. The creation of Israel is the cartographic symptom of that vindication; and in consequence the post-modern target of meta-Christian hatred.'

'Well, that's cleared that one up,' Adam said. 'Leaving the usual mess behind it, of course.'

'And so to our *moutons*. I have been approached by a prestigious university press with a view to both editing and majorly contributing to a volume of essays on – *grosso modo* – what it means, nay, what it *can* mean, to be a Jew in the post-Christian era which is imminent, if not – as I have argued *in extenso* – already upon – or indeed in some veridical sense behind – us.'

'Can you possibly be about to elucidate?'

'We live, I should argue, in a world of *reproduction* – not to say factitious – morality. Post-modernism, not least when it comes to the *recyclage du passé*, is a product of – how shall I put it? – taxidermic nostalgia.'

'By which we are all stuffed, are we, some of us?'

'Who can quite let go of the idea that God, *some* God if only the one who does not exist, still has in mind a vestigial purpose for the world? The defeat of Nazism seemed – I emphasise the provisionality of such a schema – to discountenance the notion of a final solution which would coincide with the disappearance of the Jew. Even the Church of Rome abated its complicity. If no one had *wanted* the survival of the Jews, no one in 1945 dared quite to deplore it. The result? A Jewish state.'

'Which,' Innes Maclean said, 'is never what the people who actually lived there already remotely wanted.'

'If I fail to disagree with you, *monsieur le professeur et rédacteur-en-chef*, you will doubtless feel righteously aggrieved. However, you are more accurate than you know: neither Arab nor Jew actually then resident in Palestine welcomed Holocaust survivors.'

'No? Then why did the Zionists resort to the tactics they did to get them there?'

'Correct me if I am right, but in the later 1940s, *sabras* displayed scant sympathy for the dregs of Europe washed up, in every sense, on their shores. Having failed to resist the Nazis, the survivors were – according to more than a few – bringing the blood of enfeebled starvelings into *eretz Israel*.'

'Result: Israel is the single greatest irritant in the world's oyster.'

'That bivalvular image is, if I may say so, the projection of a metaphysical calculus which has lost its traction on the psyche of the west, the higher registers at least. For the lower orders, joining up the frequent dots of prejudice and superstition will, no doubt, not cease to lead, without intermediates, to the paranoia of which you, like your compatriot Carlyle, show such venomous if witless symptoms. My preferred question is rather: where will men go now for a myth to abate the fear of moral chaos which Christianity promised to alleviate, a promise which it shows diminishing signs of honouring?'

Drawn by Samuel Marcus's strident confidences, a small congregation had formed around him. Fists clenched into a combative posture, he seemed to become at once smaller and more dominating. The brilliant dark eyes glinted with splinters of light as he derived energy from the attention directed on him.

'Communism has failed; fascism will not serve, although not all its intellectual advocates were, alas perhaps, as third-rate as wilful taxonomy affects to make them. Need I tell you that Leo Strauss's criticism of Carl Schmitt had to be of the highest quality, as that sublime anti-Semite had the nerve to confess, before he could quite pin him? My quasi-provisional answer must be that Islam alone now affects to know what is wrong with the world and what can be done to rectify it. And the head of their recipe book – as it has been said, not least in the esteemed publication which you, Innes Maclean, co-edited with such dire, some have ventured to say "hired", distinction – is the destruction of Israel. And now comes my question: where does this leave us?'

'Never speechless,' Adam said, 'one of us, at least.'

'Your superbity, Master Morris, postpones – but cannot disperse – the issue. Then again, who constitutes this "us" that it leaves? Let me pose the supplementary in the form of a rhetorical paradox: what *can* it still mean to be a secularised diaspora Jew in a world in which the state of Israel exists? When vacuum and content threaten syncretistic – not to say syncretinous – convergence, a moral black hole bids fair, or foul, to engulf the *ci-devant* civilised world. The meta-Yeatsian, quasi-Hegelian eclipse of centrality is maieutic to a conscienceless extremism which proclaims itself exempt from any need to give a reasonable account of itself. Islam thus contrives to be the *natura naturans* of the irrational. Communism without the scientific dressing; regression as progress. You may shake your head, but you do it at your peril. Remember the Chinese executioner and his "kindly nod".'

Connie Simpson had found a spoon with which to tinkle her glass for silence. 'Ladies and gentlemen, forgive me; but I want to say a very few words about *The Necessity of Chance,* the volume of truly remarkable "essays and assays" of which I am the proud, and humble, publisher and which bear the unmistakable stamp of the genius that is Samuel Marcus Cohen. His novels – those in the Noah trilogy not least – are, as you know, head and shoulders, at *least,* above those of his contemporaries and need no Arafat – I'm sorry, Ararat – on which to ground their survival. In *The Necessity of Chance,* Samuel Marcus marries unrivalled intellectual range with the . . . probing, often insolent imagination that gave us *The Field of Blood* which has so far sold two million copies hardback and has been translated into fifteen languages . . .'

'And was written in at least eighteen of them.' Adam did not know, yet seemed to recognise the voice which had whispered, with animated presumption, in his left ear.

'If there is any justice,' Connie was saying, 'and there is a subject on which Samuel Marcus is uniquely qualified to ironise – the next gathering in honour of the author of *The Necessity of Chance* will be in Stockholm and it will be to celebrate his access to the Nobel laureate which is his manifest due. Ladies and gentlemen, I ask you to raise your glasses to Samuel Marcus Cohen.'

'Hear, hear.' Adam half-turned to get a clear view of the slim, fair, blue-eyed young man, in a charcoat suit, maroon shirt, who had spoken to him.

'Adam Morris?' The lips were tight, carefully amused, and pink. They seemed to promise a limited edition of intimacy. 'Terry Slater.'

'Who else?' Adam said. 'The cleverest thing in Connie's woodwork. The notes you made on my novel were infuriatingly shrewd.'

'*Into Africa* is – ounce for pound – a far, far better thing than Samuel Marcus ever did.'

'Connie hears you, that's treason.'

'Secretly she agrees.'

'All the more reason for our red queen to cut your head off.'

'Can I ask you something? Jason Singer.'

'Is that a question?'

'It is for me.'

'Is he a good agent, are you wanting to know?'

'I know he's said to be that. Does he . . . how can I put it delicately: fuck around at all?'

'You're in love with his wife,' Adam said.

'Who told you? Tamara? Connie!'

'Your question, didn't it? I rarely see Tamara except in restaurants where she always seems to be savouring the fare with her thumbs down. She's looking very good tonight, what I can see of her, bait and hook all in one.'

'Is Jason aware how many lovers she's had?'

Adam said, 'Let's go and ask him when he gets here.'

'He has them too, doesn't he?'

'I only know about the women he had before he met Tamara. There were quite a few of those. He used to bring them for the weekend. They smiled on the Saturday, wept on Sunday, and went back on the shelf on Monday.'

'What about men?' Terry said.

'Men.'

'Jason likes them too, doesn't he? Or did.'

'Not in our house. Lady Macbeth and I know nothing of such things.'

Samuel Marcus was saying, 'As you may well divine, I am becomingly reluctant to respond at any length to the divine Constance Simpson. Let me say merely, implying, I hope *multum in parvis*, that the publisher whom a happy few of us here, lions and lambs alike, are lucky enough to share may flatter but never deceives. She carries the torch of literature in a waning light and long may she have the unflagging flair to sustain its portage.'

103

'Only Tammy's pretty sure that Jason's bifocal.'

'Has she told their children that?'

'Not particularly unusual, is it? I don't see it as a moral issue. You like him, I gather. So do I. Professionally. He's been very good.'

'But lo, here he comes!'

Jason Singer, in a black corduroy suit, looked as if he had been running, at least from his taxi. The long face was unusually bright and his red woollen tie had flipped to one side, revealing that he had failed to do up one of his black shirt buttons. 'If this isn't a record, what is? Two of my classiest authors on speaking terms with each other! Thank God, in the form of Harvey the Harv, I seem to have missed the speeches.'

Adam said, 'How are you, Jason? We were just talking about you.'

'I've got some news, Terence. On *What Is She?* Yesterday Japan, today – would you believe it? – Korea.'

'Korea. Is that vertical or horizontal?'

'I only know it's two thousand dollars. Nothing, I agree, but . . . kudos-wise it's the cream in our *latte*. Have you seen Tamara?'

Adam said, 'I have observed her doing the rounds, and no one does it more appetisingly, I must say.'

'Only we're supposed to be going to this new muncheria that your bisexual friend is opening. *Nibbles*.'

'Denis Porson, is he really?'

'He promises "Round the clock eating and running". I *think* he said "clock".'

Adam said, 'And cue the lovely Tamara Singer . . .'

'Jason, where the hell've you been?'

'Talking big buckaroos, wife; where have you? Do you know Terry Slater?'

'If you have, you have. Hullo, Terry; yes. How are you, Adam?'

'Full of admiration.'

'Are you? What for exactly?'

'A restaurant critic who can still do up her belt to a tight notch. What else?'

'I sometimes undo it under the table. Jason, you need to do up your shirt. Some men are depilating their chests these days, did you know that?'

'Saw it in the *Church Times,*' Adam said.

'How's the new one coming, Terry?' Jason said. 'Got a title yet?'

'What do you think of *The Plotting Heart?*'

Adam said, 'What's that in Korean?'

'Hear that, Terry? You've got the older generation jealous already. *The Plotting Heart* . . . doesn't sing to me exactly. Tell you what though, Terence, come and sample this muncheria with us; I've got something else I want to talk to you about. You don't mind if a brilliant young writer tags along with us, Tammy, do you?'

'Three's company,' Tamara said. 'What is it they say?'

Terry said, 'Two into one will go?'

'Might be it. Meaning what exactly?'

Adam said, '*Very* nice of you to ask me, Jason, but I'm going home actually.'

'I had heard that. Come if you want to, Adam, but I assumed – '

'Rightly,' Adam said. 'Being true to form is one of the duller forms of verity, but there we aren't.'

'Adam!' Lars Waring looked at the wine which was still on the waiter's tray and shook his head. 'Thank goodness you're still here.'

'Call me in the morning, Adam,' Jason said, while Terry was helping Tamara with her coat. 'Things to talk about.'

Lars said, 'I'm very glad to tell you that thanks to the meeting I've just come from, I have every reason to believe that *Options* has achieved critical mass, capital-wise. We have our launching pad.'

Adam said, 'I only hope that you didn't give too many hostages to somebody's fortune. No stings attached?'

'Strings,' Lars said. 'None that are binding. Which leads to a pressing question.'

'How soon can you have the other two thousand I promised

you? Amazing what trouble a croissant can land you in these days!'

'The first issue. I want you in it. Have you time?'

'But plenty of inclination. When are you planning it for?'

'Early New Year. Before the election. Does Feb seem realistic? Meaning three, four thousand words by December fifteen, latest?'

'Who else have we got writing for us? Do you have a topic in mind?'

'How about you on Samuel Marcus Cohen?'

'Not necessarily a pretty sight.'

'You know his work backwards. The forthcoming book of essays is very much your meat, I suspect.'

'And hot potatoes. I do rather admire the prolix little poseur, you know. I just may disappoint you, and myself, by saying something nice about him. Not to say "encomiastic", which he would prefer.'

'I've persuaded Gavin Pope to do a major chunk for us. "Multi-cultural Britain; or from Literacy to Tom-Tom."'

'Thanks to me, you were about to say. You have him.'

'Oh, did you speak to him?'

'I gave you his number,' Adam said.

'For which much thanks in that case. How soon do you think you could let me have that cheque?'

Joyce Hadleigh had taken a half-open copy of *The Necesssity of Chance* from the display on the chimneypiece and carried it across to its author. Her elegant trepidation turned larceny into a compliment. 'Could you sign this for me possibly?'

'It would be my pleasure, Miss Hadleigh. I have often relished your mellifluous omni-competence when it comes to quizzing the famous. You achieve the common touch without touching on the common. *Rarissime!*'

'And while I'm at it, may I ask you something?'

'Anything but my precise date of birth!'

'Israel and the Palestinians. Where do you stand?'

'You plunge with brave, not to say practised, immediacy into the *vif du sujet*. Should I be on my guard? Is this for some cleverly placed secret camera? Forgive my caution.'

'I overheard a bit of what you were saying to Adam and people, but I . . . I remain somewhat . . . confused honestly.'

'In which case, I have not lucubrated in vain.'

'Is peace ever going to be a possibility?'

Adam smiled at Lars Waring. 'On the left-hand side of the bus, you can enjoy an unrivalled view of Joyce Hadleigh in the process of prostrating herself as a wide-eyed suppliant at the altar of Samuel Marcus's salvific potency.'

Lars Waring said, 'Sorry? *Bus?*'

'I can never,' Samuel Marcus said, 'in truth, stand in either camp without the quasi-Irish sentiment that peace can never be attained from wherever each is now pitched. And then again what is peace?'

Joyce said, 'My son Peter was killed in South Lebanon. By a rocket. Four years ago this week. I don't know who to blame.'

'And may I inquire, with all due delicacy, on which side he was engaged?'

'Neither. He was a sound man on a film unit. The rocket hit their car.'

Samuel Marcus said, 'I grieve, of course, for the loss of your son.'

'But what?'

'Allow me, as gently as I may, to observe that the media too are a side. There are – this does not reflect in any way on your son – there are three sides in all two-sided conflicts today; and, I have argued elsewhere, there have been, with exponentially increasing disparities, at least since Potsdam. The Berlin Wall fell not because of politics; publicity and its garrulous organs sufficed to do what Joshua's trumpet did to the walls of Jericho.'

'I find myself wishing I could go and see where it happened.'

'Can this not be contrived? Surely some enterprising producer would relish the opportunity. Or might it be that you also do not wish it?'

'I want someone to tell me what they all want to achieve. Can you?'

'As the French *achever* makes manifest, achievement has something in common etymologically with finishing things off. In the locus which concerns us, both sides wish to kill and at the same time to be the uniquely innocent victims of their victims.'

'But who do you blame most?'

'Let me duck the question, the better to answer it. One of my favourite, furtive books is entitled *Three Impostors*. Moses was the first. I will not spell out the other venerable names for fear that some ayatollan fatwa or papal anathema may fall on my shriven head. Only the Jews lack the machinery – if not always the appetite – to kill those who disturb their illusion of unique election. Which the junior monotheisms, and their attendant monomanias, have sought to appropriate. The devices of self-righteousness cluster about the sources of revelation. The meta-Pierian spring of poisons.'

'Peter died for no good reason and no good cause and I wish I could come to terms with it.'

'How should there be terms to come to? Then again, whereof we cannot speak is the most common topic for garrulity. You make me sharply conscious that I cannot be the comforter that you may wish I was, as indeed do I. I believe I read a novel of yours while serving in the office of a judge, for the last time, I have promised myself, for some allegedly coveted literary trophy.'

'Goodnight, Samuel Marcus. Goodnight, Joyce.'

'Goodnight, dear hostess. May our sales increase exponentially to cover the lavishly generalised canapés!'

'Goodnight, Connie,' Joyce said. 'Eminently delightful evening!' She turned to Samuel Marcus and frowned. '*Generalised*?'

'As can happen with caviar,' Samuel Marcus said. 'I trawl the sediment of memory and emerge with, your novel, was it . . . *The Third Floor*, conceivably?'

'You must've got out half way! It was actually *The Sixth Floor*. Much it matters.'

'About the television trade. Wherein you spoke, perhaps without realising it, *avant la lettre* perhaps, to the very issue of why your son was where he was, if never of what happened to him.'

'I hadn't thought of that. Thank you. Really.'

'I have presumed on your intelligence, not – I must hope – at the expense of your feelings. You are a woman who deserves no less, but has some right to hope for more. The individual, one comes to see, is at once nothing in the tohubohu of things, and everything in the realm of the heart. Kierkegaard's genius was precisely in that perception. Do you have transport?'

'I genuinely hesitate to mention this,' Joyce said, as she went through the door which gallant Samuel Marcus was holding open for her, 'but they've asked me to do a TV series about Key Figures of Our Time. Who do you think really rates in that department?'

It was raining by the time Adam had found his coat and walked, his mouth soured by the party, into Brook Street.

'Taxi!' Adam was glad to pull open the door of a cab standing at the lights and make it his own before it reached Claridge's. '15, Tregunter Road, if you please.'

'Hey! I waved at him before you did.'

'I didn't wave, Innes; I shouted. Try it next time.'

'Not going to Fulham, are you, by any chance?'

'No, I'm going there quite deliberately. It's where I live, as if you didn't know. Oh, do stop glowering and get in, for God's sake, if you must.'

Innes Maclean said, 'I've got a bone to pick with you, haven't I?'

'Still got it with you, have you? That letter of mine about Lord Poobah you almost didn't publish, until I threatened to picket your office, was ten years ago. More. Everything is these days, isn't it?'

'*Options.*'

'Really? I'm not sure it's *got* bones.'

'To tell you the truth, Adam, I can't even remember what it was you were so acrimonious about.'

'I can. The British willingness in 1946/7 to recruit ex-SS men as miners in good King Clement's golden reign, and their simultaneous determination to keep Jews out, a decision which your noble patron, the Lord A., saw fit to defend.'

'How you people do treasure your albums of grievances! The philately, so to speak, of the eternally rancorous.'

'You didn't want them here and you don't approve of them there, in Israel, so – objectively speaking, comrade – you only wish that Adolf had finished the job.'

'You warned him off having me as editor, didn't you? Lars Waring. He told me himself.'

Adam leaned forward. 'Pull up just here, would you, please, driver? By the big puddle on the left. This is your stop, Innes. Off you go. Why ever would I want to warn him against a monumental shit-head?'

Innes Maclean sat there. 'And you wonder why people don't like you.'

'I like the sly "and" in there. Conjoining the spoken and the unspoken. And I'd like you out there.'

'Don't be such a – '

'Very, very careful with the next word, Innes, all right?'

'I was going to say "child".'

'Fuck you either way. I never mentioned your name to Lars.'

'It came up though, didn't it? As putative editor.'

'Good one. I have never before heard the word "putative" used in dialogue. Except perhaps by Samuel Marcus when *urbi* and *orbi*.'

'Dangerous, dangerous man.'

'Get out of my taxi, Innes, before I spoon you out. It never occurred to me that you, of all yesterday's men, could ever be editor of *Options*. I would certainly never have put money into it if it had. Does that ring true at all?'

'Look, I can't be stopping here forever.'

'It's all right, driver, drive on. You can bloody well pay your share.'

'You were going to Fulham anyway.'

'It's your cab, Innes, isn't it? You waved at it. I'll be your guest, OK?'

'If the money matters to you that much . . .'

'Prominent – well, fairly – ex-editor strangled in taxi. Long-nosed writer held. I never liked you, Innes. But then again, who does? Did you ever shag Anna Cunningham?'

'Why would Lars Waring say something that wasn't true? Anna Cunningham? No such luck.'

'You should've published her poetry in one of your posse of pissy mags. She sent it to you, didn't she? Because he didn't have the guts to tell you that he didn't want you anywhere near the mag he always intended to edit himself.'

'She's got religion, hasn't she? The Cunningham lady. I remember her at Cambridge as quite a giggling armful!'

'Seventeen did you say, guv?'

'Fifteen, didn't I? This is me,' Adam said. 'Do you want to take him on to wherever it is that you never asked us round to after you'd had dinner with us?'

'That was twenty-eight years ago. I can walk from here.'

'You could've walked from back there. What you mean is, you're determined to stiff me for the cab. Let me have a receipt, driver, would you, please?'

'You'll get it back off tax, I presume. Time all that was stopped. With any luck, Gordon will be addressing that kind of thing once they get in. I know very well what your animus is all about and always has been.'

'Good. I'm glad you're clear on that. Who the hell is Gordon?'

'You people never forgive, do you, and you never forget either? Why is that?'

'It's a living. And by all means, tell your friends I said so. I'll certainly be telling mine. Love to Fiona. I shall never forget her leopardskin slacks, as we called them in those happy days I shall be glad never to see again. Much like you, really, Innes.'

'And you wonder why you've never got where you might have.'

'Nothing sweeter than the smell of burning bridges, is there?'

111

'How was it?'

'Hateful. God knows why I went; and if He told me I wouldn't necessarily believe him.'

'No one said how much they admired your work?'

'A man called Terry Slater came close. It's his speciality. He's aspiring to be Tammy Singer's *cavaliere servente*. In the modern style: saddle up and go to town. Where *would* you go?'

'If what?'

'You were going to meet a man. It wouldn't be Claridge's, you said.'

'Almost certainly his chic penthouse overlooking Chelsea Harbour.'

'You'd risk being taped for posterity, you know that, don't you?'

'Do now.'

'Did it ever occur to you that Jason Singer was gay at all?'

'On the contrary.'

'Really?'

'I don't have the tapes, but I did dance with him one time at one of those awards shindigs we never go to. He appeared quite capable of . . . presenting arms, shall I say? Come to think of it, I could go to his place. Only thing, he might well be there. He has brown lips, have you noticed? And he tends to froth in the corners.'

Adam said, 'When I was twenty-three, I thought I knew everything there was to know about all the characters in the world. Now I don't even know all that much about myself. Samuel Marcus accused me of "superbity". You wouldn't say that, would you?'

'Never heard of it.'

'No one has. He imagines it comes from the Latin *superbitas*, but there's no such word. I just went in and checked. It's not even ecclesiastical.'

'Have you eaten?'

'Crow mostly.'

'Only there's still some kedgeree I didn't finish.'

'Lead me to it. The actual Latin word is *superbia*.'

'I'll use that then, if I absolutely have to.'

'Rachel used to say "asbolutely", do you remember?'

'I remember,' Barbara said. 'I think it's something she caught at school.'

Adam sat at the kitchen table to eat the kedgeree. Barbara brought the ketchup bottle from the fridge. 'The one thing you don't know about me,' he said, 'I never have ketchup with your kedgeree. By the way, Denis Porson's opening a new place. *Nibbles*, Tammy Singer said it was called. We ought to try it sometime after we've walked out after the first act of some play that everyone has told us we really, really ought to go to. I do sometimes wonder, Ba, which I dislike more: Jews or Gentiles.'

'Lucky I'm neither then.'

'No, no, that's me. Sometimes. I wish. Jewishness is something you get landed with and . . .'

'Are you Adam Morris the writer at all?'

'I've written about lots of other things actually.'

'And yet . . . the hero of *Into Africa* does just happen to be called Saul Nathan.'

'Never liked him. Samuel Marcus was fishing for me to contribute to some new symposium on what it means. To be a Jew.'

'Take thirty-eight, that must be. At least.'

'Do you ever think about it?'

'What is it they always say? "Must we . . ."'

'". . . have this conversation", would it be?'

'I don't care what kind of a flower you are.'

'It's going to be strange, isn't it, having Juliana in the house? In Paraguay in ze good old days, her grandparents probably had Dr Josef Mengele to say "ah" to.'

'Well, don't blame her,' Barbara said. 'She was a baby, if that, at the time, and she's now the mother of your grandson.'

'*Uncircumcised* grandson. As if it mattered. I said it first!'

'Now I remember why I got the ketchup out of the fridge.'

'You dare.'

'Never think I wouldn't, just because I don't.'

'No "e" in the Brook of Brook Street by the way. I checked.'

iv

'Four seven three oh.'

'Joyce, is that you?'

'It can't be all that much of a surprise. It is my number.'

'Only I called before and you weren't there, that's all. I got your ghost. I ran before the beep. It's Daniel. You can guess why I called. I was thinking about you. And Peter.'

'So you thought you'd ring up and make me cry.'

'Not my intention. By the longest possible chalk. Are you alone?'

'Why? Where are you? You sound close.'

'Promise not to laugh.'

'No problem there.'

'I'm at Claridge's.'

'*Claridge's*? You're not! What ever are you doing there?'

'Not the washing up. I've got rather a nice room actually, as the guest of one Carlo Pavlides.'

'That's really, really funny, because I was right next door two hours ago. At a publication party for high falutes and upwards.'

'They've flown me in because they want me to be in this new period piece, scripted by one Adam Morris. I'm going to be the decent British doctor friend of his that the main character – a South American dictator called Francisco Lopez – finally treats abominably. Three weeks in Paraguay or somewhere that looks very like it. The rest at tropical Pinewood. I end up covered in sores and bruises. Never unlikely with Mike Clode directing.'

'What do you know? You really are a famous actor suddenly.'

'Suddenly can take a hell of a long time in some cases. Joyce . . .'

'The same. Listen, before you . . . I really like *Una Vita*. Your Anglo-Italian's really . . . amazing. I ought to interview you on

Joyce's Choice. Or are you too grand these days?'

'Of course. You wouldn't like to have breakfast, would you?, is why I rang.'

'It's a bit late in the day.'

'Tomorrow morning. It's all on Carlo's tab.'

'I never had you down as a freeloader, Daniel. You used to be much too moral. For anything. Eight-thirty?'

When she put down the telephone, Joyce looked in the mirror next to the Matthew Smith to see how she was reacting. What did her smile mean, if that was a smile? She had taken a step away when the telephone rang again.

Joyce picked it up and said, 'I know: you've just realised you're sorry but you've got to have breakfast with a star.'

'Miss Hadleigh? This is Samuel Marcus Cohen. Am I inopportune?'

'Only when your words get longer than I am.'

'I contrived to wring your telephone number from our mutual friend, the Protean Adam Morris.'

'And what can I do for you?'

'On the contrary, if contrary it is. With your permission, I should like to send you a poem.'

'You don't need my permission to do that.'

'I do, however, need your address.'

'Did Adam not have it?'

'I do what I propose to do with, yes . . . trepidation. Yet . . . you will, I hope, see why. I have found myself thinking about your son. I confess I wished to have it from your own lips. Your address.'

'12b Albert Mansions, west eight.'

v

When the time came for her to leave the apartment on Veteran Avenue, Clifford Ayres helped Rachel to pack Bill Bourne's books and manuscripts into four large cardboard boxes which she despatched to the librarian of the college where Bill and her father had been undergraduates together. At the end of the semester, Clifford put her bags into his Chevrolet pick-up and drove her along the San Diego freeway to LAX.

'Are you looking forward to London?'

'Not a whole lot.'

'But you don't figure on coming back, do you?'

'Not my call,' she said. 'Depends on Harrison Q. Harris. If he offers me tenure, who knows?'

'I do; because he won't. You're much too pretty for a maiden gentleman with a regular fresh carnation in his buttonhole. I don't know what happened exactly to change your mind. But I know something did; or someone.'

'I just haven't decided what I want to do with my life, Clifford, is the truth. That's why you probably won't believe it.'

'After Bill died, I turned colour, is what I think.'

'In my eyes? I don't think so. After my dad came out, is what you really and truly think.'

'You suddenly got scared. How come?'

'Of hurting you maybe.'

'How about what hurts is you not wanting to?'

'I can't spend my life with you, Cliff, any more. I don't know why. If you do, then maybe you do.'

'Like what we did that weekend. Is my guess. Up at Lake Tahoe with Bill. Could be the decisive factor.'

'But you'd sooner blame my dad.'

'It's like he was still around.'

'What happened up there at the lake house, that was . . . for Bill. And he's . . . gone. It's gone with him. You could be right though: it's also still around. Like you and me were three people still. His eyes still on us, is what maybe . . . changed things. I didn't think so at the time, it seemed fine. But now . . . we're kinda compromised, even though nobody is ever going to know we did what we did. We'll know, is the truth. Simple as that.'

'Unless it's simpler: black man, white woman, makes you feel what you feel. The minute you stop –'

'Except I don't,' she said. 'Because I don't think of us in those terms. I never did.'

'So how about your father? Does he?'

'We don't discuss those things.'

'Silence has a big mouth sometimes.'

'Listen, Cliff, he thought you were great. And very smart. He did. He totally accepted who you were, as an individual, in my life and . . . on campus generally. Like with Mitch Ambrose. You think he couldn't tell you apart? He could tell you apart. I hate to hear you even hinting differently. Not least, because it changes how I feel about you.'

'Doesn't seem to matter too much how you feel.'

'Unworthy, OK?'

'Like what happened at Lake Tahoe, is that?'

'You want me to be ashamed. You want me to look all hot remembering what . . . we all did. Yes, you do. I don't feel it. Correction: I didn't, but now I do a little. Because I can see the replay in your eyes. I thought we were somehow . . . being generous, to Bill, but somewhere in there, you were being what you don't want my dad to think you are; that is, what you do want him to. Don't look that way, Cliff, because truly, it's not puzzling. And it's not just what I would say. It's what I damn well do say. Somewhere along the line, you want things to be like Mitch Ambrose says they are; you play being opposed to him but that's what you're doing, playing; and players are all just a little bit complicit, like Iago and Othello are.'

'Finished?'

'Absolutely not,' she said. 'Absolutely and totally not. Damn. Damn your smile. This is not a moment I wanted to be cute, at all.'

'Freud would take a different view possibly.'

'Proving nothing whatever. You want me to be loyal to Sigmund? I don't carry that kind of obligation.'

'You can finally afford to be mad with me. What about exactly?'

'It's coming out, OK? Our baby finally.'

'Our baby.'

'Conceived by the lake. Did he take pictures, Bill? He swore he wouldn't.'

'Why would he swear that if he wasn't going to, is that what's going on here now? Is that what you want to hear?'

'You took pictures,' she said. 'I can see them when I look at your eyes. And I really liked you, Cliff, I really did. And like was better than love, just for a little while back there. A good part of it, at least.'

'British Airways,' he said. 'Right through there. Just the way you should go, always.'

Rachel kissed him, hard, on those lips and decidedly did not close her eyes when he looked down at her. She took the pain and the condescension and the attempt at indifference and still had her arms around him until she felt him rise against her and then she released him, and herself, and latched her backpack over one shoulder, picked up her bags and walked towards the terminal without looking back. She fanned aside his reflection on the glass of the door.

The London plane was delayed for forty minutes, during which Rachel read one of the stiff books she had brought from the apartment. By the time the flight was called, there was a fat enough portion of it left for her to read herself to sleep on the plane. As the plane climbed and turned eastwards, she looked down, without noticeable emotion, on the tilted Pacific below them.

'Good afternoon, ladies and gentlemen, just to let you know that the latest weather report indicates our flight to London, Heathrow, will take approximately eleven hours. I hope you can all relax and enjoy your meal and then get some sleep and . . . I'll try not to wake you up with too many announcements.'

'What takes you to London?' Rachel's neighbour, a young man in a jeans jacket (over a ribbed cotton sweater) and chinos, with tooled leather boots, took his cue, it seemed, from the captain's chattiness.

Rachel turned her page. 'Sorry? Talking to me?'

'With no great originality, I'm afraid.'

'Christmas, you might say. Polite word for unemployment.'

'What are you reading?'

Rachel looked at the cover of her book and then showed it to her neighbour.

'*After Virtue,*' he said. 'Heavy!'

'And then some. Avoids taking sleeping pills. Haven't read it, have you?'

'Elements. Don't worry; I won't spoil the ending. My name's Jonty Logan.'

'Short for Jonathan?'

'I wish I'd said Jonathan now. I keep meaning to shake off Jonty and I never contrive to do it. Sticky stuff, names. And you are . . . ?'

'Rachel. Morris. My father calls me Raitch. I kinda dread the day he doesn't any more. Why would I tell a stranger a thing like that?'

'Avoids having to tell them anything else. Life is an exercise in reluctance, followed by regret.'

'Someone must have said that.'

'It's getting late. They've said pretty well everything. English, are you?'

'Somewhat.'

'No Englishman's ever entirely anything, is he?' He had to be in his late thirties. The black hair and the pale blue eyes with long dark lashes suggested Celtic blood, like Bill Bourne's. 'He's basically an unreformed Aristotelian Catholic, isn't he?'

'Excuse me?'

'Alasdair MacIntyre. Thomas Aquinas in modern dress. Am I right? He thinks it all fell apart when virtue was privatised.'

'You've heard different?'

'If they put it together again, what then?'

'All the king's men are never going to work that, are they? And his horses won't help a lot.'

'Moral chaos or Holy Inquisition. Take your pick.'

'And your shovel. And then head for the hills. Are you a Catholic? Ex, possibly?'

'On the contrary. I'm a lot luckier than you are, aren't I?'

'Are you so? How come?'

'I'm sitting next to you and you're only sitting next to me.'

She read for a while, then – without looking up – she said, 'OK: what is the contrary?'

'My parents were . . . try Plymouth Brethren. You're Jewish, right?'

Rachel said, 'Only my profile.'

'No, it isn't. Your intelligence and your . . . snap.'

'Let me warn you: I don't crackle and I rarely pop.'

Jonty said, 'Bloody MacIntyre's book is a sulk, not a morality. Two hundred pages of pious pout passing for plausible philosophy. Am I wrong?' He opened an Elmore Leonard paperback and read a few pages. 'Ask me, virtue is social not personal. We can't do it on our own. Like sex. Not and have it mean anything.'

Rachel read to the bottom of the page and then slapped her book shut and looked up at the control panel above her head.

'You should be grateful,' he said.

'That you're wearing clean socks? I am.'

'Oh do you mind? I couldn't resist the boots, but they tend to the strangulatory. Socks are supposed to be clean today, but I can always . . . put those bloody stretchy jobs on they give you.'

'Up to you.'

'Was I supposed not to ask? If you were Jewish?'

'Ask anything you like, as long as you don't mind if I don't answer.'

'That's not an offer I'm likely to refuse. What've you been doing in California? Studying? Trying to be a movie star? What?'

She opened her book again, glanced at him, and resumed reading.

'Yes, I damn well do,' he said. 'Obviously. Because who wouldn't?'

'Do you though?' She closed the book, with a sour face. 'Do what exactly?'

'Try, think you're beautiful. Do you now seriously want to go and sit somewhere else? Your mother must be quite a looker.'

'I like the window or I would.'

'I can't have spoilt it for you, can I? Alasdair's book. No one reads *After Virtue* with the expectation of a twist in the tail. What made you buy it anyway?'

'How about I stole it?'

'Yes? I've done my share of book stealing in my time. Not only books actually. Truth to tell, I've also picked a pocket or two.'

'I didn't *steal* steal it. I took it. From the books of the man I was . . . living with. Who died. Bill Bourne.'

'Could that possibly be the same Bill Bourne that wrote a book about the *miglior fabbro* himself? Ezra Pound.'

'Could there possibly be another one?' Rachel said.

'You *lived with him*? He was old enough to be your father.'

'But he wasn't,' she said. 'How come you ever heard of him?'

'I'm a bit of an old Ez fan. What was the attraction exactly?'

'Brains; roughly.'

'Seldom anything to take your clothes off for. You think you're annoyed with me. I think it's with yourself.'

'Try both,' she said. 'I hate old Ez.'

'Did you ever,' he said, 'try both? I'm surprised girls don't do it all the time. Unless they do.'

'Hints are never going to be the kind of things you take, are they?'

Jonty said, 'Face it: it's your fault.'

'Is it?' she said. 'What?'

'That you excite . . . try, interest.'

'Meaning you think you do; and I'm failing to be excited or interested.'

'Rachel Morris. Where do you get it from? Take it that I'm referring to the sharpness.'

'You're accustomed to being fresh with women. You're not a movie producer, so presumably you're some kind of a professor. Used to sophomore pushovers. You've read *After Virtue*. The blurb at least. So . . . philosopher, are you?'

'Up there with Ludwig! You look even better when you're

nettled. You're on the green with that one; see if you can roll in the putt. You're doing severe and thoughtful with your lips. I like that. Very promising.'

'You're an inter-disciplinarian non-Oxbridge academic . . . on the run from an English identity that isn't exactly your size. Hence the Venice Beach wardrobe and the New Mexico bootees.'

'Plunk! Straight in, the lady!'

'Stanford?'

'Santa Barbara. Visiting professor. I thought I'd hate it. And now it's over . . . I have withdrawal symptoms.'

'Not noticeably.'

'I do though. I feel as if I'm going back into a tight little island. And driven to confess it to strange girls.'

'You've had a measure of success in the strange girl department.'

'Immeasurable,' he said. 'Some were stranger than others.'

'Only not today. Not this evening anyway.'

Jonty said, 'No? Because you know what's happening, don't you?'

'If you imagine a remake of *Brief Encounter*, I have to tell you it's not.'

'Then why can I hear Rachmaninoff's Third Piano Concerto?'

'You can't. It's the Second.'

'Which proves you can hear it too.'

'You have very neat . . . how about footwork? But I am truly not available. Truly I'm not.'

'The repetition gives me reason to hope. Implying self-cancellation.'

'Reinforcement,' she said, 'in this case. Reason never hopes.'

'The cur can still have his reasons,' Jonty said.

'I'm putting up the shutters, OK? Putting on the shades. Whatever.' She was wrestling her blanket from its plastic envelope. 'I need to sleep. A long period of silence on your part would be much appreciated.'

'Raitch . . .'

She did not respond. He reached and caressed her right breast, as if he had done it many times before. She opened her left eye and slapped his face, hard enough for the man across the aisle to hear, and blink and turn his head, despite the earphones.

Jonty said, 'That's the first time in my life that anyone did that to me in quite so – all right, "timely"? – a way. The first time ever, in truth. But why should you believe that?'

'Damn you to hell,' she said, 'if you really want to know. And back.'

vi

Joyce stood in the doorway of the Foyer Reading Room until the Maître d' approached her. 'I'm supposed to be having breakfast with Daniel Bradley.'

'Of course, Miss Hadleigh. What a pleasure, as always, to have you with us.'

She was careful not to notice the people who noticed her and leaned, whispering, towards each other, as she walked through the room to the corner table where Dan, in intelligent spectacles, was reading the *Guardian*. He threw the paper on to an adjacent ledge and stood up. 'Joyce! You're looking much too smart for me.'

'Good heavens, you're bearded!'

He kissed her nicely, and professionally, as he never had before. 'The script demanded it,' he said. 'What do you think?'

'Brings out the corsair in you.'

'The *senior* corsair you're too polite to say. I'm having the works. Works for me, works for you; what do you say?'

'Seniority suits you. And showbiz. Being a star takes the starch out. Dear God, I was all set to be pale and sad and now . . . I want the works. Disgraceful, isn't it?'

'You can be pale and sad and still enjoy the amenities. Same again for the lady. I like my bacon well done, do you?'

'Why do they never take the rind off even in the best places? Dare I ask: are there any raspberries?'

'Of course, madame.'

'Everything plus raspberries for the lady.'

'Does it change at all?'

'What's that?'

'How you feel.'

'It does rather. For instance, only recently I've found I want to go to where he was killed. It's been growing on me.'

Daniel said, 'I find I don't actually want anything to do with the past at all. I'm growing out of it rather.'

'Why are we having breakfast?'

'I wondered how you were.'

Joyce said, 'You wanted to tell me something. Prove something then.'

'I don't think I need to do that, do I?'

The waiter returned with orange juice, granola, prunes and raspberries.

Joyce said, 'Where are you living these days? When you're not at Claridge's.'

'I've got a house in a little Puglian hill town called Locorotondo. Down on the Adriatic. Quite remote, more like Greece than Italy, the region: still pagan underneath. Hence full of rather aggressive churches.'

'And you're not lonely down there?'

'Part of the attraction. I've also got a couple I . . . live with. It's a very . . . flexible arrangement. Pia and Daniele, funnily enough. They're quite a bit younger than I am; full of beans therefore. They run a little restaurant I put them into, *tavola calda* style, which is convenient when I'm there. They've decorated the place with murals. Pia also make ceramics.'

'You're quite one of the Medicis these days!'

'To think I might still be a headmaster if I hadn't been accused of something it never remotely occurred to me to do! I thought life and sex had something to do with sincerity. Now I realise: only bad sex is sincere. The better it gets, the less it has to do with anyone in particular. I suppose I called you because I wanted to apologise.'

'For being unduly kind.'

'Falsely genuine, more like it. Now I'm an actor I can be genuinely false. Myself, you might say! I'm sorry for you. I'm not sorry for me. Peter was yours. Never mine. The man you married, and who married you, he no longer exists. I wanted you to know.'

'Free then, am I? Or is that you?'

'Both possibly.'

'So you won't ever call me again, will you?'

'Here comes the bacon. How were the raspberries?'

When they had finished breakfast, Daniel escorted Joyce to the entrance to the hotel. As the doorman opened the door of the taxi to her, she held out her hand and Daniel smiled and took it. She was surprised, as she parted from him, to feel a pang of desire; it doubled, almost perfectly, with dislike.

The following morning, Joyce saw a dark blue envelope on the mat under the letterbox in her flat. Its single page contained a handwritten message. 'Dear Miss Hadleigh, I ask that you read the enclosed lines aloud, while standing in front of a mirror. They were discovered, hidden under the sole of a child's shoe in the camp archives of Majdanek concentration camp. The author was nine years old. Elzunia is the Polish for Elizabeth. She left word that it was to be sung to the tune of a nursery rhyme. I press your hand. Samuel Marcus Cohen.'

Joyce went into her sitting room and stood in front of the mirror and cleared her throat, worked her lips and then read the lines which she had been sent:

> Once there was a girl Elzunia,
> She's dying all alone now,
> Her daddy, he's in Majdanek,
> Mummy in Auschwitz-Birkenau.

'Are you awake at all?'

'Depends.'

'Because I just wanted to ask you something. How long, roughly, should I leave it before I can plausibly tell you that I've fallen pretty well totally in love with you?'

Rachel said, 'A bit.'

'Till we've landed?

'And cleared Customs, I should.'

'Will it do me any good, do you imagine?'

'Improbable.'

'I watched you sleep. It was lovely.'

'Sneaky,' Rachel said.

'Little bit sneaky.'

Adam had considered driving out to Heathrow to meet Rachel's plane, but Mike Clode made a pre-emptive call late the previous evening. In the event, Rachel did not arrive at Tregunter Road till close to half past noon. She knocked and rang the bell at the same time.

'Raitch! Thank goodness. We actually called the airport. Ba was afraid you'd decided to cut. She's gone to the shops. Busy beats worried.'

'They had to lose my bag, didn't they? Misplace my bag, I should say. They recommended calling later. Knowing very well that you never get through to anyone, so I hung in there.'

'And two hours later they found it.'

'Three, by my count. It was right there on the ground by the belt all the time. Some helpful pleb had dumped it in a corner. How are you, dad?'

'Ashamed. That I didn't come out to meet you. I had a break-fast . . . would you believe meeting? Carlo the Pav and company. You look — as they will all say these days — brilliant. Amazing even! He added. Fitting Ossa on Pelion in one trite moment.'

'California,' she said, raising her hands to shape her hair. 'Soon wash off, I'm afraid. Are they here yet? Tom and . . . Juliana and . . .'

'Alexis. No. Tomorrow.'

'Nervous possibly, are you?'

'At least you're not a stranger, Raitch. Well, not too much of one.'

She made some kind of a face and suddenly she was snorting with an emotion that made her smile and almost weep at the same time.

'What?' Adam said. 'Honey, what?'

'Christ knows,' she said.

They listened to the key in the front door and then Adam was taking plastic bags from Barbara's hands.

'You made it finally!'

'How are you, Mum?'

'Fine. When did you last eat? You must be hungry. What's so funny?'

Rachel said, '*Shema Yisroel!*'

'How funny is that?'

'Pretty funny actually, in the circs.'

Adam and Barbara drove in the Mercedes to the airport in order to meet Tom and his wife Juliana and their son Alexis at Heathrow. Tom was wearing a long brown leather coat and brass-buckled half-boots. Juliana was in a green cape, high black heels; her blonde hair was in a loose bun. Eight-year-old Alexis's curls shone like a halo.

'Hullo, hullo and . . . hullo. Good to see you, Alexi? Juliana. How very nice of you to come all this way!'

'Not at all,' she said, in a more pleasant voice than Adam had expected. 'It's a pleasure to see you again.'

'Car's . . .' Adam pointed and then led the way. 'You look very . . . elegant; and then some, to tell you the truth.'

'Ah, the truth,' Juliana said. 'A little soon for that!'

Tom said, 'So: how's my Mum?'

'Brimming with all the clichés your father would hate to hear paraded.'

'Still terrorising you then, is he?'

'Some things never change. Others do. He's never terrorised me. Alexi's at least three inches taller than last time.'

'He serves overarm now. Pretty well too. Especially when he foot–faults.'

'Like son, like grandfather,' Adam said.

As they walked to the car, Adam looked at his son and tried not to find him a stranger. Tom looked handsome, and fit, but it was as if his behaviour was as carefully chosen as the twill trousers and the leather coat, shinier than anything Adam had ever worn. The gear and the haircut, neatly but not too neatly layered, made it clear that Tom could afford the most expensive brand of modesty.

When they found the car, Adam said, 'Come in front with me, Juliana. Two men in front's terribly suburban.'

Barbara said, 'You're busy?'

'Pretty busy,' Tom said. 'Every retired company director seems to be grabbing his Seve golfbag and rushing to buy a villa in the south of Spain these days. We're just starting up another big new development near Cadiz. Two hundred villas with pools, three golf courses, a dozen tennis courts.'

'Are you playing at all?' Adam called back.

'Golf, hardly at all. Tennis a bit. It's quicker. I've got Xavier Sanchez to beat me when I have a moment. You have to come down again, have a hit with him.'

'I'd probably never touch the ball.'

'Join the club! As a matter of fact, Xav's very tactful. You'll never guess he's deliberately hitting it to where you are.'

Barbara, 'How about you, Juliana? Are you a tennis player?'

'I prefer to ride.'

'Of course. You did that in . . . in South America, didn't you?'

'Paraguay, yes I did. A long time ago now.'

Adam said, 'How many languages do you speak, Alexi?'

'Only Spanish and English really.'

Tom said, 'Plus a little French, and some German, don't you, Alex?'

'Only sometimes.'

Adam said, 'Have you been to Germany recently, Juliana?'

'Three months ago I was there for a while.'

'Juliana's been doing some interesting work over there.'

Adam looked at her.

'Finding things out about . . . the past of their families for people who want to know about it.'

'Yes? What sort of people are those?'

'All sorts,' Juliana said. 'Like liquorice.'

'And what kind of thing?'

'Family histories. The kind of things that . . . haven't been talked about very much over the years. I'm a sort of . . . therapeutic archaeologist, you might say.'

Alexis said, 'Do you have a tennis court?'

'Afraid not. I go to a club, when I go. I can take you, if you stay long enough.'

'No need; I play tennis all the time.'

'Lucky Alexi!'

When they had returned to Tregunter Road and the bags had been taken upstairs, Adam opened a bottle of Perrier Jouet. As he poured it, he was reminded of the significance of the initials PJ and looked at Juliana. She smiled carefully back. They drank the champagne, out of Venetian glasses, in the sitting room. Christmas packages lay like brightly wrapped boulders under the tree. Later, in his study, Adam wrote in his notebook that the conversation seemed to be all about the things it was not about: skating without ice. Perhaps he was alone in thinking so, but he didn't think so.

As supper time approached, Juliana went into the kitchen with Barbara.

Alexis was upstairs with a box of his father's old Dinky toys and a platoon of mutilated Action Men. Adam and Tom were left alone in the sitting room, like uneasy finalists.

Tom said, 'I don't know which of you and Jools is more nervous than the other.'

'Very difficult for her, I know. I'm trying to make it easy. Which makes it even more difficult probably. Trying to get things right is the usual way of getting them wrong.'

'You haven't changed much, dad.'

'Odd, isn't it? You and me. The way we . . .'

'Yes, it is. Promptly followed by no, it isn't. Fathers and sons is a pretty old story. Remember Noah?'

'*No*. I've read a trilogy about him, though, and his sons, which is more than you have, I'll bet. By Samuel Marcus Cohen.'

'Never heard of him.'

'Really? Perhaps I ought to live in Spain. Is there room?'

'Anytime. You've never really forgiven me, have you? The Reverend Miguel Sung and all that. I still don't really understand why I did what I did. Might help if I did, possibly.'

'Where's it left you exactly?'

'As you might say, when cornered: I don't do exactitude.'

'I try to,' Adam said, 'but only when I'm writing.'

'Life's something else.'

'That's probably what I've got against it. The butterfly you can't pin down. Are you happy at all?'

'Happy. At all? Yes. Yes, dammit.'

'We're very glad you wanted to come; *said* you wanted to. She's being extremely . . . improve on "nice" for me. Juliana. Very good-looking woman. Dignified without being . . . *dignified*. Hint of . . . something more.'

'She'd seriously appreciate a chance to talk to you. Seriously.'

'I'm available.'

'Only she doesn't know how to start. How's Rachel doing?'

'Ask her yourself. You'll probably get a fuller answer. She'll be here for supper. She looks wonderful. I was surprised, after the flight.'

'Maybe she's got a secret love.'

'So does Juliana,' Adam said. 'Look wonderful. That might have been better timed. Never mind. She popped out to see some friends, Rachel. She's written a remarkable book on Catullus and other antique Romans. Not easy to find new things to say in that department, but she manages it.'

'Get her to go for a walk, dad, will you, or something? Juliana.

Give her a chance to be alone with you. Please. But not . . . as if you'd . . . planned it. It'd mean a lot to her.'

'Of course. Of *course*. Heavens, I'd like to.'

Although difficult to honour, Adam discovered a certain savour in Tom's request that he should contrive to be alone with Juliana. His performance as carver, pourer of drinks, teller of jokes seemed easier because it was, in some way, an imposture. As they tore open the careful parcels on Christmas morning, he looked at Juliana and did not look at her. He waited all day for his moment to be alone with her, but never managed it. Only on Christmas night, while they were all bundling crumpled wrapping paper into a plastic sack, did she catch his glance with a wince of recognition. The pale brows contracted and she tilted her head, like a question mark. At the same time, a blink of light flashed, like apprehension, in her eye. He thought of the deer he had hit when driving the Mercedes home from Gourdon.

'Juliana, I don't know why, but I was wondering have you ever been to Richmond Park?'

'I don't think so, no. I am quite certain not, to tell the truth.'

'Only in the morning I need to deliver a belated present to an old friend of mine, a film producer, lives out that way. Italian. It's very . . . old England. Deer and horses. Only . . . on Boxing Day, shouldn't take long. If you felt like coming with me.'

'Yes, please. I would like this.' She continued to look at him. 'Very much.'

Later, when everyone had kissed everyone, as if after a show that had been artfully performed, and promised that the turkey was perfect and all the presents were exactly what they wanted, they went to their rooms, as sated as actors by the sincerity of their imposture.

When she had closed their bedroom door, Barbara looked at Adam, who was still wearing the new maroon cashmere sweater that she had given him, as he protracted his show of casual familiarity.

'Went as well as we could possibly hope, don't you think? Stuffing was fabulous.'

Barbara said, 'So what's it all about?'

'What's that?'

'Oh come on. Your rendezvous, for God's sake. With Juliana.'

'Oh that. Nothing. Nothing.'

'Hmm. Two nothings! What do they make?'

'We shall have to see, shan't we? When we get there.'

IV

Juliana came downstairs on Boxing Day morning in trim black trousers, shin-high black boots and a long dark crimson, turtle-necked alpaca sweater with a shining black belt. Adam had put on brown corduroy trousers and a thick brown cardigan, big buttons to the top. The day was clear and chill. At breakfast, Barbara asked Alexis whether he was up for teaching her to play football on his new Nintendo. Adam guessed the generosity it required of her. Rachel and Tom were still having breakfast when Adam and Juliana (who now put on a slim suede coat, with a fur collar, and a white knitted hat) set out, as casually as Adam could manage, to deliver Bruno Laszlo's Christmas present.

As they got into the car, Adam was conscious that the blue-black Mercedes 280C was no longer the latest model.

'It's shameful really.'

'Yes? What is that?'

'You've been married to Tom for – God, can it really be eight years?'

'Nine.'

'And this is just about the first time I've been alone with you.'

'And you don't quite know what to say.'

'And I don't quite know what to say. Your English is . . . astonishing. Perfect, really. That's what gives you away, as not being naturally English: the clarity of your consonants. How do you like living in Cordoba?'

'Is that what you've been waiting to ask me? I like it. In truth, we are outside the city.'

'We lived in Andalusia at one time. Barbara and I. In the early Sixties. Very early. On the coast. But we used to drive up to Cordoba. The Mezquita is one of my favourite buildings. Pity

Charles the Fifth had to ruin a beautiful mosque, which he himself admired, didn't he, by cramming an overdressed Christian cathedral in the middle of it.'

'I like the back streets up around the little statue of Moses Maimonides. The orange trees against the white walls.'

'I still find *The Guide for the Perplexed* more than a little perplexing.'

'Do I understand you?'

'I was . . . showing knowledge . . . of Maimonides's masterpiece. The title anyway. But I don't have to. Does Spain feel like home to you? In a permanent sense?'

'*Vamos a ver.* I'm not sure anywhere does. Or has to.'

'How many languages do you speak?'

'A few. Comes of never belonging anywhere in particular, probably, when I was small. Not German.'

'Your mother is . . .'

'Belgian. *Was* Belgian. Whatever that is. Whenever that was. She's been in Paraguay for such long time I doubt she'll leave it now. Yehuda Halevi . . .'

'Excuse me?'

'Have you ever read him?'

'God help me, I'm not sure I've ever heard of him.'

'A Jewish poet who lived in Andalusia, in the eleventh century. I understand him only in translation, but I like to sit and read him in the Juderia. He wrote love poems, but also about how he longed to go back to Jerusalem, where he had never been and where the Crusaders – he calls them "Edomites" – had just killed all the Jews, and the Muslims too.'

'I've never remotely had that desire,' Adam said. 'Is that a liberation or . . . a defect? Probably. Yehuda . . .'

'Halevi.'

'I must try and get hold of some. In Hebrew originally, presumably.'

'He was very influenced though, by Arab poetry. Just as flamenco was by Jewish music. Everything is an amalgam, except for lies, of course. Lies can always be pure.' Juliana was looking out of the window when she said, 'I've brought something . . . bad into your family, is the truth, isn't it?'

Adam said, 'I don't think that at all.'

'No?' She looked at him. He was watching the road with attention, although there was little traffic. 'Her grandfather was a full-blown Nazi. Isn't that what you think of when you think about me?'

'Not the first thing. Was he? Full-blown?'

'Worse perhaps. He was an insincere Nazi who never belonged and so he never repented.'

'How did that one work?'

'No doubts; no beliefs, that was Rudi. He was never loyal; so he was never disloyal either. He used the Nazis, to get rich, and they thought they were using him.'

'And weren't they? Didn't they: to get their money out?'

'Of course.'

Adam said, 'Did Tom ever meet him at all?'

'Money – you know what they say – "has no smell", don't they? Tommy saw him maybe. When he was a guard at the hotel. No one had any idea what he was. Tommy, I mean.'

'And what was he?' Adam said.

'Your son, for instance.'

'Not that anyone would notice.'

'I'm not sure he cares so much about those things. Not too much, perhaps. The war, I mean.'

'Some money smells quite a bit. Freud might say that's what we like about it. There's an English novel, *Humphry Clinker*, in which the rather shameless leading character, a rich man, enjoys having a pail of his own shit stirred under his nose.'

'I have not read this.'

'By one Tobias Smollett.'

Juliana said, 'You don't know all that much about Tommy, do you, Mr Morris?'

'Very little. I'm well aware. Can you contrive to call me Adam possibly, do you think?'

'Contrive . . . ?'

'I used to think I did. Know Tom; quite well. But that was . . .'

'When he was being what you wanted him to be.'

'Also when he was being the direct opposite. I could understand that too, but . . . It's strange, Juliana. I've just written this film about Paraguay . . . in the old days. Francisco Lopez and Madame Lynch. You spent years where it all happened and I've never been there, just . . . researched it. Which makes me the expert. I feel the same about . . . the past. Even my own. I was never quite there when it happened. Much you care, but this is Putney Bridge. Where the Boat Race starts. Did you ever meet Josef Mengele?'

'He was before I was born. And he was only a very short time in Hohenau. The German town a lot of . . . people lived in in Paraguay. Nineteen-sixty, he came from Buenos Aires after the Israelis captured Adolf Eichmann. He was afraid they would get him too. Mossad; the bogeymen! Then he went to Brazil. After that to Bolivia, I think.'

'Your grandfather. Rudi. How much of him did you see?'

'He came and went; he went more than he came, it seemed like. He had many businesses, many lives, many women, Rudi. He was always very clean, very smart, as if he came from a better place. Always properly shaved and . . . groomed. He had many children possibly. He was also very . . . gracious always, to me, as a little girl. He did not care so much for my father. Father was so . . . what? Modest. No ambition, except . . . not to be the son of my grandfather. He carried the guilt which his father never did, poor Viktor, and the fears. He was ashamed of what he wasn't; and still is, I expect.'

Adam said, 'This is Wimbledon Common. It always reminds me of an old radio joke, a sort of mock commercial: "She's young, she's beautiful, she uses . . . Wimbledon Common!"'

'And what is the joke?'

'True. When you were a little girl, you lived in . . .'

'Yes. Hohenau. And then we moved to near Asunción, where – '

' – you had the cheese factory.'

'He still has it,' Juliana said, 'my father. And I still smell it sometimes. A clean smell, but not one you want to smell all the time exactly. I hate yoghurt. My mother too, hated it. And stainless steel. She opened a little motel, near Encarnacion, close to the Paraná. The river – very wide – between us and Argentina. She is more successful than Papa. My father is not too much of a man, to tell you the sad truth. He has tried so hard not to be something that . . . he isn't: anything.'

Adam said, 'You preferred your grandfather. I probably would too, is that what that smile tells me?'

'We can't always *contrive* also to dislike what we hate, can we? Or love what we like. Even when we like it very much. My grandfather was a beastly man. It was especially beastly of him to be so . . . charming. He was good at getting what he wanted; and he wanted many things. Including little girls who ran to see what he had brought them. He knew how to seduce them just as much as anyone else. You are not at all sure, are you, what you want me to be, or what you want to think of me? Or is that the same thing? You aren't even quite sure if you want me to like you. Perhaps it would be nice if I liked you more than you really like me. Perhaps that's always nice; to have other people and they don't have you.'

'I do like clever women,' Adam said.

'Your daughter is very clever, I think.'

Adam said, 'How come it was so difficult for you and Tom to get out of Paraguay?'

'OK,' she said, 'it wasn't *that* difficult. But people were very afraid of what . . . anyone who went away might tell people: the newspapers; Mossad! So if anyone threatened to leave, whatever reason, it was frightening for the ones left behind. They were all sleeping dogs, you know, or the children of sleeping dogs.'

'And what sleeping dogs do best is lie.'

'Yes, it is. You're not one of the gentlemen who prefer blondes, I think.'

'How did your grandfather manage to get out of Germany after the war?'

'He contrived,' she said. 'By being out before it *was* after. He was always going everywhere. No one was surprised that he went or that he came back. They never suspected that he was anything but . . . what he wasn't, because he never was. There was no secret with him. He could be a patriotic Nazi because what he was not *was* what he was best of all. Like an actor; who is unconvincing only when he is being himself. My grandmother, it was much worse for her; he never really wanted to see her again. When she arrived, she was like . . . an accusation.'

Adam said, 'You made Tom believe he was being heroic, when you got out, is that how it was?'

Juliana said, 'I wanted to leave Paraguay; Tommy wanted to take me. Heroic? I don't know about that.'

'I remember him saying that you had quite a hairy time.'

'It was more romantic when it had hair on it, maybe, but yes . . .' Juliana looked out of the window, as if Putney Vale cemetery was a beauty spot. 'You could say that we played a game which also at one point . . . was not a game.'

'You knew it was a game; he didn't.'

'And just possibly vice versa,' she said. 'That was the kind of game it was.'

'And are you glad you played it?'

'Of course. Of course. Tommy is a good father. We have a good life. Thanks to . . . many factors.'

'My brother Derek not least . . .'

'Of course,' she said. 'You love your wife?'

'Very dated of me.'

'Even though she is not a Jew.'

'This is called the Robin Hood Gate. No idea why really. Robin Hood, if he ever existed, operated in Sherwood Forest, at least a hundred miles from here.'

'Tommy. What is he?'

'Tom? Don't ask me. Ask Tom.'

'I'm not sure he knows.'

'Is that my fault?'

'I don't know. Is it?'

'Look, to me, he isn't even Tommy,' Adam said. 'Ask me if this is Richmond Park, and yes, it is. Trees, grass. Not very green. Deer; coming up! Over there. Dapples like targets. Richmond Park was where Henry the Eighth pulled a bow when he wasn't pulling birds.'

'Just when you think you know English . . .'

'No, no,' Adam said, 'just when you think you know anything. Pulling birds is slang, for running after women. Obsolete probably. I'm not sure I ever used it till today. Odd. The people you are with change the things you say and they never guess it could be anything to do with them. Do you think we should have a walk? Can't come all this way and then not get some fresh air, can we?'

ii

After they had finished breakfast, Rachel said, 'What are you going to do now?'

Tom said, 'Something that doesn't involve you, is that what you're hoping?'

'Only I was thinking of going and seeing someone for a bit.'

'Do I know him?'

'No. Nor do I really.'

'Sounds good. Off you go then. Will you be back for lunch?'

'I might; I might not. Don't mind, do you?'

'Go, for God's sake,' Tom said. 'I haven't seen you for months, why would I have to hang on to you now?'

Rachel walked down to the King's Road, crossed it and went down Tite Street to Swan Walk, a row of pretty cottages with front doors of various bright colours. Jonty Logan opened the yellow door of 7A wearing white Moorish slippers and a silk robe.

'This is nice,' she said.

'Not mine. Nor's the gear, obviously enough. Belongs to a

friend of mine I was at Colchester with; historian. Ben Pinto. He's in Italy researching, so he says; he's supposed to be doing a book about Carlo Levi. Hullo to the *Mezzogiorno*. And doing a treatment for a TV documentary, of course.'

'Good. That he's in Italy, I mean.'

'Have you had breakfast?'

'Lots.'

'That only leaves bed then really, doesn't it?'

'You think?'

'Ready when you are,' he said.

'You really are too.'

'I love you,' he said.

'Oh that's all right,' she said. 'No need.'

'I love you, I said.'

'Has this place got an upstairs at all?'

'You have no idea what you do to me.'

'I have *some* idea,' she said.

'I truly wasn't sure you'd come.'

'I truly wasn't sure I should. Wrong. I was pretty sure I shouldn't. I had a strong feeling right away, that you were trouble. Why else would I be here, to tell you the truth? What is it about you?'

'"Me chawm," as the poet said; George Barker. You can't resist being irresistible, is more likely the truth of it. Do you know his stuff at all? I rather like it. I'm a lot less important to you than you're clever enough to make me think.'

Later, Rachel said, 'You're too bloody much, you're too bloody much.'

'You're altogether more than that,' Jonty said. 'I love you, Rachel. It doesn't matter whether you believe me or not; I'm done for.'

'To cap a cliché with a cliché: you don't know anything about me. Or why this has happened.'

'I know a little bit,' he said. 'For instance, I know you used me. Don't think I don't know that. It doesn't matter why. I could tell by how much you enjoyed it. It was a relief; am I not right? Thought so! Whatever it was for you, I'm extremely grateful, for me, as you very well know. At the same time, I can see through all that to what you really are.'

'Can you just?' she said. 'And you? What are you really?'

'Greatly reduced from the number you first encountered. I was quite pleased with myself at that point.'

'Delete "quite" and I'd agree.'

'How can a woman have intelligent *breasts*? They're beautiful, but they're also wise.'

'Bullshit.'

'No, no. I don't even want to hurt you, you're so . . . who you are.'

'Do you usually, like hurting girls?'

'Hurt hurt? No. Unless they want it, and then it doesn't hurt, does it?'

'Is that a warning? Or a promise?'

'Forget I said that . . . I'm not that person any more.'

'Who are you then?'

'How about someone who wants to be with you more than anything in the world, and forever? Which means that last week I didn't exist. Look at you. *And* you're clever. The nightmare no one wants to wake up from.'

Rachel said, 'Look at you again, already!'

'Your fault,' he said. 'What happens when I look at you.'

'Does it? You've done a lot of drugs, haven't you?'

'I've done some.'

'Some is always a lot. I haven't; done them. Aside from hash a few times, which didn't do a lot for me, and then very, very slowly. The man I lived with did more than . . . I ever knew when I started.'

'Bill Bourne, are we talking about here?'

'It's certainly true of Bill.'

'Indicating that he's not alone on the score sheet.'

'He drank a lot too. I liked that rather less, to tell the truth. Drinkers always want you to do it with them, and I can't work when I drink. Bill could, all the time.'

'But you stayed with him,' Jonty Logan said. 'Perhaps you were why he did it so much.'

'Thanks for that,' she said, 'but I wasn't. I see what you mean about hurting girls.'

'Oh it's not limited to girls. It's true of most anything I admire. Why are you putting that on?'

'How about I'm getting cold?'

'I'd never've guessed. The sweater's fine. But don't put anything else on, will you? I love you like that. As if you didn't know.'

'Bill had terminal cancer. He drank because of it and because of drinking, all his life, I mean, he had cancer. The music goes round and round. I suppose, in a way, he liked doing things I didn't entirely enjoy, and liked me to, but I did enjoy *him*. He taught me more than anyone ever did, and partly because it was *him* I learned it from. The fact of his . . . person. He changed me more than I know or, maybe, want to.'

'Men,' Jonty said. 'Those're your drug.'

'I can do without them,' she said.

'Because you can always get them when you want them. You use them when you want to. That's what druggies do.'

Rachel said, 'While we're at it – '

'And we do seem to be that,' Jonty said.

'And as if it mattered: I was actually with two men in California. I may have loved both. I may not have loved either. When Bill died, that – a little to my surprise – and very, very slightly to my relief . . .'

'. . . killed the other one, did it?'

'One *licensed* the other, is what hit me, once I was on the plane. I felt it before, but I didn't know why. It was complicated by . . . other things. Before Bill died, I thought it would have to be either or; turned out it was both or none.'

'And that's why you hit *me* on the plane. That hard!'

'That was pretty amazing,' she said, 'wasn't it? I really shocked myself. I also enjoyed it.'

'And look where it got you,' he said.

142

'You invited it,' she said.

'Now you're getting there.'

'Are you going to turn nasty on me?' she said.

'When I love you?'

'That's often the time, isn't it?'

'The clever woman always knows more than she should if he wants to be happy. The double white line is the one we like to cross.'

Rachel said, 'Are you still using?'

Jonty said, 'Finished. Promise.'

'As if they were two different things. You'd promise if you hadn't.'

'But more sincerely, surely. With a tear or two.'

'*Experto crede?*'

'Oh good heavens, yes. Trust me.'

'Up dike and down dale,' she said.

'I only said it to provoke you.'

'And to amuse yourself.'

'You're playing with giving me up. Seeing how much it might hurt.'

'Which of us?'

'There's always that to it. Your body's more generous than your heart, Rachel. Has that ever occurred to you?'

'God, yes. And now what do we do?'

'That "we" is the best thing you've said so far. Wrap it up and I'll have it for Christmas.'

'All gone Christmas,' Rachel said. 'I ought to go too.'

'I hope that means you're not going to. This isn't much of a pad, but . . .'

'No, it's not,' she said, 'and no, I won't. Move in. Gay, is he, your friend?'

'Ben? He may well be a vegetable. He's a man with a conscience. He has a nostalgia for the Italy in which Jews were persecuted but not very often murdered. Puglia suits him nicely. Plenty of pretty, sad ghettos. Do you want to get married?'

Rachel said, 'What're you going to do? In England. In the way of work?'

'Live off you, aren't I? Or preferably on you. Is that the time? No, it isn't! One of my old professors I'm in touch with, he thinks he might have something for me. Especially when the Tories lose the election.'

'And if they don't?'

'There has to be some university in need of an impressively qualified intellectual cross-dresser. Failing that, there's always journalism, the only truly modern art. "A sum of destructions", was Picasso's phrase, and doesn't that cover it perfectly though, the field he wasn't talking about? Journalism is society's wrecker's ball; we all want to swing it.'

'I ought to run a mile, shouldn't I?' Rachel said. 'Probably two. The more I know you're the kind of man you are . . .'

'I don't believe in kinds of men. Nor do you.'

'The ones you know you shouldn't trust; and then you always do.'

'I want you more every second I look at you.'

'Blue eyes, black hair, white skin, soft voice, hard . . . heart; *you* are the nightmare, aren't you?'

'It's more than generous of you to say so.'

'That's what I'm afraid of,' she said.

iii

Adam said, 'Every year the English dream of a white Christmas. Instead, they get days like this: bright sunshine, clear skies. Which are much better, but no one *ever* dreams of them.'

'Tommy reminds me sometimes . . . you won't like this.'

'Suggests it's likely to be true.'

'Of someone who is . . . how do you say?'

'I suspect you know pretty well how we say most things. Especially the things we don't.'

'On the run. He wants me to be the one with a past. But

I'm really not. He is, but he doesn't know what it is.'

'And that's our fault. Mine and Barbara's, you think. Especially mine.'

'That's so English: things always have to be someone's fault.'

'The English have only one surviving fine art: the court of inquiry. Tom told me that your grandmother was raped, many times, before she got out of Berlin after the Russians arrived.'

'That's what I told him.'

'Meaning it's not true?'

'No? They raped everyone they could find. Young children. Old women. I don't know about boys very much.'

Adam said, 'And we don't care any more than your . . .'

'You were going to say "friends".'

'Very likely. In Paraguay. Minded what they did.'

'They were pleased, in a way. About what was done to Germans – the women like my grandmother, the fire raids on Dresden and Hamburg – those things made them innocent, victims.'

'I was referring to the things they did when they were the masters of Europe.'

'Oh! The things . . . *they* had done, those things had to be some kind of a . . . do I dare to say "joke"? You think they were fanatics; most of them were overgrown schoolboys and all those things they did, killing, stealing, strutting, they were – what do you call them? – pranks, don't you? They were also savage pranks.'

'Schoolboys are often monsters. Bullying is the one sport pretty well anyone can be good at.'

Juliana said, 'Nothing gives people more in common than all of them having the chance to pretend the same thing.'

'Which was?'

'In Hohenau? Being normal. They could smile; be polite; laugh; ride horses. They had picnics and christenings; and funerals. It gave them something to play at being all the time: nice people, with nothing to hide, living in a sunny place where they behaved like . . . model citizens. Under a dictator – with a nice

German name – who asked only that they pay their taxes and help him . . . develop his country.'

'Home from home!'

'For my grandparents and their friends, being reminded of the past was sometimes a pleasure, sometimes a persecution. It depended on who did the reminding. Nothing is only what it is. What do you think Alexi is?'

'Very bright. Very . . .'

'English?'

'English. Not . . . the first thing I'd say about him. But . . . son of an Englishman, why not? Does it matter?'

'We all have to be something.'

'Especially if we can't be ourselves.'

'You're still not sure, are you? If you want to end up liking me or not liking me after this.'

'Liking might be more difficult than not.'

Juliana said, 'Sometimes you are very like him. Tommy.'

'Only wish I had his backhand,' Adam said.

'You say hurtful things and expect them to please people. I am wrong, of course: *he* is like *you*.'

'He's done a lot of things I never have, and probably wouldn't dare. Too late now.'

Juliana said, 'You're thinking of Robert.'

Adam said, 'Robert.'

'Your old friend from school. That Tommy knew in Buenos Aires. Very well, I think. Before he came to Paraguay.'

'Robert *Carn*. Not much of a friend, Robert, actually, though certainly, I suppose, at this point, old. In your eyes anyway.'

'He had great charm, that man. He had the gift of seeming to be self-sufficient and then of making an exception for your sake.'

'You met him yourself, did you?'

'When we arrived in the bus from Posadas, seventeen hours, in Buenos Aires, we stayed for a short time with Roberto. Everything seemed to amuse him, but only a very, very little. That made it seem exceptional that he should smile the way he did. He was like a welcoming wolf, Roberto.'

'Juliana, I really have to take this present to this man I have to take this present to. Who lives . . . five, ten minutes from here. Perhaps we should . . .'

'Have I told you something I should not have?'

'You haven't told me anything, have you?'

'And should I not have?'

The Mercedes was canted against the verge. He touched her shoulder as she got in. She looked back and the light was on her face. He started the car and eased it into the careful line of traffic going towards Sheen Gate.

'Tommy thinks I'm the one who has secrets. You do too, don't you, think so? Or ought to have? The Nazis in the woodshed. Plus a grandfather who may well have left so far undiscovered millions. Perhaps there is a message hidden somewhere and I can turn, all of a sudden, into the Countess of Monte Cristo.'

'Is that really a possibility?'

'Great expectations?' she said. 'Would that be nice? Would it make me more . . . interesting?'

'I suppose – not that I've thought about it till now – that there might be some comedy in . . . seeing you and Tom lapped in ill-gotten clover. Not all that much though. What would you do with it, a fortune?'

'It will not happen. I would never keep a penny. You don't believe me. Because I have blonde hair and blue eyes. Anyway, we don't need it, do we? Tommy is not a Jew. Am I right?'

'Not in orthodox eyes, no; but in Nazi ones . . . probably. Certainly.'

Juliana said, 'I wish I had told Rudi, my grandfather, that he was. Tommy. A Jew.'

'And what would he have said?'

Juliana said, 'He would have smiled a certain smile of his, the one with ice in it. That was Papi. And then shrug, and say probably, "So?" It would have amused him, I think, that I might think he would give a damn. He was alone in the world, whoever he was with. That was the price he paid. The only one. I wonder what he'd say if he knew what I've decided to do now.'

'Which is what?'

'This is what I have been wanting to tell you: I'm going to convert.'

'You're going to become a Roman Catholic?'

'On the contrary.'

'The contrary. A rational human being?'

'A Jew.'

Adam's foot touched the brake pedal. 'Ah! For whose benefit, is that?'

'Mine,' she said. 'Because then I will know who I am. And then so will Alexi. If he wants to. That way, we shall always have somewhere to go.'

'Or not. That's where I go: nowhere in particular. It's not that easy, you know, to become –'

'Oh I know that. I've already started. I'm learning Hebrew even.'

'Are you really? More than I ever have.'

'Reading back to front. It comes of living in Cordoba, to tell you the truth. Yehuda Halevi was not the kind of Jew anyone ever was again after . . . the end of the *convivencia*, which itself was not at all as nice as nice people like to imagine. He dared to say things that no one dares to say any more. His contempt for Christians and Muslims, for instance, the usurpers and plagiarists and vulgarians.'

'Listen to you! You're already rather more of a Jew than I am.'

'You admire the Mezquita and all that . . . candy-striped arcading. Me, I prefer the little synagogue in the back street. Have you ever been there?'

'Have I been there? "*Antigua sinagoga Ebraica.*" The old custodian used to say. In the 1950s, when I was there. He lived next door and he had just two teeth. Maimonides must have preached there. And they probably gave him a hard time.'

'I go and sit in there and study my Hebrew and read Halevi. Blanched walls. No images. No cross. Above all, no cross. Only ghosts. Do you think I'm mad, doing what I'm doing?'

'But I do envy you rather,' Adam said. 'If that's any good to you.'

iv

'You've done something strange to me; what you did has. That's why I asked you to come and see me. I have to admit, I was just a little surprised when you agreed to. You know why. I haven't been able to get it out of my head. I don't know whether I feel better or whether I feel worse. Both perhaps. You smile. You understand. I'm not going to ask you what made you send it to me. Perhaps you were being kind; perhaps you weren't. Perhaps it comes to the same thing. You smile again. It's not a particularly nice smile, is it? Could just be that's what I like about it. You've done something to me, and I don't quite know what. Do you? Put me in your power. Under your wing? Same thing. I read the poem to myself once a day. I rather dread finding that I've turned into a kind of post-Holocaust Ophelia and start reciting it to myself all the time. Except there's one strange thing: it's only — what? — four lines, but whenever I look away from the text, I can't ever remember what comes next. It's as if — I'm telling you things you know! — the tears I can't quite shed are blinding my mind, not my eyes. I don't know if you know what people think of you, or whether you care. But you have a slightly . . . sinister reputation. Especially when it comes to women. But — I may be very foolish to say this — you sending me those lines, they make you seem . . . I'll try accessible. Small. And touching. You don't frighten me. And that's why I wrote to you. I never expected you to come. I thought you were probably in America somewhere by now.'

'I go next week. Committees of scented ladies of a certain agelessness will take me to their cosmetically enhanced bosoms. The Via Olorosa. Hurrah and alas in close conjunction, as so often when one is faced with the conspicuous generosity and jargonised responses which – save at the highest levels, and maybe at the lowest – are the mark, as Alexis de Tocqueville so presciently observed, of man's best hope.'

'I've never really felt right in America,' Joyce said.

'You are a famous person on these shores. Over there, you have yet to make your *poussée*.'

'I like it when I don't understand you, but I still don't. It makes me feel young probably.'

'You have yet to make your presence felt, shall we say? Yet your qualities could well be as much in demand *outre-mer* as they have been, and remain, here in this small corner.'

'You've no idea how insular a person I am. Parochial even. Underneath. I hide her, but she's always there.'

'This confession from the renownedly smartest woman in London. With the most recognisable tones.'

'Even my voice comes from the tailor.'

'The dread of authenticity is, I presume, the fuel of your urgent, yet insular ambition. Like the Reverend Dodgson's Red Queen, you cannot stop running for fear that you will catch your foot in your own roots. What you say in that voice is, however, not available off the peg.'

'I'll tell you something funny,' Joyce said. 'Not at all funny.'

'That is a delightful painting; by Sir Matthew Smith, if I am right.'

'Aren't you always? I bought it a long time ago. I think of him as just plain Matthew Smith.'

'The Fauvisme, some over-reacher has said, of Stratford Matty Beau. Were you advised as to the purchase?'

'I just liked it,' Joyce said. 'Do you want tea or anything?'

'Tea? No. You were advised by yourself, which argues for more accuracy of taste than you care, or choose, to admit to. What is at once funny and not funny?'

'I've never shown the poem, or read it aloud, to anyone else.'

'But you are now going to read it to me.'

'Why would I do that? When you know it better than I do.'

'But not in your voice. That will make it new to me. Come, read it to me.'

'I'm not sure I can.'

'Hence my insistence. Read it to me and I will take you with me to America. The one is not conditional on the other, nor a consequence. It is a conjunction. *A vous de jouer.* It is for you to choose.'

'How many times have you been married?'

'Three. So far. Not that all my liaisons have been marriages. As you may well imagine, or indeed know. Documentation is available. I am at the moment a grieving, yet tearless, widower. Thus eligible for consolation.'

'And having me read that poem will . . . console you?'

'Not at all. It will lend it, oh yes, by all means smile, *muscle*.'

'Strange: I want to and I don't want to. Read it.'

'But you will. For me. To whom the same thing applies.'

She picked up the piece of paper with the poem on it. It shook while she read it.

'It seems unbearably long.'

'The retort to Theodor Adorno is there in those four lines. But here is the thing which Adorno represses: the answer – no, the sequel – to the death of that little girl is, and here the unspeakable declares itself, the sequel is not vengeance, not – to avoid re-opening the wound we both recognise – territorial: it is desire. The unquestionable which owes nothing to argument or morals or thought. Desire. Only one man has seen that intimate link and seen it in the light of what he saw in Auschwitz itself: one man, in the inner ring of hell, making love – and here lust and love are indeed the indistinguishable one which moralists would deny that they can be – as if that alone were defiance enough, and who shall say it was not? When one fucks, Joyce Hadleigh, one is not fucking in the presence of the Lord, one is fucking Him, or Her. One is doing the one thing, because it requires two, that He or She can never do. Sex gives the lie to divine omnipotence. Hence each monotheism seeks to discountenance it in the eyes of the Lord. You see fit to smile.'

Adam drove into the tight private road, parallel to the Upper Richmond Road, along the frontage of Ranelagh Court, a large, rectilinear stack of 1930s flats. The cars already parked there were two BMWs, a Lexus, three VWs (two Golfs and a Passat) and a Range Rover, not of the latest design.

Adam said, 'And now, if you want to come up and meet a genuine film producer, slightly down on his luck, this is your big chance.'

'Then I take it. Of course.'

There were three entrances to the flats. Number 36 was at the far end of the block. Adam pressed the bell on the panel and stood in front of the electric Judas window that enabled the tenants to see as well as quiz their visitors.

'Yes?'

'Bruno, it's Adam.'

'You push the door.'

They went up in the new lift to the top floor.

'Bruno. How are you?'

'I cannot complain, otherwise I would.' Bruno now had a very large stomach. The top button of his grey trousers was undone under the loosened brown belt. He was wearing a rumpled grey shirt with a black jacket and monogrammed leather slippers. The thin hair was tight, as if moist, against one side of his scalp, wild the other.

Adam said, 'This is Juliana. Bruno Laszlo. The last of the old brigade.'

'My big chance,' Juliana said.

Bruno said, 'I must ask you: where did you find her?'

'Under the tree, of course. Very nicely wrapped, as you can see. She happens to be my daughter-in-law. Bruno, I brought you a very small gift.'

'You are working with Carlo again. Come in. What have I got to offer you?'

'I did some work on the *Eliza Lynch* script he's doing with

Mike. If it's good enough, they'll make out I had nothing to do with it. You know what those people are like.'

'You have your ideal Eliza Lynch wiz you right here. The eyes, I must say! You have to be an actress.'

'Today everyone does,' Juliana said.

Bruno Laszlo had lived in Lowndes Square when Adam first knew him, but it was thirty years since he had had a success. Although he had continued to produce – or to be about to produce – other films, none had made much money. The Ranelagh Court flat was eclectically furnished: Adam recognised a dining room table and chairs which had been props in *The Woman In Question*. A sprawl of Italian newspapers was on the floor under the bookshelves next to the fireplace. It looked as if, when Bruno turned the pages, he never flattened them again. The cushions on the couch were depressed; two rungs of the greenish, braided curtains had jumped their rail and the material, with its faded lining, drooped on to the windowsill.

Bruno said, 'This is a very beautiful book. Italo Svevo, I must tell you, is my favourite author. After you, Adam, of course. What can I offer you?'

'Nothing. Truly. We're on our way home.'

Juliana said, 'Forgive me, but . . . can I possibly use your . . . ?'

'Down the hall,' Bruno said. 'The second on the right. The right? The left.' Bruno stood in the middle of his room frowning, as if the place was not wholly familiar to him. 'My God, I must tell you, Adam, she is just my type.'

'I must tell you, Bruno, she's everybody's type. Are you all by yourself?'

'I have a housekeeper but she has gone to wherever it is to see I don't know who.'

'What happened to Sharon?'

'After Magda died, she went back to her husband, or the man she left for her husband. Maybe both. I don't know. She is grey now.' He breathed in deeply and let out only some of what he had drawn in. 'So: thanks to you, Mike Clode cannot now direct *Life and Loves* till I don't know when, if then.'

Adam said, 'Then that's when we'll do it.'

'I am sorry like hell you never directed a film.'

'I'm quite sorry myself, but if I'd really wanted to, perhaps I would have. Too late now. *Eheu, fugaces* . . . and all of that.'

'Was he such a nice man, Horace? *Non ci sono convinto.* I won the Vatican prize for a Latin poem, did you know that? In 1937. Out of all the schoolchildren in Italy. My father gave a big party in our apartment in Torino. And two years later, less, he was dead; the family businesses were all confiscated and I was a refugee in London. Wizzout a penny. Did I ever tell you what happened the first time I went wiz a woman after leaving Italy?'

Adam said, 'Remind me.'

'In Torino, we went often to the brothels, you know, young men, Italy in the 1930s, what else could we do? Maria's, it was a sort of . . . boys' club; the best kind: wiz girls. So, in London, 1941, I was all alone, miserable like hell. Freezing cold night. In the blackout, you can imagine. So I saw this girl in a doorway, you know, and I went up to her and I said, "Good evening." And you know what she said?'

'What?'

'"It's sree quid." Which was a lot, I must say. But . . . I had some money my family had in London, luckily, so . . . We went to her room, gloomy like hell, I must say, and she said, "Give me the money." I gave her the money and she lay down on the bed wiz all her clothes on. Like that. Legs so. I couldn't believe it. I said, "Look, for God's sake . . . in Italy, when a young man goes with a girl, you know, we have a bit of a talk and a laugh togezzer and – after all – in Italy, a man and woman, we take our clothes off and we enjoy ourselves." Guess what she said. I tell you: "Welcome to England, ducky."' Bruno jerked his head as Juliana was coming down the corridor towards them. 'She is in love wiz you, I think.'

'Doubt it.'

'I swear to you. You lift your . . . little finger and . . . you'll see. You start wiz your little finger.'

Adam said, 'We must go. And Bruno . . . next year, we must

154

make that movie. Before you ask me to revise the script again.'

'But first I want to give you something.'

'I don't want you to do that, honestly.'

'I have it for you in my mind a long time. Up there. Top shelf. I get it in a second. Easy, I stand on the chair.'

Adam said, 'No look, Bruno, let me – for God's sake – '

Bruno took off his slippers and climbed on the arm of the armchair under the bookshelf, but still could not quite reach. He put one foot on the mantelpiece and heaved himself up by the edge of a high shelf. 'You know who was Curzio Malaparte?'

'Mussolini's favourite writer. With a house on Capri. It wasn't his real name, was it?'

'An evil genius, Kurt Erich Suckert; a transplanted bastard, like me, also like Italo Svevo, but a genius, I have to say. And his masterpiece, *Kaputt* – '

Bruno was pulling, with the tips of his fingers, at the tight top shelf. He worked a volume free but then it came out too fast and fell on to Adam's head before bouncing on to the floor. As Adam crouched and turned away, and Juliana was making a disbelieving face, Bruno's silk-stockinged foot slipped from the polished corner of the mantelpiece and, in an avalanche of Dante, Moravia, Pavese, Anatole France, Bruno was hanging by one hand from the top shelf and then his hand slipped from it and he fell, first against the corner of the fireplace and then on to and off the arm of his chair. Somehow, on the way down, he managed to say, '*Kaputt* . . .' Then he crashed on to the floor. He gave one huge sigh, it seemed, and then he was white and open-mouthed, as if he had surprised himself.

'Bloody hell!' Adam was still holding his head.

Juliana said, 'Oh my God! My God!'

'Jesus Christ. Bruno. *Bruno*!'

Juliana said, 'No, no. Don't. Don't move him.'

Adam loosened Bruno's tie, noticing the coffee stain on the grey shirt, the spines of stubble on the sag of his throat, the white skin, the open eyes. Juliana straddled Bruno and punched down on his chest, again and again, and again.

'Are you all right?'

Adam said, 'Me? Of course.'

'That book hit you on the head quite hard.'

'Yes, it did.'

'Nothing's happening. He's not breathing that I can tell.'

'We'd better . . . call an ambulance. Dear Christ, please let this be a joke.'

Juliana said, '*Kaputt* and then . . . *Kaputt*, but really! It's too much, I think. I'm sorry.'

Adam said, 'Please don't do this, Juliana. Laugh. Because this is someone . . . you don't know him, but . . .'

Juliana said, 'Now you understand, yes? How quickly something is nothing. Nothing at all. Now you know how they all lived after the war. No trouble. Do you want to kiss me? I would like you to. Kiss me, yes, why not, why not? You want things to mean something? Things don't mean anything. There you are: look, look.'

Adam was saying, 'Yes, hullo. Ambulance. We need an ambulance. There's been an accident. Indoors, someone's had a fall. Yes. I'm calling from . . . from 36, Ranelagh Court, there's been an accident, and I very much fear . . . someone is dead. My name? My name is Adam Morris. No, I was visiting the . . . the gentleman and he . . . he had a bad fall. S.W., S.W. 14, I think it is. On the Upper Richmond Road. Soon as possible, please.'

He put the telephone back, looked at Bruno and looked away. How could a dead man's expression seem to be amused, conniving even? Juliana reached to touch Adam's jaw with the tips of her long fingers, and then her nail was picking at the corner of his mouth.

'All we can do is wait.'

'Yes?'

'Barbara will be worried.'

'*You* will be worried; but will she? She will not. Trust me.'

'If we don't get back for lunch.'

'Oh. Oh dear.'

Adam said, 'My brother told me that Tom killed somebody. When you were escaping from Paraguay. Is that true?'

'Derek should not have. But it doesn't matter.'

'Killing somebody? Doesn't matter? That's very . . . *modern*, Bruno would say. Have said.'

'Look, it was not . . . connected with . . . escaping. Except in the sense . . .'

'You and my brother . . . how do you get on?'

'Now you are curious? Derek is very generous, also quite . . . demanding. When it comes to Tommy. We get on very well, all of us. Look, it was Tommy or him, the man in Asunción. He didn't want Tommy to take me away. South America, these things happen.'

'South Kensington these things happen too, probably. What things exactly?'

'All right: he tried to stop Tommy taking me away. He came at us with a gun and Tommy . . . defended himself.'

'I see. Do I?'

'I think you see. *I* see. Why this is so important now; because it is not, is it?'

Adam said, 'What man was this exactly?'

'Everyone had guns there, many guns. The man thought I was . . . for him. Let's say.'

'He was your lover.'

'Oh, lover . . . He liked to fuck me. You wouldn't understand that.'

'What was his name?'

'Much it matters! Wolf Schmitt.'

'Like the California beer.'

'Excuse me.'

'Wolfschmidt. It's a beer they have in California.'

'I wouldn't know. But that was his name. The name he used anyway.'

Adam said, 'And Alexi – '

Juliana looked at him. 'You should not think what you are thinking. It is not true.'

'And if it were, what does it matter? Is that where we are?'

'I will never tell Tommy,' she said. 'And anyway . . .'

' – he knows?'

'Not at all,' she said. 'He *almost* knows. Which . . . keeps us . . . together.'

'I imagine. Dear God, I keep expecting Bruno to . . . say something. Not true. I feel . . . as if he's waiting for me to say something. Can it be "Sorry"? The thing being, I always thought he was a kind of joke; the kind that dispensed money if you stood on his toes. Damn and blast it, you know? I feel as if . . . I don't know, I missed something.'

'You did. The ambulance is coming now.'

'I'd better go down. Do you want to come?'

'I stay here with him. In case he needs anything.'

'I don't know anything much about you, Juliana, but I'm willing to bet it's all true.'

vi

'We didn't stay,' Adam said, 'because there wasn't anything to stay *for*. I didn't know who to contact, or even if there was anyone. One minute you're taking someone a Christmas present, the next you're getting ready to go to his funeral. I suppose it'll be the same with one's own. God may be a comedian, but He's rarely a very funny one.'

'You never really liked him all that much,' Barbara said, 'did you? Bruno.'

'But I did somewhat love him, I realise. If only because he was such fun to imitate.'

'You always made him sound funnier than he actually was.'

'Even when he was . . . lying there . . . I wanted to . . . not laugh exactly. I wanted it to be something silly that he could have done and then have undone. I always dreaded him calling and now . . .'

'You do know you've got quite a large bump on your

head, don't you? I've got some arnica in the bathroom cupboard.'

The telephone was ringing. Adam said, 'I still wouldn't be surprised if that was him. Hullo.'

'Adam? Mike. Terrible, terrible thing. I can hardly believe it. Shocking. Incredible. Heart-breaking. Tragic.'

Adam said, 'Are you doing a synonym-check by any chance? If so, how come "devastating" missed the cut? Are you not devastated? Everyone else is, always; totally in most cases. Will your life ever be the same again? You bet it will. I doubt if it's all that different now.'

'All right, all right; callous sod, aren't you? But it does make me wish we'd at least got round to doing *Life and Loves* with him though, poor old Brunowski, before he shuffled off the mortal coil.'

'No reason why we shouldn't still do it. Once you've finished massacring extras in Paraguay.'

'Are you writing an obit at all, old son? You should. You know all the stories.'

'Only the ones that aren't fit to print. I could call the *Telegraph*, I suppose.'

'He deserves that much after the way you treated him. He'd still be alive if it weren't for you probably. While we're at it, Ad; about our friend Carlo . . .'

'Tell me.'

'He seems to have gone off message rather. I thought you might know what was going on.'

'Since when did the scribe know what's going on? You're the ranking Pharisee around here. If you don't know, who does?'

'Last thing I heard,' Mike said, 'darling Julia'd raised a few of her usual impossible last-minute demands. Hot and cold running champagne at all hours in her Winnebago. She does love you though.'

'Well, that's all that matters.'

'Must come of not really knowing you too well. She hasn't called you, has she, at all?'

'No one's called me and I haven't called anyone. At all. Not recently. Except the ambulance service.'

'The thing is, Carruthers, it's very quiet out there tonight.' Mike was doing his best, not bad, imitation of Roger Livesey. 'Too quiet.'

'I thought that was my line,' Adam said.

'Slow on cue, you miss your chance.'

'Story of my life.'

'I don't like it, old son. I don't know what it is exactly, but I don't. One bit. Keep me posted, Ad. We're in this bloody jungle together. Remember that.'

'And when and where is the funeral? I take it you were about to ask.'

'"Keep me posted" was supposed to cover that. Obviously.'

'Not the way you did it, maestro. Would you mind trying it again?'

'*Keep me posted*. Honestly, Adam. When you've killed people, it's time to grow up. I might have known, mind you. Everyone says she's a bitch.'

Adam wrote a six-hundred word obituary of Bruno Laszlo for the *Daily Telegraph* and dropped a self-induced tear on the finished copy. On the first Wednesday of the New Year, he drove, alone, to the crematorium where a few dozen people, subdued by the chilly sunshine, shook each other's hands or kissed cheeks before going into the so-called chapel to watch Bruno's coffin slide into the Harrow Road entrance to the underworld. Jill Tabard, who had starred in *The Woman In Question*, was adjacent to Adam, but not close.

'*Facilis descensus Averno . . .*'

'Trust Adam Morris to say something no one can understand.'

'Easy the descent to Avernus. Virgil. Bruno'd understand.'

'Bruno isn't here,' Jill said. 'Nor is Mike, I notice.'

'Who's the youngish man in the black knitted hat with the ill-advised pompom that everyone's being so nice to?'

'That would be Bruno's son. Eddie.'

'God help me, I never knew he had one.'

'Nor did he, all that often.'

When there seemed to be nothing more to be done, most of the audience moved out of the beige room, past an incised plaque commemorating the opening of the premises by some minor royal, and edged towards the car park. Once on the pavement, Jill turned the other way and so was facing Adam, but not looking at him.

'Jill . . . darling.'

'Yes.'

'Is something wrong?'

'Wrong? Because someone we both knew is dead? Why should it be?'

'You're being very . . . terse.'

'I'm not saying you weren't quite right, of course.'

'Well, I nearly always am. Except when I'm wrong. About what exactly was I, *not*?'

'Me, weren't you? Being too old and nothing like breasty enough to play Eliza Lynch. Things you say do have a way of getting back to people, but how could you be expected to know that?'

Adam said, '*What?* When did I ever say that? When did I ever *think* that? Who told you I did? As if I can't guess. I don't need to guess.'

Jill put her arm through his. 'Oh darling, why is everybody in the business *such* a bastard?'

'As Bruno would say . . . I don't know what he'd say. Probably "Dere are worse things to be, to tell you de truce."'

'So now you've got Julia.'

'*They*'ve got Julia,' Adam said. 'If they really have. I've got no illusions about being of their party or privy to their plans. Mike told you that I'd said that about you, presumably.'

'He had to be honest, didn't he? Top-of-the-range bastard.'

'Makes you almost love him, doesn't it?'

'Aren't you the clever one?'

'How's Septimus?'

161

'Fifteen. Five feet eight, and counting. You know he got a scholarship to Eton.'

'The word is out. Does he like it?'

'Loves it. Denis *adores* it. He goes down to house matches with champers on ice in the boot and knows people's nicknames and everything. Seppy was man of the match last week. Denis practically did a lap of honour. Have you been to *Nibbles* yet?'

'We don't seem to go out as often as we used to.'

Jill said, 'Darling, I don't know if I'm supposed to tell you, but Carlo slipped me a copy of the script of your *Life and Loves* to read.'

'At my suggestion. You'd do Joannie wonderfully. Better than anyone I can imagine.'

'You are sweet. It's a beautifully written part.'

'That's code for "not for me", isn't it?'

'Trouble is,' Jill said, 'once an ageing Mum, always an ageing Mum. However glam you make her. Of course, some might say, I *am* an ageing Mum, but . . .'

'Life can be that kind of a bitch, kiddo.'

'Spoken like a man who thinks he's exempt.'

'Thinks, no; imagines, slightly.'

'Writers!' she said. 'You do have two bites of every cherry, don't you?'

'Which gives us two chances to break a tooth; and rarely get a lot of cherry. How did you get here?'

'Cab.'

'Confident that some kind sir would run you home. Nothing ageing about you, Miss Tabard; nothing that's visible to the naked eye. Lucky for you I'm going your way. But then who wouldn't be?'

'Still got the Merc.'

'Still got the *same* Merc, it says in my script. Which way is your way actually, these days?'

'I'm staying with Denis in Lamb's Conduit Street. I'm not sure it's living. But he's very sweet. We're not exactly Adam and Eve, but we can comfort each other with left-over apples.'

'Lamb's Conduit Street. Flat? House?'

'House; bang next to a pub. And I do mean bang. Frequently. But he couldn't resist it, could he? The street, I mean, not the house. Says it all, some of it.'

'What happened to Norman Segal?'

'Norman Segal. He went walkies, did Norman: blamed me when Carlo kicked him off *Eliza Lynch*.'

'After you'd done everything you could to get Carlo to keep him on it.'

'And then some.'

'Oh God, did you really?'

'I thought Carlo was having a heart attack, but apparently it was a good time. Much good it did anybody except him. Oh, darling, what does it matter? You're such a monogamist. Why do funerals make me horny?'

Adam said, 'Can't help you there.'

'Strange, isn't it, the lure of doing something one ought to be ashamed of? It's right here and then down on the left. Come on up and have a second-hand nibble. Den brings home tons more than we can eat.'

Adam said, 'Do you know, I will? They make *me* hungry. Funerals.'

Jill let them in by a black door just beyond a short fence with a sign on it asking 'Patrons' to respect the pub's neighbours.

'Look what I found at the cemetery,' Jill said, as they went into the first-floor drawing room.

Denis was sitting at a desk by the window at the side of the room, comparing designs for a new menu through rectangular shell-rimmed half-glasses. 'Adam! *Quelle joie!*' He jumped up. 'The *neige d'antan* as unblemished as ever!'

As they embraced, Adam said, 'How are you, Denis?'

'My fettle seems fine for the time of year. Always allowing for a touch of the Gibbons, dear. Declining, but not yet falling; but never look too closely. As for you, your sere isn't even yellow yet. How do you do it? No need whatever to say, but be warned: it will be taken down and used, pitilessly, as evidence against you.'

'Adam's hungry.'

Denis said, 'And shall be served, *instanter*, if not sooner. One Rupert Nisbet called, Miss Tabard, and craved immediate audience. So I should keep him waiting if I were you, but then if I were . . . the world would be a different and prettier place. Not altogether a bad idea. But I ramble.'

'I'll count to ten.'

'Maud isn't here, so come into the kitchen instead, Adam, and savour a taste of yesterday.' Denis led the way into the steel and vinyl kitchen, with its centrally suspended storage spaces and side-by-side ovens. '*Entre nous*, who or what is Rupert Nisbet?'

'Casting director, can he be?'

'Hope so, dear. How's Bra?'

'Holding up.'

'I think you just may've used that one before.'

'Unworthy then, unworthy now. True nevertheless. She's very well. What she'd do for a kitchen like this one!'

'She doesn't have to, if she doesn't want to. I can talk to the people who put it in for me and they'll do the same for her, in the nicest possible way. Do help yourself to whatever stimulates the phagocytes. It rarely takes much in my experience.'

'We're looking at fifty grand plus, aren't we? For a kitchen like this.'

'Debatable, dear. My pleasure to play the Armenian on your behalf. Twenty per cent orf for cashypoo. I shall never forget the way you both – '

'Ancient history. Time you did. Forget it. It wasn't much.'

'Ah, the bad old days. You know something? I miss them more and more.'

'Do you hear from Gianni at all?'

'He's a *paterfamilias,* dear. Sent me a *Buon Natale* card featuring self, wife and four raven *ragazzi* of various ages. Plus his *buco's* just posted its first star in the Michelin. Just the kind of salt my wounds need, dear. No, I wish him all the luck in the world and not ever such a lot more. Truth to tell – and it must *not* become a habit – Gianni's not what I miss. One bit. I have a very accommodating young *sous-chef* who lives in Ribbon Dance Mews, if you can believe that. More apt than convenient, but you can't have it all, and you're lucky if you get even a *soupçon*. Young*ish*, I should've said; action man: shaved top and bottom. But I do so miss the good old bad old days. My friends, the ones who've survived, they all have "relationships", dear, and "civil partners" and I *do* know what all else, because they will keep telling me about them. I only ever wanted uncivil ones. Whatever do they keep in their closets these days? Ultra-fluffy spare towels and dinky duvets I presume, because absolutely everything that used to be locked away is now out in the middle of the floor. The love that dared not speak its name has become the most garrulous sweetheart in town. You know what it's killed, of course, don't you, all this outing and abouting? The sweet sin of it all, dear; Sodom's now turned into a garden suburb full of people in sleeveless vests doing press-ups and cleaning the motor. Talk about cities of the plain! Couldn't be plainer, most of them! Not mother's idea of fun, one bit. What we got off on was fear. Leicester Square isn't really Leicester Square without Mavis and her big blue van. You have to be a period piece like yours truly if you don't want to be seen as sincere and faithful and *responsible* and politically pi. You know my best treat these days? Catching people who come into *Nibbles* and try to put oysters and things in their plasticated bags. And then letting them off, like crackers. We had a woman last week who tried to steal some of our signature lobster soup in her douche bag.'

Adam said, '*Bisque dat qui cito dat.*'

'For all I know, you're absolutely right. I'd've had the lady for Christmas if I hadn't already spotted her using the mayonnaise spoon for the vinaigrette. Back to Stoke Newington with you, madam, and serves you right if Eric's home when you get there!'

'Septimus is well, I gather.'

'And straight. So the girls tell me.'

'They don't.'

'They don't have to, dear. He'll probably round on me in the end, and then I shall know that I haven't failed him. The one fear I've still got. Apart from Madam Mortality.'

'It won't happen.'

'That's what I'm afraid of.'

'No, it isn't,' Adam said. 'And it won't. Got to go. Happy New Year, Den. Lovely nosh. More power to your dildo.'

'That's a low blow, but it's better than no blow at all.' Denis kissed Adam, courteously, very near the mouth. 'On we go, dear. And never, *never* ask what happens to the hindmost.'

Adam turned right into Red Lion Square as the lights came on. A fox was crossing, unhurriedly, from the short pavement and went through the railings into the greenery. When he got home, he told Barbara about it. 'The wild tends to be just a little smaller, and neater, than you expected. Guess what.'

'Must I?'

'Not when I tell you what it is: Mike couldn't even come to the bloody funeral. Oh I know what you're thinking: he didn't kill him.'

'I wasn't thinking that at all and you didn't, so don't say you did. Rachel's got a new . . . follower.'

'Explains . . .'

'That she wants us to meet.'

'That's quick. Why? Does she want us to?'

'Seems he's a great admirer of your fiction. Does that help? Jonty . . . Logan. He was a pupil of Gavin Pope's at Colchester. Used to be ultra-left; now he's New Labour, whatever that is.'

'Socialism with a nose job,' Adam said, 'served with sun-dried tomatoes and the hint of a wink from the head waiter. Reminds me: Denis sent you some éclairs which I left in the boot. I don't know why I haven't told you this before but . . . Juliana's converting to Judaism.'

'Dear God!'

'Apparently so. Maimonides put the 'fluence on her.'

'Who?'

'This Hebe she came across in the south of Spain. Do you know how much Tom's making these days?'

'Plenty, I presume.'

'And he never has to do rewrites. I probably should've gone into property.'

'I always wanted you to,' Barbara said. 'And then I could've left you; and found a violinist to live with. You're almost telling me something and you don't quite dare. What? And why?'

'Might it be because I don't quite – just not *quite* – know you well enough?'

'Boring!'

'The only charge that gives me the chills. Why would she choose to be Jewish? If you asked me to, what would I say honestly?'

'Alexi, am I right?'

'What about Alexi?'

'I obviously am.'

'I meant –'

'I always had a tiny little suspicion it was cuckoo time. Now, it seems, the eggs's got feathers on it. Does Tom not know, do you imagine?'

'I was the only one who didn't, is that where we are?'

Barbara said, 'You're such a moralist all the time, anyone would think you were the one who had something to hide.'

'I wish. Does it affect how you feel about him? Alexi.'

'I'm not sure how much I do. Or did. Or will. I think . . . they were probably . . . being kind to us. Coming here.'

'As if . . . someone had told them that one of us was dying. I wish she didn't call him Tommy.'

'Someone knows you're home.'

Adam picked up the telephone. '*Allo*. No, sorry: hullo.'

'You'll never guess what's bloody well happened.'

'And I don't suppose I shall ever much care,' Adam said. 'You're now going to ask me when Bruno's funeral is; as if you didn't know bloody well that it was today.'

'Of course I bloody well knew,' Mike said. 'Why do you think I went to Golders Green?'

'No idea. Visiting Evelyn Waugh's birthplace, were you?'

'That's where I thought it was. And it wasn't.'

'Yes, it was.'

'The funeral.'

'Do you know something? Even after all this time, Mike, I almost believe you're telling the truth.'

'Look, I'll come to the memorial service, all right? Promise. Was Jill there?'

'We both missed you. Like anything.'

'I'll even say a few words,' Mike said. 'I'll be too choked to say more. Adam . . .'

'Still here.'

'I've always thought of us as friends. From way back. If not before.'

'You're cramming on an awful lot of sail suddenly, skipper.'

'One thing before I say anything else: I love the script, OK? *Eliza.* I don't know what you've heard from whoever but it's not true: I don't want to change a word. Apart from a few . . . I certainly do *not* intend to get another writer in.'

'In other words, Carlo wants to, is that what this is about?'

'On the contrary. You'd never have been on it if it weren't for me. I'm not asking for thanks, but I do think . . . I'm entitled to a little loyalty.'

Adam said, 'You do do choked very well, I must say. What's going on?'

'Do just one thing for me. After all these years. One thing, would you? Call Carlo.'

'And say what?'

'Take some soundings.'

'Why can't you? No one swings a better lead than you do. I don't even know where he is.'

'I thought as much,' Mike said. 'I thought as much.'

'Second one was better,' Adam said.

'You're talking to a drowning man, you callous bastard.'

'What have you got to drown about, Mike, exactly? You own more rubber rings than anyone I ever met.'

'I still haven't had anything on paper, you bastard. From Carlo.

168

Oh I know: more bloody fool me. All right: you know who's arrived in London and is now staying in a river-front suite at the Savoy?'

'No idea.'

'Sorry, but you said it a shade too quickly.'

Adam said, 'No . . . idea.'

'Only Jake Leibowitz. Has he called you yet?'

'I haven't spoken to Jake since I turned him down on *The Siren's Song*.'

'Big mistake. Which even you can be guaranteed not to make again. Deny it. You know who's behind all this? Julia. And you know something else, don't you? Never give people their first big break, Adam, because they never, never forgive you. They'll wait *decades*, literally, to give you the shaft.'

Adam said, 'Mike, I promise you – '

'Do you just? Well, unfortunately, you're bang wrong. Because guess who's Carlo's number one gin-rummy partner these days.'

'Pass.'

'How about Daniel Bradley?'

'Dan?'

'Ever since he avoided going to clink and fled the country, he's gone from strength to bloody strength.'

'He did not flee the country: he was acquitted. Rightly. And he's now – '

'I know what he is now,' Mike said, 'so don't tell me: a bloody good actor making up for lost time. In all directions. Prominent senior citizen of Shagsville, I'm told. Bloody idiot, I could've made him into a major star right after Cambridge and he knows it. I loved that man and this is how he rewards me. There's a plot for you. The one man I ever really cared a damn about – apart from you, Adam, goes without saying. Call Carlo and tell him he'd be making a big mistake, will you do at least that much? You do believe I went to Golders Green, don't you? Adam?'

'I'm trying.' Adam was making winding-up motions to Barbara. 'You're probably wrong about the whole thing, Michael. In which case calling Carlo is the last thing I should do.'

'Unless I'm right.'

'In which case, there's no point in calling him.'

'And that's what you call friendship, is it? That's what you call friendship.'

'I call Carlo and the next thing I know you'll be telling Jill that I got you fired.'

'Jill won't even talk to me. The menopause and effect.'

'She'd still be brilliant in *Life and Loves*.'

'Think so?' Mike said. 'Know something: you could be right. Know something else? Time we made the best bloody movie either of us has ever made. Play it right and Carlo'll set it up just to avoid having to face either of us ever again, unless we all win Oscars, in which case . . . loveya, kiddo! With Jill as Joannie.'

'You've just realised you always loved her, haven't you?'

'Why do you have to be such a bastard? But it's true: I have, always. You know what's wrong with *Eliza,* don't you?'

'If it's the script, that's not the kind of kiss I was looking for.'

'Knowing Jake, it'll go so far over budget Carlo'll have to sell a chunk of the Cayman Islands to stay in business.'

'Meanwhile we'll be home free.'

'I've always, always wanted to make *Life and Loves.* You know that. Your best script ever. And Jill'd be wonderful. I actually always did love her, you know that, don't you, Adam? Deep down. You wouldn't call her, would you, for me? Some women, a very few, get better as they get older. Barbara all right?'

V

On the publication day of *Into Africa,* Adam Morris was again due to be the guest on Alan Parks's long-running radio programme, *Book Now.* After breakfast, he went into his room and opened the novel again, in the furtive hope that, scanned with dispassionate partisanship, it just might still seem as good as it had before the critics were invited to do justice to it. He winced twice, and smiled once, before he looked out of the window and saw the ticking taxi which the producer had sent to take him to Broadcasting House.

In the foyer at B.H., Adam sat reading the fat proof copy of *Thank Christ,* which Alan Parks had sent him and which he had brought for inscription. When its author came out of the lift, Adam slipped it into his briefcase and stood up.

'Good to see you, Ad. How are you?'

'I could try "apprehensive". You look – '

'I know I do, but fortunately it doesn't matter; this is radio. Shall we repair to the quizzing place? They've dug us a studio in the lower basement. The doghouse being too good for runners in the superannuation stakes, apparently. What've you got to be apprehensive about? You know I'm a pussycat these days, bent only on allaying the mange of time.'

Adam said, 'Samuel Marcus pronounces it pissy-cat these days, I imagine.'

'Just because I made it known that Our Greatest Living's latest fabulous fabrication was a litter of shavings held over from his previous excursions into incest, lesbianism, jackbootiquery, transexuality and all the other forms of itching powder we can most of us get plenty of at the vicarage?'

'Your opinion wouldn't have anything to do with him being about to marry a certain Joyce Hadleigh, would it?'

'A presently *very* certain Joyce Hadleigh, seeing as they're joined at the hype. I don't know which of them is more welcome to the other. She started a little late, did Joycey, in the celebrity stakes, but she's undoubtedly worked her way through the field like a good 'un. If she can saddle up and ride Samuel Marcus all the way to Stockholm, good luck to them both, he lied. Soon after which, your friend Sammy will be Sir Samuel and her surgically renovated ladyship will be asking us all to her three times twenty-first birthday party; some of us.'

Adam said, 'I don't expect to make the cut myself.'

As the lift doors opened to the basement, Alan said, 'How's Barbara?'

'Well, thank you. And Shirley?'

'You know Donald died, of course, don't you? Our poor little tuppenny bun, as Shirl called him sometimes.'

'I thought I wrote to you, both.'

'So you did. I could give you a list of people who didn't, but why would I do that? You foinds out who your friends are when you foinds out who your friends are, isn't that the sorry truth though, some of it? Poor little chap lived longer than we ever expected and it was still very hard for her to take. You see that?'

They were close together in the narrow, false light of the corridor leading to the studio.

'See what?' Could it be that Alan was drawing attention to the liverspots on the back of his hand?

'You do,' Alan said. 'Exhibit A: it's known as a teardrop. I mention Donald and . . . stormy weather. I haven't exactly been a model of fidelity over the years, far as Shirl's concerned.'

'Have you not?'

Alan pulled the heavy door. 'You're as tactful as you are transparent, Ad. But here's the funny thing: ever since Don died I've been . . . you name it, if it's got a name. No, not that one; not sorry for her; not one bit. No, nor yet relieved. Oddly, the opposite: I actually miss the poor little bugger. Avoided him when he was alive and now . . . I look at her, Ad, and I love her. Desire isn't of the essence, but . . . mysteriously enough, even

172

that's . . . try: resurgent, as it hasn't been for a decade or two. Not in any conjugal sense.'

The door was open only a foot. It gave access to a little booth with doors leading both ways from it. 'And does Shirley . . . ?'

'Reciprocate, are you wondering possibly? After the way I've treated her? Have you been an unfailingly faithful husband or are you not quite the dull dog you seem?'

'I don't do revelations.'

'Do you do antique croissants? Because come on in in that case; there'll almost certainly be some. Yes, and welcome to the *café d'Antan*. The Ron-Dave-who of the intellectuals. And what about Barbara? Is it true what I don't hear?'

Adam said, 'Which is what?'

'That's always the question. Along with when and where and other notoriously tough ones.'

'We shall not go down the path to the rose garden, you and I, nor yet open the gate.'

Alan said, 'Our lovely producer'll be in in a minute. You knew all along, didn't you?'

'Remind me.'

'Simon Hobbs.'

'Simon Hobbs.'

'Son of Anna of the same name,' Alan said. 'What used to be Cunningham. And now is again. The poet lady who was all the raj when we were first undergladuates . . .'

'Anna. Of course I remember Anna. Only our best living poet, if you ask me. Yours and mine and to hell with Innes Maclean. Is she still alive? Those lines of hers, "I once was someone else/ People still mistake me for" – '

'Still resonate? Wasn't it the truth though? And isn't it still? The moving finger writes and, having writ, does a bit more of the same, only rarely as good. Simon's her now grown-up son.'

'And what's he got to do with Barbara?'

'Barbara? You tell me.'

'You were fishing.'

'Never go anywhere without my rod, pole or perch. Shirl's the only one I know about; who knows Simon. Since he was . . . not quite fifteen. And, yes, in case you're wondering covertly, knows him in the full frontal biblical sense is what has recently broken . . . cover. She could probably have gone to gaol if somebody'd found out at the time. Corrupting a minor. Imagine being corrupted by a woman like that when you were fourteen. Very heaven, am I right? She met him at some kids' birthday party and . . . miserable, runty, buck-toothed little chap, apparently, at the time, she took a shine to him; of course. Call it pity, penance or cradle-snatching, it stayed shiny, and rocked, for nearly twenty years. Even after he was married. Colour her Camilla, or not.'

'And you never guessed.'

'I was a bit busy at the time,' Alan said. 'You know me. A tracked vehicle steered by its own tracks, as the driving licences used to say. So occupied covering my own muddy trail I don't take time to notice anybody else's. She didn't tell me till Don died.'

'And . . . what was . . . your reaction?'

'Try believing immense relief. I don't think anything contributed more to what I suddenly came to feel about Shirley than . . . finding she had a secret love. I felt she'd let me off. Generosity. That's how it hit me: just the particular ton of bricks I needed. If God exists, He has my thanks, and my phone number, if He ever cares to get back to me. The millennium may well be His last chance. Mad maybe, but I was . . . grateful to her, Shirl. Having Simon – the secret and the pleasure – was what gave her the strength to love Donald the way she did, all those years. Amazing, but I found I loved her for that. That and this and a squeeze of the other; because who knows what lubricates the rusty lock again and turns, not to mention stiffens, the tired key? Suddenly, you're back into the rose garden with a bolt to shoot. She's a great woman I happen to have married and I didn't realise till . . . If you care to know why I'm now officially reclassified as a pussycat, that's why.'

'So that's why you look different: you're a happy man.'

'Who loves his lawful wedded wife. Not easy to handle at my time of life. Hence the symptomatic tear. But, lo! the lovely Leila has entered the control room. Hi there, Leila.'

'I'll be right there, Alan. Hullo, Mr Morris.'

'Oh Christ, she's a Mr Morriser! Which reminds me: your book, will you sign it for me?'

ii

'Only me.'

Barbara said, 'Darling! How lovely to see you! Should I have known you were coming?'

'To tell you the hideous truth,' Rachel said. 'I needed somewhere I could throw up again in a hurry if I needed to.'

'Come in! Make yourself at home. Throw up. Are you in trouble?'

'Adam all right?'

'He's fine. He's doing this broadcast. Narcissus has his pool before him, as he – and you – might say.'

'They always tell you pregnancy isn't a sickness; so why am I throwing up?'

'It'll pass. Do you want something?'

'God, yes. I wish I knew what. I don't honestly know who to talk to.'

'To eat, I meant. About what?'

'Tell me something honestly, Mum. Jonty. What do you think about him, really?'

'He's very charming.'

'And Adam?'

Barbara said, 'You should ask him.'

'Should I not have married him? Speak freely.'

'Invitation to never being forgiven. I truly don't know who should marry whom, *ever*. You can only tell by the results.'

'He's very . . . *chawming*, isn't he? Jonty. Is it genuine, do you think?'

'Oh darling, don't keep trying to make me say things you're afraid to say for yourself.'

'I would never do that.'

'The things we would never do are the ones we want other people to.'

'Consciously, I mean.'

'And then we blame them for doing them.'

'You had doubts.'

Barbara said, 'I wanted you to be happy. You looked as if you were and . . .'

'An ox sat on your tongue, as Aeschylus would say. Are you happy or were you when . . . ?'

'What's wrong, Rachel?'

'. . . you were my age.'

'I'm not sure I ever was,' Barbara said, 'even when I was.'

'I always *thought* you were, you and dad. Happy. You made it seem so easy, and so natural. When we were small . . .'

'We did our best.'

'Not altogether nice of you, possibly. To make it look so . . . natural. Do you think he's clever? Jonty. Do you?'

'What do I know about clever?' Barbara said. 'Suppose you tell me what's happened.'

'You know *all* about clever. How many men have you known, Mum, in your life?'

'Early pregnancy is not a good time for dispassionate assessment. Men can get quite . . . distant when it comes home to them that their boyish days are numbered. Is that what's happening? If so . . .'

Rachel said, 'I think he's using again.'

'Using.'

'I don't know what but . . . I'm sure of it. We've got this joint account and . . . it's gone down recently; with a bump. I got this fattish advance for a book about Roman women. Lays of ancient Rome, as dad put it – '

'Not where he can find it again, I hope.'

'I woke up this morning and I looked at Jonty and – I seem to

176

have done it again, Mum, I seem to have bloody well done it again.'

'And what is it? And when did you do it before?'

Rachel breathed in through flared nostrils. She could imagine the relief of telling her mother about her pregnancy in California and all the things which she had promised Adam she would never reveal. That was the cramp that held her hunched in her chair, tears stalled in her eyes. 'You know what it's like with men,' she said. 'You get into things long before you know what kind of thing you've got into. You don't know the tenth of it when you start, do you?'

'Then again the unknown's part of what we want, isn't it?'

'And it's always got less to do with them than they imagine, doesn't it? And then we blame them.'

'Using what exactly, do you suppose?'

Rachel was reaching for Kleenex. 'Once they've used heroin, that's always . . . the one they go back to.'

Barbara said, 'Have you ever . . . ?'

'Not yet. It makes people very sexy; did you know that?'

'Sorry, but I don't know anything much in that department. It makes me feel very old. We once smoked pot – they called it then – at a party in the south of Spain. Someone brought it over, in a paper bag, from Morocco. Before plastic. Bags.'

'And did you like it?'

'It made everyone very slow, and deeply, deeply boring. I remember a not young, unhandsome man called Sam asking, very seriously, if he could show us his erection. And your father said, "Show it if you must, but don't pass it around." Which seemed funny at the time. Or was it ten minutes later? Pretty well the same thing.'

'They do like you to do it with them,' Rachel said. 'Like alcoholics. I'm going to make a mess of it, Mum, life. I can see it coming, and going. I looked at him this morning when I woke up, the way I always have, smiling and happy, honestly, I thought I was, and I looked at him looking at me and it was . . . like being with someone who was dead. I know what you're thinking: it's not about Jonty, it's about Bill, but it isn't. I don't blame you, but . . . was it ever, ever like that with you?'

'No. Never.'

'He is clever though. And I do love him. When he's there. He said he loved me. He said a lot of things. Still does. He's good at that. And he likes dad's books, and company. A lot. And I am going to keep the baby and what I would like, very much, that's a glass of water. You haven't got a water biscuit, have you? He still hasn't got a job. He says he's writing a book. But he never shows it to me. With some Marmite on it, possibly?'

iii

'Are we all set? Because shall we do this now?'

Alan said, 'Ready when you are, Leila. So . . . listen, Ad, it's the time-honoured routine: when the green light flashes I shall morph into a completely strange monster and introduce you as if I'd never met you before and we take it from there, on the way to becoming bosom buddies within a matter of seconds.'

'Or seconds out.'

'Might be a cleverer way of putting it, but I'll forgive you.'

Leila was saying, 'Ten seconds then, studio. Green light coming . . .'

'Deep breath and . . . here we go.'

'. . . now.'

'Good evening and welcome to the one hundred and somethingth edition of *Book Now*. My guest this evening is Adam Morris, now − if he doesn't mind my saying so, and it's true even if he does − a highly seasoned, not to say veteran practitioner in the business, and pleasure, I trust, of composing novels that − unless I'm much mistaken, and when did that ever happen? − are calculated to amuse and incense that rare brand of readers who can manage words of two syllables and up without moving their lips or scratching their hirsute and recondite recesses. Let's start with an excerpt, shall we, Adam? Chapter one, verse one.'

Adam took a deep breath, steadied himself, and began: 'When recruited as a mercenary to stage a coup in Zianda, Guy Fielden does not *wish* to be captured, tortured, executed, but he entertains a regular fantasy that he will be. Fear does not inhibit appetite; it is part of it. At school, two decades before, he had been a monitor who watched, and winced, with folded arms, as the head of the house laid into a bent boy. Fielden now feels a similar, appalled complicity with Major "Bob" Farrer, the leader of the mercenaries to whose strength he has been recruited for "top money". Guy is amused to call Farrer "Mister Kurtz" to those who do not take the reference. The major's first question, after a day of burning and shooting, is "Now who's for dinner?" Guy hates him and he would, he fears, die for him.

'Once a choirboy, Fielden's *imitatio* is not of Christ Himself, but of the robbers crucifed with Him: Guy dreams of being the other felon, paired with Farrer, in the crucifixion. His schoolboy Christianity craved "purity", the white symptom of corruption.'

Alan said, 'There you have it, some of it. This one seems to break new ground, Adam, taking place, as it does, not only in your customary patch of British West Hampstead but also in what was once British West, and Central, Africa before Harold Macmillan's wind of change laid everything flatulent. Africa is a place you know well, of course, as a result of your long service as a flak-jacketed hired gun.'

'I spent about three weeks, gunless, in Keenya, now known as Ken-ya, a longish while ago, doing some mostly unused rewriting on a movie, and I went to a literary gathering of the kind you so regularly ornament, Alan, in Georgetown two years ago now. That lasted about ten days. I don't get more hired than that.'

Alan said, 'And yet you have the nerve, and – I have to concede – the verve, to pass yourself off as a master of the meta-colonial arts and a proficient operator when it comes to the bush telegraph and adjacent activities. Hilda Heaven, your lubricious African tart comes – if I may appropriate a subtle culinary term – highly spiced and tastily upholstered, before proceeding to bare essentials. She has no shortage of what our greatest lady novelist

chose, in a recent masterpiss, to designate as "curved rounds".
Presumably, strictly between you and me and the tabloid press,
ever avid to pick up on a peccadillo, you've had a wealth of field
experience as a long-standing subscriber to the in-and-out club?'

'My novel is about the life of Saul Nathan, a North London
solicitor, who is asked by H.M.G. to go to Africa – '

'Give us that bit.'

Adam cleared his throat and assumed his impersonal voice.
'Saul specialises in tax affairs. He honours Sartre's recom-
mendation in "assuming" his Jewishness: he agrees to be what he
cannot escape being said to be. He honours what he cannot avoid
by choosing to inhabit an identity wished on him by others. One
can decide to be only what one is not. Such an existential decision
implies a vestigial, colourless second self which chooses the role to
enact. Saul may assist others to avoid tax, if they wish to, but only
by breaching the spirit of the law while remaining within the
letter. He himself honours the spirit too, a cook who never
swallows his own best recipes.'

Alan said, 'As *alter egos* go, he's pretty thoroughly altered, that
I'll grant you, but you know and I know – and even my auntie
Flo, who's a game old bird, she knows too – that an author can't
rely on his characters to know things he doesn't. Unlike the
divinity, you have to take responsibility for what you create.'

'The Africa that Saul Nathan sees, and I write about, is limited
to what he encounters and tries to deal with on two equally
hurried flights, commissioned by H.M.G., at an interval of twenty
years or so, first to try and save three black men from white so-
called justice and then, much later, to save a white man, whom he
happens to have known at school, from black so-called justice.'

'What you're telling me implies that the Africa, past and
peasant, that you describe, or rather imagine, is – dare I say it? –
schematically contrapuntal? Seems I do!'

'And no one says it better than you.'

'Appreciate that! Melodramatically even. Right, so: the first third
of the book is set in something not a million miles away from good
old Ian Smith's whiter-than-white Salisbury, as it was before

Robert Ebagum won all our hearts; and the second in, well, it could be anywhere run by some contemporary upstart tyrannical ex-sergeant turned field marshal with the name of Winston Churchill Abrahams, couldn't it? Any specific stogie-sucker in mind in that department?'

'Winston's an amalgam, you might say.'

'If I said he was a quasi-stereotypical caricature, would you be quick to mount your well-exercised high horse and gallop off in all directions?'

'Good old Stephen Leacock!' Adam said. 'I prefer conflation.'

'Nothing to worry about, I'm told, if it's treated promptly. You don't have any qualms about depicting friend Abrahams as a bloodthirsty buffoon who boasts of fancying roast leg of missionary when he's peckish?'

'Might it not possibly be that he's kidding when he tells Saul that? He also reminds Saul that before the Great War, the Belgians, on King Leopold's orders, killed six million Congolese and got paid by the number of ears they collected. By the standards of European civilisation, Winston's a . . . how about pussy-cat?'

'You've been accused of having a reactionary go at the large number – so Tariq Tariq insists in the Workers' Revolutionary *Standard* – of hard-working, anti-corruption African governments that are struggling bravely to cope with the consequences of villainous white supremacy.'

'Man can be a savage beast,' Adam said. 'No matter what his colour. And also a heroic one, at times; think of the scene where the Ziandan police inspector Johnson saves Nathan from a mob that's righteously sacking the U.N. mission.'

'"Gungadin meets Uncle Tom", is how one impartial critic and old friend of yours, and mine, describes the gallant, locally coloured officer of the law.'

'Most of my white characters are infinitely nastier than any of the black ones. And a lot less fun.'

'Your Saul Nathan,' Alan said, 'he's somewhat heroically unheroic, I'll give you that. Especially when it comes to the rather ignominious anti-sex scene with Hilda Heaven. I did like it when he noticed how pink her heels were. Not a thousand miles from the Adam Morris that I see before me, your Mr Nathan, can it be?'

'Eight hundred and sixty-three. Miles. Minimum. Saul's a composite figure, who does all kinds of things I never did or will or could.'

'But he does stand in for you, and maybe for me and a host of other crouch potatoes: the outsider insider, showerproof in most weathers, but praying to the God we don't believe in that the deluge won't hit us yet a while. Saul's decent and he's . . . *moyen sensuel,* to name but a fool very like both of us, if you'd care to have this dance with me, and he's a commentator very glad not to be down there on the pitch with the muddled oafs who actually play the game. But are you not just a little too eager to score at both ends and never get tackled yourself?'

'Winston's a parody drawn from life, but then so is Douglas Douglas – '

Alan said, 'That's the glassy-eyed character breakaway president in the first part, based on one Ian Smith, if anyone's memory goes back that far – '

'Who hanged three men who had just been reprieved by H.M.G., thus using, and parodying, the old machinery of British justice to back the interests of an upstart white minority. Ancient history at this point, but – '

Alan said, 'Let me quote you a little more from the Leavishite review by an old mutual friend of ours, well, old anyway; and I'm not all that sure about the mutuality, Innes Maclean: "Adam Morris's Africa is a black and white show without the song and dance, a confection too neatly zebra-striped –" Innes is on fire and safari at the same time "– to carry the mark of anything but Mr Morris's customary desire to have things both ways: the moralist and the clown, the progressive and the reactionary, the hare and the hound." That's a whole lot of "both" he's crammed in there, master Innes. But doesn't he have a point?'

'He does,' Adam said. 'And it's always the same one: he has to be the only literary pundit with perfect pitch. He's been like that ever since he became the youngest fogey of them all, as I think you were witty enough to call him.'

'If not the first. Plagiarism is the badge of all our trade. At one point, while stuck in some benighted airport, waiting for the first and final call, Saul Nathan permits himself to wonder whether H.M.G. will award him a gong if he manages to save the black guys, which he doesn't, or maybe *because* he doesn't; not that he imagines anyone will be grateful, but purely because Whitehall will want to remind Douglas Douglas that he remains well and truly bogged in the do-do. Have you reached the stage of beginning to wonder if you'll ever get to join the O.B.E.s and C.B.E.s and similar antique gloominaries? You've got the big seven-oh looming up ahead. Just the kind of quavering candle that might grace your antique cake.'

'Never occurs to me.'

'No ambition whatsoever to take tea and Cherie's retro butties at Number Ten?'

'I'm not sure those things add too many cubits to anyone's stature, are you?'

'Me, I'll go on relying on my soap box till the last syllable of recording time. I was interested in . . . this passage, if you'd care to read it for us.'

'"Nathan is married to a lapsed Catholic. Mary is shackled to the shade of a faith in which she no longer believes, somewhat as Nathan is to Judaism. One of their sons, Christopher, was born with spina bifida. The other, Aaron, now runs a fish restaurant in San Diego where no reservations are taken. His line is always busy."'

'So Saul Nathan, he's the saviour who can't save the sum of things for love, any more than Guy Fielden and Major F. can for money, isn't that the ultimate irony behind *Into Africa*? The white man is the burden, is that where we are today? And worse to come tomorrow.'

Adam said, 'That's for you to judge.'

'Because when he comes home, safely as he imagines, to

London, having saved an old friend, whom he doesn't altogether like, from a fate he doesn't entirely deserve to escape – irony on irony, Saul discovers that he has been denounced, in one of the mags we both know and write for, as a crypto-fascist who's managed to do for a white man what, some twenty years earlier, he failed to do for the three blacks. And in addition, the nubile intern he's been giving extra-marital tuition to has blown . . . the gaffe to the tabloids. Instead of being a hero, Saul finds himself dumped by his wife, shames his kids and winds up being disbarred or whatever it is that sends solicitors down the swift Hebrus to the municipal dump. Henceforth, you tell us with some glee, he has to operate with a black mask over his face, so to speak, or not to speak, Nathaniel Hawthorne-style, working as a ghost brief writer – what the French call a *nègre*, you're fancy, unless it's generous, enough to inform us – for an alcoholic Old Etonian ex-competitor who embezzles old ladies' money and get away with it, not to mention her, often to Monte Carlo. So finally, and well into extra time, Innes Maclean would argue, more than a few people in your novel wind up manifestly hung, very well drawn and, in Saul's case, none too comfortably quartered, in Ultimissima Thule. Egg on every face. Just the stuff to give the droops, some might say.'

'If you say so, Alan.'

'Dare I add, unless it's subtract, that I savoured every disgracefully overdone moment of it? If anyone's looking for political incorrectness, Adam Morris, thou art the man!'

Leila's voice came through from the control room. 'Thank you both very much. Super stuff. I just need the intro from you again, Alan, and it's the one hundred and thirty-eighth edition actually.'

Alan sipped some water, re-addressed himself to the micro-phone and did the intro again, twice. He was signing Adam's proof of *Thank Christ* when Leila came through the door.

Adam said, 'Are you sure that was all right, Leila? Not too abrasive?'

'Abrasive's fine, as long as it's . . . fine.'

'Not abrasive enough, probably,' Adam said. 'One never says

what needs saying, for fear people'll hear it. Where are you from, actually, Leila, originally?'

'My parents are Palestinian,' she said. 'They now live in Beirut.'

Adam walked down Regent Street to the London Library, where he spent half an hour construing an article which Rachel had had published in the *The Journal of Roman Studies*. Its topic was triangularity and mirror imagery in Catullus's poetic contrivance. Adam smiled at his daughter's thanks to him for his 'valuable suggestions' with regard (the phrase was nicely apt) to poem 51, the version of Sappho, which – as 'Mr Morris has pointed out to me' is doubly duplicitous, since the masculine Catullus holds a Latin mirror to Sappho's Greek, and then, 'within the poem itself, the phrase "*sedens adversus identidem/ et spectat et audit*" breaches, by its very expression, the exclusivity of the face-to-face it celebrates. Catullus, the poet, cannot refrain from intrusion; his complicity, even with the character to whom he gives his own name, is disjunctive. He supplies two adverse points of his own triangle.'

Since it was too late to do any work before lunch, Adam decided, for the sake of his virtue and his waistline, to walk at least some of the way home to Tregunter Road. Hoping and dreading that *Into Africa* might be reviewed in it, he bought the first edition of the *Evening Standard* from the man outside the Ritz. When he reached Hyde Park Corner, he took the long pedestrian underpass to avoid having to cross three streams of traffic in order to reach Knightsbridge. Few people took the same route. Adam's footsteps echoed as he addressed himself to the long bore of the tiled tunnel. It reeked of what streaked the walls nearest the entrance.

He was reminded, by the tedium of the walk, of the futility of a morning spent in measured self-advertisement. Towards the middle of the traverse, a busker in a drab overcoat and flat cap was backed against the tiles playing *Liebestraum* on the violin. Adam felt in his pockets for change. He was throwing a pound into the empty violin case with the blind man's collapsed white stick in it, when there was a large presence at his side. He seemed to hear the approaching footsteps after the big black man was actually there.

'Excuse me, sir, you look like a generous man.' Now that it was too late, Adam made to walk on briskly. 'No, no, sir, listen to me, please, because . . .' There was a hand on his arm now. 'Did you drop this by any chance, sir?'

Adam continued to walk, but he felt like a dreaming dog which moved its feet but gained no ground. 'I wasn't carrying anything that I know of.' He had to look back though and there was the tall man, in a long, open khaki coat with a lazy belt, track trousers and grimy sneakers.

'Five pound note, man. Are you sure? When you blew your nose.'

'I don't remember doing that. I doubt if it's mine. You found it, you keep it. Your good luck.'

'Wait a minute, man, wait a minute. Perhaps I am *your* good luck. What's your hurry?'

'Would you kindly let go of me?'

'Check your pockets, old man. Make sure what you've still got or haven't got.'

Adam said, 'I haven't got anything. If you want the newspaper, you're welcome to it.'

'Are you afraid of me, old man? What are you afraid I'm going to do to you?'

'I asked you not to touch me. Please don't.' Adam had moved only a few yards from the violinist, who continued to play *Liebestraum* with repetitive indifference. 'Keep the money by all means.'

'Am I hurting you? I'm showing you respect; you should show me respect. I have a story I would like to tell you. A personal tale.'

'Very nice of you, but – with due respect – it's not my bedtime.'

'Oh, do you still have a bedtime? Congratulations. I need another one of these to go with this one. So I can pay the rent for my children. Have you got another one?'

'I told you: if that one was mine, you're welcome to it. I don't have another.'

'What's the matter with you, Grandpa? You look as if you are going to cry. Not many people about at this time of the day. I happen to know that. Don't be frightened. And don't look at him, he can't do anything because he's only got one leg. And he's blind. I could very easily take his money, but that would be a bad thing to do, am I right?'

'Let go of me. I did ask you.'

'Have you still got your wallet with you all right? You'd better check. Likewise the credit cards.'

'Take your hands off me. Now. Please.'

'Please is nice. Please is polite.' The man's breath was against Adam's ear. 'But it's not as good as a donation. You look a Christian man . . .' Adam twisted away from the heat of him and then loud fast footsteps were coming and, before Adam could be sure whether they came from the left or the right, there was an impact.

'There you are, you black bastard, serve you right, fucking monkey.'

The black man fell backwards, tried to regain his balance, tripped over Adam's leg and fell, with a yelp, to the concrete floor. The young man, in jeans, T-shirt and leather jacket, was already running towards where Adam had come in.

Adam called, 'Hey, wait a minute – wait a minute – thank you, but – hey!'

'Train to catch, rabbi. I'll 'ave that kiss another time.'

Adam started to walk on. It seemed unwise to run, and undignified.

'Hey, man, where you going? He's broke my bloody elbow. My bloody elbow's broke. You are a rabbi and you going to leave me? Look at this.' The man was sitting, knees up, one hand holding the other arm against his chest. 'At least help me to get up.'

'Look, stay there,' Adam said. 'I'll get some help. Don't move.'

'What did you want to do that for? Move? You've broken my bloody ribs too and all. It hurts when I, when I breathe, it hurts. Call an ambulance.'

Adam said, 'I will. I haven't got a telephone.'

'I'm not going to take it off you, man. You still afraid of me? You broke my bloody elbow. I can feel the bone. Look at this. Look at the blood. Look what you done.'

'I didn't do anything. I'll . . . go and call an ambulance.'

'I know what you'll do, you'll go straight home; you won't do nothing. I'm in pain.'

Adam had not gone far along the tunnel when a policeman came down the steps from outside. 'What's going on here?'

'Guy fell down and broke his arm. And he may be damaged elsewhere.'

'They broke my bloody arm, the rabbi and the other fellah – and my rib, broke 'em too, feels like. All I done was try and give him back some money he dropped. And this is what he do. This is his thanks. Arrest him, officer, before he does it again!'

Adam said, 'Look, just . . . take care of him, OK? He needs an ambulance.'

'I'll have your name and address, sir, if I may.'

Adam said, 'I was walking through the underpass and he started – '

'Your name and address, sir, please.'

'The guy's had an accident. Nothing to do with me. I don't want to make any trouble for him. Adam Morris, 15, Tregunter Road, that's S.W.10.'

'Have you got your driving licence with you, sir?'

'I'm not driving,' Adam said. 'Driving licence; I don't know. Have I? No. I have my card from the London Library; do you want to see that?'

The black man was sitting with his knees under his chin, holding his broken arm with the other hand. The violinist was groping with blind fingers for whatever had been thrown into his case.

'Hyde Park Corner underpass number three, injured man needs ambulance assistance. Non-lethal. Black male, I would say twenty-eight years old.'

As if he had taken thought and chosen it from a large repertoire, the violinist resumed playing *Liebestraum*.

Adam said, 'Look, I don't feel particularly well. I want to go home now.'

'We'll be getting in touch with you, sir, in due course.'

'In touch? What for? Someone crashed into the man, nothing to do with me, and he fell over and hurt himself. No one ever gets in touch after I phone up when yobs leave junk in our front yard.'

iv

Adam flagged a taxi in Knightsbridge. He sat in the back with the newspaper on his knees. When they reached Tregunter Road, he asked the cabbie to stop on the corner. He closed the cab door quietly and walked up to number fifteen and opened, and then closed, the front door as silently as he could.

'Adam?'

'Only me.' He walked across the hall and into his room and shut the door.

'Adam.'

'Don't worry. I'm all right.' He sat at his desk and opened the *Evening Standard*.

Barbara was outside the door. 'What's wrong?'

'Nothing. Don't worry.'

'Am I really supposed not to come in? Have you had anything to eat?'

'I'm not hungry. You can come in.'

'He hated the book.'

'Who did?'

'Two-faced bastard. Alan Parks presumably.'

'No, no, Alan was . . . Alan was fine. I haven't looked at this bloody thing yet. Probably haven't reviewed it, anyway. If you're not a journalist you never get notices these days. Innes bloody Maclean. Trust people you went to Cambridge with. Ha!'

'You look strange.'

'Do I? How?'

'And sound it. Unusually . . . white. Are you ill?'

'No,' Adam said. 'I'm old.'

'Everybody's old,' Barbara said. 'Do you need the doctor?'

'I'm OK.'

'You're manifestly anything but.'

'Anything but is exactly what I am. Always was.'

'Are you in pain?'

'Don't go away. Sit down, Ba.'

'I was going to get you a glass of water. Something's happened. What is it? What did he do, or say, that upset you, Alan?'

'Alan? Nothing. He was actually rather touching. He cried.'

'At the book?'

'No, no; not on the air. Over Donald and Shirley and . . . the human condition, I suppose. One tear, but a genuine one.'

'And?'

'Sorry, but if I cry, it'll be buckets.'

'Cry about what?'

'Strange,' Adam said, 'but they all want you to have a secret lover. *You*, I mean.'

'Do they? Why?'

'I could try: people do so hope other people aren't as happy as they seem.'

Barbara said, 'But then so do you, sometimes, don't you? Hope that. Might put some pepper on the boiled potatoes, isn't that it? I'm too good to be true; if I am. Don't bother to cry about that.'

'I'll wait for the spilt milk.'

'Something happened. What? You're bound to tell me sooner or later. If you really didn't want to, you wouldn't have closed the door like that.'

Adam said, 'If I'd taken a taxi home, it never would have. I was being moral. I should have known better. False economy and doctor's orders. England today.' He sighed and opened the paper to the Arts Section. 'Oh God, look at that, they've given *Into Africa* to one of those people with initials instead of a first name. Always makes them bitchy, for some reason. Thought so: he finds the scene with Hilda Heaven "gratuitously erotic". And he's lucky to get it. He thinks it tells us "more about the author than

the author well knows". But on the other hand, he has to admit
. . . not a lot but, he defies anyone not to read this book "without
a mixture of uneasiness and relish".'

The front door bell rang and then the knocker was rapped.

Barbara said, 'Are you expecting anyone?'

'That'll be the cop shop,' Adam said.

'The what? Why?'

Adam said, 'I'll get it. Routine inquiries. Clichés on wheels.
Mit flashing lights already.'

'What happened?'

'I didn't rob a bank. No such luck.'

Adam opened the door to two men, one in plain clothes, the
other in uniform.

'Mr Adam Morris?'

Adam led them into the living room. Barbara stood in the door
of his study, her forehead creased with sour surprise.

'I'm Inspector Harold Siddons. This is Detective Constable
McIlwraith. Begin at the beginning, shall we? Your full name
is . . .?'

'Full. Adam Ellis Morris. I never use the Ellis, but there it is.'

'And this is your permanent residence, is it?'

'This is my house,' Adam said, 'and here I am. Does that cover
it?'

'And your occupation would be what?'

Adam said, 'Would be . . . I'm a writer.'

'Retired then, are you?'

'Not according to the tax man.'

'As a rabbi, that would be.'

Adam said, 'Look, I am not and have never been a rabbi.
That was a . . . try "joke", by the joker who did not stay to
speak his name. Which someone has turned into a . . . try "job
description", shall we?'

'Journalist then, would be more accurate?'

'Not at all. I write books. And things. Films.'

'Your age being what?'

'Good point. Do you not want to sit down? I do rather.'

'Are you all right, sir?'

'My father had a schoolmaster, at St Paul's actually, who used to say to his class, when exasperated, "My boys, my dearest wish is to die before you". I begin to understand how he felt. It's how I feel. Except that I should like to survive it, of course.'

'Are you taking medication at all, sir?'

'Should I be? I was attacked in the underpass – threatened anyway and – by a large man who caught hold of me, not very violently, I have to admit – '

'We'll come to all that, sir.'

'What else is there to come to, quite frankly?' Adam sat there, both hands under his jaw, panting just a little more, so he liked to imagine, than he needed to. 'Did they take care of his arm all right? That chap? It looked quite nasty – '

'Mister . . .' Siddons checked his notebook '. . . Idun is in hospital. He had a very nasty experience, but his condition is not giving cause for concern. I'd now appreciate your version of events.'

Adam said, '*Version?* That sounds as if there's some kind of doubt or . . . competition; is there?'

'Just tell us what happened, in your own words, if you would, please.'

'My own words.' Adam blew a little air into the room, the ghost of an expletive. 'I'd been doing a broadcast, at the B.B.C., and I was walking home through the underpass and I was approached, quite menacingly actually, by this . . . large youngish man. Am I allowed to say he was black? He was black. He came up from behind, asked if I'd dropped some money – which I don't think I did, in fact I'm sure I didn't, and he used this as a way of pestering me for . . . more money . . . he held on to me when I tried to walk on and . . . I was somewhat afraid he was going to attack me.'

'Afraid why? It doesn't sound . . .'

'Then I've told it badly. I just may not be at the peak of my powers at the moment. Because he was very persistent, and rude. I asked him politely to leave me alone.'

'Rude how?'

'His manner and his words, and especially the way he touched me, they suggested that I was afraid of him.'

'Which you weren't?'

'I was afraid of what he might do. Is it unknown for people to be mugged by large young men in underpasses?'

'Were you aware of his colour?'

'I was mainly aware of his *size*. I *noticed* his colour. What kind of person would I be if I hadn't noticed it? There's a famous novel about a black man, in America – '

'Rude *how* was he, exactly?'

' – called *The Invisible Man*, about a black man whom no one ever seems to see. All right: he called me "old man". Contemptuously.'

'And how old are you?'

'What's it got to do with anything? Quite a lot, I suppose. Sixty-eight. How old are you?'

'Was he rude to you in any other way?'

'He asked me to turn out my pockets – pretending that I might have lost something. Actually, of course, because – so I feared, irrationally and with, you will probably say, racism aforethought – he wanted me to show what I'd got on me. When I didn't choose to do that, he was very – persistent, to put it mildly.'

'To which you reacted how?'

'All I did was try to get away from him and he sort of . . . blocked me off and became more and more insistent . . . and then this man, a young man, in jeans and a T-shirt, shaven head, came charging down the underpass, seemed to see what was . . . going on and . . . veered across and cannoned straight into Mr . . . what's his name?'

'Winthrop Idun.'

'Winthrop Idun. Who fell over, heavily, and, it seems, broke his arm.'

'And this young man who you called to – '

'Excuse me? I never *called* to anyone. I never even saw him coming.'

'Mr Idun says you called out to this young man – and meanwhile called him – Mr Idun – something . . . racially abusive.'

'I don't remember saying a single word.'

'Really? Only you said just now that you asked Mr Idun – '

'I asked him – to leave me alone, yes, but – that was before – '

'"Get this obscenity black bastard off me."'

Adam said, 'I've never said anything like that in my life.'

'You were . . . distressed.'

'That isn't something I say when I'm distressed. It isn't something I say at all.'

'Mr Idun, in his statement, remembers differently.'

'Mr Idun remembers falsely.'

'Whereupon – '

'Whereupon! Jesus Christ!'

'You disagree?'

Adam said, 'Not easy to disagree with whereupon. I'll almost certainly disagree with what comes next. Whereupon what, supposedly?'

'Whereupon – '

'Dear God . . .'

'Do you want a glass of water, sir?'

'I do not,' Adam said. 'Thank you.'

' – this young man changed direction, ran violently into Mr Idun who tried to get out of the way. Whereupon – '

'Now we're coming to it.'

' – you tripped him and he fell heavily to the floor, causing the injuries previously mentioned.'

'I tripped him?'

'You don't question that.'

'That *was* a question. As posed in the interrogative mode. I did *not* trip him. In the sense of doing anything active. He may have tripped over me as he fell but I *did* nothing. I was taken totally by surprise.'

'After calling out – quite understandably, it may have been – for someone to come and – '

'It damn well would have been understandable, but I didn't:

call out. This young man arrived like a . . . bolt from the blue, you might say. Running for a train, he said. Whereupon, he ran full tilt into Mr Idun and off he went.'

'You'd never seen him before then?'

'Before? What does *then* mean here?' Adam scratched his eyebrow. 'No.'

'Would you recognise him if you saw him again?'

'I shouldn't think so. He looked much like any other young . . . man of his . . . quality. You might categorise him as a sensitive Millwall supporter.'

'And you'd never seen him before?'

'Inspector Garrick.'

'Siddons.'

'Siddons, of course, I'm sorry. Do you seriously imagine . . .'

'It's not my business to imagine anything, sir.'

'Can you seriously believe that I . . . *arranged* for this to happen? That I . . . *procured* this . . . other young man to . . . come down the stairs. Charge along the underpass and . . . knock . . . Winthrop – was that his name – to the ground. I was attacked, for God's sake; not very seriously, but attacked nonetheless. Ask the violinist if he heard me saying anything, have you done that? There was a violinist in the tunnel.'

'The violinist in question is blind.'

'And that affects his hearing, does it?'

'He was playing at the time. He denies hearing anything.'

'*Denies*? In other words, you prompted him, did you?'

Siddons said, 'This is not helping your case, Mr Morris.'

Adam said, 'My *what*? I do want a glass of water actually. Two possibly. I was . . . I was threatened and I did nothing except – whereupon – '

'If you wish to bring counter-charges against Mr Idun, sir, that's a matter for you.'

'I don't want to have anything further to do with Mr Idun, who will, I trust, make a full recovery. *Counter*-charges? Meaning what? I hope you're joking. I'm certain you're not.'

'Mr Idun maintains that you called out to this young man

you say you'd never seen before – inciting him to attack Mr Idun – '

'You cannot be serious.'

'I'm paid to be serious,' Siddons said. 'And I am serious. This is what is being alleged. And that is why I am here. Whereupon he was subjected, so he says, to a violent assault in which you actively participated.'

'Mr Idun actually *said* "actively participated"? Do you have him on tape saying that? Or did you say that and he repeated it? Or didn't.'

'I shall assume, entirely for your sake, that you never said that, sir. Because I don't think it would be helpful to your . . . case for you to be seen and heard to take an aggressive attitude to this inquiry.'

'So you said before. And I . . . don't think a member of the public who's been threatened while walking peacefully along should need help or have a case to answer. Inspector Siddons . . . Mr Idun is a large young man who came up to me, from behind, in the underpass and did what . . . I suspect he's done a few times before – '

'And why would you suspect that, sir?'

'Why would I suspect that? I read the newspapers, I watch the box. Why would I *not* suspect that? If someone you don't know, who is also rather large, came up from behind you and grabbed your sleeve, what would you – ?'

'If the gentleman honestly thought you'd dropped some money and, unlike quite a few people, some might say, he chased after you, wanting to return it – '

'The way he went about it, it was obviously a dodge.'

'Obvious? Why? If an old lady had done the same, would you still be claiming that you'd been . . . "threatened", I think you said.'

Adam said, 'Are you charging me with anything, Inspector?'

'Not at this stage. At this stage, no.'

'So nothing that's been said so far can be used as evidence, do I have that right from a lifetime of attention to blue lampoonery?'

'Detective Constable McIlwraith will type up what you've said, sir, and if you agree it's accurate, it will form part of the background evidence – '

'In other words, you're prepared to take Mr Idun's word against mine.'

'Which I should not, is that what – ?

'That is what. That is very much what. In fact – '

Barbara opened the door as if she had quite forgotten that there was anyone in the room. 'Oh, I'm so sorry . . . While I'm here, would any of you gentlemen like a cup of tea?'

Siddons said, 'Very kind of you, madam, but we shan't be long. The gentleman would like a glass of water though.'

'This is my wife. The reason Inspector . . . Siddons, Siddons thinks I'd like a glass of water is that these gentlemen seem to have in mind to accuse me of assaulting a huge . . . guy in his twenties and . . . thereby, not to mention whereupon, conspiring to break his arm on purpose with malice aforethought. Part of life's rich comedy series. The unfunny part.'

Barbara said, 'My husband came home in a state of shock. I don't know what you're threatening him with, but it seems to me totally wrong when someone is clearly in a vulnerable state – '

'No one is threatening anyone, Mrs . . . Mrs Morris. We had a few questions and it seems – '

'Tendentious questions, that should be,' Adam said. 'Because they'd already made up their minds – '

'Adam . . . don't, all right? Please. Just don't. I'm going to call someone.'

'Try the Prime Minister. He's a straight kind of a guy. No, try – '

Barbara said, 'Sit down and relax. I know exactly who to call.'

'Ba – '

Barbara turned and frowned at Siddons. 'Excuse me, but what rank do you hold again?'

'Inspector.'

'*Full* inspector? Really? I see. Thank you.'

Adam said, 'What happens now? Am I going to be arrested?

For walking in the Hyde Park underpass in a way that threatens the Queen's peace? For inciting large men to try and con me into handing over my money and my credit cards?'

'You need to calm down, Mr Morris.'

'I have no doubt that this poor, victimised black man has a mother with chronic asthma and, despite his fluent Ph. D, has been trying in vain to find work worthy of his credentials.'

'You said "black man". Why?'

'It could have to do with his colour. Have I got it wrong?'

'But you wouldn't call me a white man, would you, Mr . . . Morris? If you had to describe me.'

Adam said, 'Listen, I happen to have – no, don't listen. Because I'm not going to say anything more. Arrest me if I do. Look, I've written . . . To hell with what I've written. But I still have.'

'I'll have Detective Constable McIlwraith type up a statement and if you agree that it's a true version of what you say occurred – '

'Are you proposing to give Mr Idun this address?'

'Give it to him? No, sir.'

'But he's going to have access to it, isn't he? Bound to have.'

'And I daresay, at the end of the day, you'll have his.'

'I'll be sure to go round and threaten him as soon as I have, won't I?'

'You appear to be a mature and educated man, sir.'

'That puts me in my place all right.'

'All these books. Forgive me asking, is that a genuine Oscar?'

'I'm sure any of them are. Genuine. Take a bite if you like.'

'This broadcast you say you were doing . . .'

'I *was* doing. Never mind about it. I was probably . . . trying . . . a little fatuously to . . . impress you, let's say, with my . . . respectability.' He smiled, reassuringly, he hoped, at Barbara as she came back into the room with his glass of water. 'Am I seriously liable to be charged with doing deliberate physical damage to Mr Idun?'

'I can't say at this stage. On the other hand, he has the right – to bring charges or to . . . pursue the matter of damages in the civil courts. I can't speak for Mr Idun. Either way, we'll be in touch.'

'Whereupon – '

'That might possibly be the case. Thank you for your co-operation. I'm sorry if I caused any additional distress.'

'Handsome of you to say so, inspector.'

Adam went to the front door with Siddons and McIlwraith and shut it quietly behind them. When he turned back into the hall, Barbara was standing there. He frowned and shrugged. 'What can you do?'

'I already did it,' Barbara said. 'Derek's on his way.'

'*Derek*? Why?'

'Because I called his office and asked him to come.'

'Very nice of you, but my bro's the last person I want to see. I don't actually want to see anyone. Least of all myself in the mirror. I look like a ghost, and it has very little resemblance to Anne Boleyn.'

'How about I do? Want you to. Before you talk yourself into serious trouble with the police.'

'I'm the bad guy? A man, a tax-payer even, who dares to walk home from St James's Square is a man who deserves everything he gets, is he? I could actually go to gaol. Could I? I could. Let this be a warning to men of previously good character who suddenly decide to beat up someone half their age and twice their size. More than, in both cases.'

Derek arrived in a large black Lexus with opaque windows. Wearing a lightweight black silk suit and white-collared blue shirt, black and silver tie, he was sitting in front with the driver. He embraced Barbara at unusual, consolatory length and patted Adam on the shoulder. 'You seem to have been true to form, Ad: said a lot more than you needed to or should have.'

'It's a living,' Adam said. 'Of a kind. Can't compete with worthwhile activities such as turning southern Spain into one big Gerrard's Cross, of course. It's very nice of you to have come over, possibly, Der, but I do not need a lecture at this point.'

'But before you shoot yourself in more feet than most normal bipeds possess, you need to get hold of what my old mentor Charlie Chernoff used to call "a good yock". I've got someone in mind.'

'Who charges five hundred an hour and takes two or three of them to write his own name at the bottom of a form letter written by a stooge. I don't need anyone. I'm completely innocent and I can argue my own case. So what else is new?'

'Do you want some coffee or anything, Derek?'

'I'm fine, Barbara. This man who attacked you, my advice is that we should at least go through the motions of bringing charges against him.'

'Let's just let the whole thing go, can't we? Good of you to come, Derek. I mean it. And now better if you go as silently as you came.'

'I'm here for Barbara,' Derek said. 'Think of her. The way you're behaving . . .'

'It's wonderful, isn't it, how quickly the victim becomes the accused? Kafka, thou shouldst be living at this hour. I was aggressed, as they will say these days. Would never have happened if I'd been playing golf at Torreroja, or Tory Roger as your many friends call it.'

Derek said, 'This isn't bringing out the best in you, Ad. At least I hope it isn't.'

'OK, so what do we do?'

'Leave it to me, old son. I'll get someone to go and see Mr – what's his name?'

'He's an Inspector. Siddons. Harold. Had to be.'

'No, no,' Derek said. 'The man who broke his elbow and things – '

'Idun. Siddons. Idun. *Yidden*. It's all getting a bit tight in the centre of the park, innit?'

'We'll take him a nice spot of medicine. He'll feel better in no time.'

'Do that and he'll come back for more.'

'I don't think so.'

'If anyone hurts him, it'll come straight back on me.'

Derek said, 'Balm in Gilead never hurt anyone. I've got pots of it.'

'I know that,' Adam said. 'Everybody does. Private jet yet?'

'Tom suggested that. Easier to rent one when you need it. What were you doing in the underpass anyway?'

'Comes of not having a car and a driver,' Adam said. 'Exercising. Real trouble is, I never really learnt to defend myself. dad always wanted me to be a boxer. He had great faith in the good old British straight left. Never to be confused with New Labour. If the police bring charges, and it wouldn't surprise me, *at all*, it'll be all over the bloody press, some of it. I shall end up being run out of the country on a rail: your kinsman, Adam Morris.'

Derek said, 'The guy's doing what these guys do. You'd probably find, if you could ever pull it, that the bloke who ran into your attacker was a mate of his an' all. Chances are, they set people up all the time.'

'And the police don't know that?'

'They *know* it; they just can't say they do. Relax, Ad, I wish you would.'

'I probably ought to take up golf.'

'You definitely ought to. It's never too late until it is. Tom'll fix you up with a villa right on the course. Barbara can spend some time at the pool, go shopping, enjoy bevvies with other men's third wives . . .'

'Look, Derek, you haven't done me anything except favours.'

'And you can't forgive me, can you?'

'Including making my son richer than I am, haven't you? I've yet to see the figures, mind.'

'Tommy does all right. Juliana makes sure of that.'

'Does she? How does she do that exactly?'

'Julie doesn't have any hang-ups about what she wants, for herself and for Tommy. She's been through a hard school. Alexi's a hell of a good tennis player, by the way, these days. Won the under-sixteens at Sevilla this year. And little Leo . . . you should see him, Julie's got him in the pool already. Six months old.'

'Julie's a new one, isn't it?'

'People call her that down there. As well as Juliana; sometimes. And Jools.'

'Whose idea was it to call Leo after dad? As if I didn't know.'

'Commemorating dead family members is quite traditional among the people you don't choose to have too much to do with.'

'The guy called me "rabbi", the Millwall supporter who took out Mister Idun for me.'

'Could be useful. Proof he doesn't know you. They used to call Jimmy Hill "the rabbi" in the old days at Craven Cottage. They'd love you to go out to Torreroja, spend some – '

' – quality time, would that be?'

'Anything wrong with it?'

'Apart from its hollow ring? Not a *salchicha.*'

'Suit yourself. Only I can't think why you don't take advantage of what we'd be more than happy to give you. Tom and I – '

' – and Julie, no doubt.'

Derek said, 'What the hell's the matter with you today, Ad?'

'Can that be the time?' Adam said. 'Nice watch, that one.'

'You're welcome to it.'

'Seriously, Der, thanks for coming over so promptly. I do appreciate it. Barbara appreciates it. You're confirmed as the captain of the club, defender of the faith, *e pluribus unum* and I only want to say – '

Derek said, 'Sometimes I truly – '

'I know,' Adam said, 'but let's not make this one of them.'

'Tom worries about it too.'

'And Juliana, of course. And the boys will soon be worrying about it too, in the juniors, no doubt.'

'Like it or not, and I know which you'd choose, I've watched Tom turn into a very able executive, very imaginative, dedicated and honest. I'm not ashamed of having made him into a passably rich man either, even if you do think, and you do, that I – '

'Put the scissors in right there, Der, I should.'

'I did not steal your son.'

'Steal him? Of course you didn't.'

'Implying that I bought him.'

'He's a grown man and he owes it all to you. Worries about what, does he? And the rest of them?'

'If you don't know, I'm not telling you. I didn't buy him. He had qualities I needed and I gave him a job he was glad to have. And he likes and he's done really well at. Now tell me where I went wrong.'

'Has she really done it, Juliana?'

Derek said, 'Done what?'

'Converted to Judaism.'

'She told you, did she?'

'Do you want a drink or anything? I should've asked. It was the way he called me "old man" that really got to me. Idun. I wanted to kill him, is the truth. Did they circumcise him, Leo?'

Derek said, 'Why not? I'll tell you who called me last week.'

'You know something?' Adam said. 'I almost hope they bloody lock me up, do you know that? Somewhere along the line, it's just the kind of thing that ought to happen. I can just imagine the lecture from the judge about people of my age who go around deliberately provoking large, disadvantaged men by dropping moolah in their tracks and then breaking their bones. Well worth three years in the slammer. Take him down. Ideally, I shall turn out to have been at school with the judge. Fix it for me, Der, why don't you? Make him an anti-Semite, that'd thicken the soup. And while I'm in the Big House, you can be wonderful to Barbara just like you are to Julie, persuade her to bury her troubles in eighteen holes a day at Tory Roger.'

'Do you know something? This is a sad, sad day, Ad, for me. I want to forget it as soon as I can. And I think you'll want me to when you look back.'

Adam said, 'Who? Called you last week.'

'Your friend Lars Waring.'

'Did he really? And are you going to do it?'

'Do what?'

'Put money in his mag.'

'He was after us to do some advertising. He was very frank about it; they're asking over the odds rates from people like us because they need the revenue. Which we're happy to go along with, up to a point. But then – '

'You got talking and . . .'

'Yes, we did, and he told me you were involved editorially and, well, he made *Options* sound like a – '

' – good deed in a naughty world? So how much are you putting in?'

'Lars and I're planning to have a talk. I'm sure he'd like you to be along. Don't go and don your tragic mask, Ad, for God's sake. Nothing bad's going to happen. I actually thought you might be pleased. I should've guessed otherwise. He sent me the issue with the piece you did about Hannah Arendt and Marty thingummy. Very . . . Sunday best, I thought.'

'You know what I'd really like to do, Derek? Sell up and go. Go down to the cottage in France and never again do anything I don't want to do. What do you think this house is worth? Nothing here I really care about.'

'What've you got here then, three thousand square feet roughly?'

'If you say so. What's that worth? A million.'

'Whatever it is,' Derek said, 'it's going to be worth a lot more in three to five years.'

'How about tomorrow?'

'Tell you what,' Derek said. 'Granted you'll never want to speak to me again, I'll give you two/five for it. Today.'

'Derek, don't say things you don't mean.'

'Not my habit.'

'Because two/five . . . you'd better be careful.'

'There is one condition.'

'You have no idea how tempted I am. What?'

'You'll have to leave everything in the house, just as it is. And I do mean everything.'

'OK. Apart from the books and . . . the pictures . . . and . . . you know, personal stuff.'

'Apart from nothing. Including the Oscar. It doesn't mean anything to you. Why would you want to keep it? Don't worry: I won't read the books or look at the pictures, I'll just leave them there to impress people.'

'Very funny,' Adam said, 'Does Tom know?'

'Not meant to be funny. About what?'

'You and Juliana. Julie.'

'You should see somebody, Ad. I mean it. Preferably today.'

'I have. I've seen Inspector Siddons and I've also seen you. Thanks for coming. I mean it.'

'And going,' Derek said. 'Which I am, believe me. Life isn't anything like what you think it is, you know that, don't you? It's not fair, it's not square; and if it were, it wouldn't be worth living, old son, and it would never, never have a funny side. Are you all right? I love you, Ad, because I don't spend a lot of time worrying about whether I'm right to. Forget Mr Idun. It's shit under the bridge. I know you like to collect that stuff; personally, I prefer to be done with it.'

'Your middle name's Gungadin, Derek, isn't it, basically?'

'You do work at losing people, Ad, don't you? It's really and truly nothing like as difficult as you seem to think it is.'

v

Rachel asked Adam if he would come to the British Museum with her to go round the Elgin marbles. *The Burlington Magazine* had commissioned an article from her about Lucullus, the predatory connoisseur who, after his successful campaign against Mithridates in Anatolia, in 88 B.C., was the first general to start shipping looted Greek statuary, in large quantities, back to Rome.

The Parthenon marbles seemed to Adam to be greyer than the last time he had seen them. 'It's as if the marble itself was sulking, isn't it? Poor old Elgin, he saved them from being turned into quicklime or whatever it was the Turks had in mind, and he's been vilified ever since, starting with Byron, who couldn't bear anyone to be more talked about than he was.'

'Everybody steals everything they can, seems to be the basic rule, doesn't it?'

'Unless buying it is easier. Which in this case it was. I'm very happy for the Greeks to have these damn things back, any time.'

Rachel said, 'Mum told you all about what's going on, presumably.'

'She told me what she told me. What're you going to do about it?'

'Give him notice, I expect. Happens all the time, they tell me.'

Adam said, 'And the baby?'

'Have it, aren't I? I can't do it again, dad. Nice irony, I expect you're thinking – having a baby with a . . . flake like Jonty after not having one with Clifford who was at least . . . was "supportive" the word I used? You bet it was. Too late now. He's pretty well cleaned me out. Jonty.'

Adam said, 'We need some advice from the wise centaur. I wonder what Derek would do.'

'All I wish is he'd give Jonts a job. And a good talking to.'

'Would that help?'

'If it was conditional on him going back into rehab? Like anything. You know what's silly, don't you? I still sort of love him and I still don't wish . . . I'd stayed with Clifford. So there is that. What there is of it.'

Adam said, 'You didn't tell Barbara, did you, about – ?'

'Would I do that, when I promised you I wouldn't?'

Adam said, 'How rich is Tom these days, any idea?'

'None at all. He's got everything he needs, it looks like.'

'And not all that much else? Do you . . . communicate at all?'

'Not hugely. He wasn't there most of the time when I was . . .'

'No. What do you think of Juliana?'

'I don't. Should I? She looks . . . good. She seems . . . how about "capable"?'

Adam said, 'Capable of what?'

'Probably. You think she conned Tom, don't you, when they

were getting out of Paraguay? Don't worry about it. He doesn't mind.'

'Did he tell you that?'

'Call it an informed guess.'

'Does he mind about her and Derek? What does your guess inform you there?'

'You don't have any idea just how selfish I am, do you, dad? I've never thought about it.'

'Then promise me you never will.'

'Without a moment's hesitation. I can't even see it matters, whatever it is. She fucks Derek, is that what you're telling me?'

Adam said, 'I probably shouldn't have said anything.'

'Almost certainly not. Because now – '

Adam said, 'I know. And I'm sorry. Let's go and have some crappy lunch. As far as I'm concerned the Greeks can have the bloody marbles if they really want them that much.'

'Yes,' Rachel said, 'and in return, they could always give most of Thessaloniki back to the families of the Jews they nicked it from when they didn't come back from Auschwitz.'

'I can always talk to Derek, if you want, about giving Jonty a job . . . He'd probably be very good on the editorial side.'

'No one who likes your novels can be all bad, dad, can he?'

'We'll hang on to that,' Adam said.

'With both hands we will; and tight.'

'Are you going to be all right, Raitch?'

'I'm like you: I'm going to do my work, no matter what. And bitch and bind while I do.'

'Like me?'

vi

A week later, Adam received formal notification that Winthrop Idun had decided not to press charges and that the police proposed to take no further action on this occasion. He took Barbara to *Nibbles* in order to celebrate his restored faith in British justice. When they returned home, they found that thieves had broken into 15, Tregunter Road, through the basement window. The steel mesh had not resisted their professionalism. The loot included Adam's Oscar. When questioned in the morning, a neighbour remembered seeing two well-dressed white men loading suitcases into a Volvo estate. Since they were laughing and chatting quite loudly, she had assumed that they were members of the Morris family.

VI

On the second Tuesday in March in 2003, Adam was invited to lunch by his brother Derek. Having set himself to walk healthily across the park from Knightsbridge, he elected not to take the underpass on his way to the cul-de-sac off Mount Street where the offices of Derek's company, A.O.M., and its subsidiaries, had expanded from their original single floor to include the whole of the discreet, renovated building. Automatic glass doors opened with sidling courtesy. A man in a black peaked cap, sitting behind a marble desk in the foyer, instructed Adam how to use a blank plastic swipe card in order to be taken directly to the unnumbered top floor.

Schindler's stainless steel lift doors opened into a soft grey-carpeted ante-room. Adam walked past the waiting area, where financial publications overlapped on a side table, towards two wide mahogany desks. Each had a black metal wing with twin computer screens on it. Only one desk had a secretary behind it. She stood up, a pretty, black-haired girl, and said, 'Oh, do please go on in, Mr Morris, Mr Morris is expecting you.' She leaned back and across and knocked, with gentle knuckles, on one soundless leaf of a heavy wooden double door and then sprang the lock.

Derek's office filled a wide corner of the building, with two windows on each of the outer walls. In the nearer half of the room, two pale suede sofas and a trio of squared, similarly upholstered armchairs surrounded a low double-decker glass table with a modest Henry Moore reclining on it. Three Epstein bronze female heads conferred on a spread-eagled console under the slatted wooden blinds of one of the windows. A suite of bold gouaches, depicting the story of Candaules, his queen and the upstart Gyges, was ranged, three one side, four the other, on the pinstriped grey flannel walls on each side of the double doors.

Derek was sitting on the desk, shoeless in fuzzy white socks, as he finished a phone call. He wore jeans and a yellow polo-necked top under a dark cotton zippered jacket. The still thick hair was shiny and slightly curled. His pedestalled desk had dark, flat equipment on it.

'Hullo, Ad.'

'How are you, Der?'

'Isn't it silly?' Derek said.

'Oh good heavens yes, most of it. And the rest is much worse. Nice padded pad you've got up here.'

'You and I making appointments with each other, I meant.'

'Or, more accurately, your secretary calling to remind me that I had one with you. But who's counting, old son, who's counting?'

'I couldn't call you myself. I was in Sumatra. And I didn't want to come all the way back and find you'd stood me up.'

'You should've sent a car for me and I'd've be here already.'

'That would've pissed you off too. It's your secret talent, isn't it, taking offence where none's intended? You people are all the same. But here I am and here you are, and it's truly *wunderbar*. How's Barbara?'

'Fine. I'll leave the dandy to you. You look very . . . stylish. And well. Sends you her love.'

'You must do something right,' Derek said. 'Or she must. I always envy you those arty leather jackets of yours. Where do you get them? Or is it always the same one?'

Adam said, 'Outlet store, L.A. This little number cost me all of sixty bucks. It's yours for a hundred. And nice to see you. And now why am I here?'

'Never get over it, will you?'

'The barrel? I'm rarely anything *but* over it.'

'You're the only man I know who actually goes out *looking* for barrels. Why do you do that?'

Adam said, 'It's getting a little late in the day for wondering; or

210

anything else. I used to be childishly proud when they put my birthday in the paper. Now that it feels as if it happens more and more frequently, it stings like an accusation.'

'But then what doesn't with you?'

'You tucked that one neatly away wide of square leg. How are things? You're manifestly not short of them. *Sumatra?*'

'You're right,' Derek said, 'it's unmanageably far away, even for a potential paradise for the Pacific rim brigade. I want your advice.'

'Talking of advice, do you know that Gavin Pope's now costs a thousand an hour? Probably why you'd prefer to have mine.'

'He's worth it. Gavin has the knack of making things that previously seemed incredibly complicated turn out to be very simple.'

'Bring him the Gordian knot and ten seconds later he hands you back a neat ball of string? No wonder they're making him a lord justice or whatever they're making him.'

'And those books of his are all over the airports.'

'Unlike mine,' Adam said. 'Thanks for letting me know. All round the wicket you're scoring already. Ah my Compton and my Edrich long ago! The Large Mound Stand, what wouldn't I do to be sitting there now?'

'Very suggestive "Large Mound Stand",' Derek said, 'when you think about it.'

'And all for one and ninepence.'

'Still functioning, are you, Ad, in the up-guards-and-at-'em department? What would you like to drink?'

'Oh,' Adam said, 'anything beyond my means that you happen to have on tap.'

'How about I insult you with a dose of boring old Bolly?'

'That'd be very acceptable, as they will say.'

'So . . .' Derek pressed open the mirror-fronted refrigerator under the grey and white marble ledge that ran along the solid wall to his right. He took out a pearled bottle of Bollinger and extracted the sighing cork with a pair of hinged steel brackets.

'You were right, weren't you, not to accept my offer? Try disapproving of a drop of that.'

'Cheers, Der, and many of them. Offer of what?'

'Two point five mill, wasn't it? For Tregunter Road. Your house.'

'They never got me my Oscar back, you know. If that was what you were after. When we were burglarised. The cops. And no muffled voice on the phone ever offered to sell it back to me for a pony or two. Who the hell would want to keep it, when it's got my name on it?'

Derek said, 'Because I bet you it's worth three/five, four million in a year or two. The house.'

'Do you still want it?'

'I never wanted it. I was just trying to show you what an idiot you were to pretend that you were down and out. Almonds? We grow our own, in Almeria. It's OK: no salt.'

Adam said, 'Advice about what are you after? Not planning to write a novel, are you? Or is it a screenplay?'

'What do you think about honours?'

'I told you: I don't.'

'Have they never offered you anything?'

'I'm not a member of the London literariate. I *almost* am, which proves it. A mandarin who was very nearly a friend of mine said to me when I won the silly Oscar, "You'd better get used to the idea that your books will never again be judged on their merits." Since then I've been the not particularly fat man outside, signalling wildly to be let in. But not so's anyone would notice, of course. Listen, the only honours that mean anything are for gallantry, and the most gallant thing I've ever done was help an old lady with her two-ton suitcase at Victoria station, when no one else would. In 1972, that was. I got the hernia award. They – whoever they now are – have not chosen, nor will they, to offer me so much as the time of day.'

'If they did, would you take it? The C.B.E., for instance.'

'I hope not,' Adam said, 'but they won't. And don't tell me you can get me one wholesale, will you? Please.'

212

'You do like to think of me as the kind of Jew you imagine you're not, don't you?'

'Look, Derek, thanks for the champagne. I honestly don't need lunch. Or the C.B.E.'

'Only they've offered, unofficially, to make me a lord.'

Adam said, 'Of *course*, they have. May I say *mazeltov* within these four suavely trousered walls? Unofficially. What're you going for? Viscount's nice.'

'Viscountcies aren't on offer. Last thing I ever had in mind. And it doesn't mean anything any more, does it? But I have given them a lot of money, one way and another. All for good causes. Including the Labour Party.'

'And they're willing to forgive you? I've often thought about going out and buying a hat so that I could take it off to you.'

'They'll all say I bought it, won't they? The peerage.'

'Bastards! Just because you paid for it.'

'Fuck off, Ad, occasionally, could you, possibly? You think money makes me . . . what would you say? Impervious, I expect. It doesn't. I don't know why you came.'

'Try: I was invited; to lunch. From Sumatra already.'

Derek said, 'You're quite right: have some food; and *then* fuck off.'

'They'll also accuse you of buying the Labour Party. Expect a cabal of the leftiest righteous to prepare your *auto-da-fé*.'

Derek pressed a silent button and, a few seconds later, the door opened and a trolley with clever, spherical wheels was pushed into the room by the same pretty girl who had greeted Adam.

'Thank you, Bernice.'

'You're welcome. Anything you need, Mr Morris, I'll be outside.'

'What about your lunch?'

'I went earlier. Rosalie's back now, by the way, if you need her.'

'Why would I, when I can have you, Bernice?'

Bernice looked at Derek but did not smile, and then at Adam, and did, and then went out.

Adam said, 'The man covered with women, that's you and Drieu all over.'

'Bernice saw the film of *Life and Loves* three times. Who's Drieu when he's at home?'

'Better if she'd read the book,' Adam said. 'Some old frog *fachot*.'

'Yeah? She did read it. And loved it. Do you ever care what you say to people?'

'Only when they're not Jewish,' Adam said. 'Get her back in here. I can have her for lunch. I've had lobster before.'

'I'm sure she'd love that.'

'I wish I was one of those men, but I never will be now.'

'I envy you, Ad, and you know it.'

'And I envy you and I don't know it, is that how the number goes? Even if you do elect to have a title.'

'I suppose it all comes back to the old, old question.'

'Bound to.'

'Is it good for the Jews?'

'Nothing is,' Adam said. 'Nothing will be. Least of all what's happening at the moment. It's a story older than the hills. I only wish there *was* a bloody international conspiracy; apart from Christianity and Islam, I mean. But on we go, some of us, isn't that the truth? Is ermine kosher at all? Should you check?'

'Being the way you are won't get you out of anything, you know.'

'Are we doing the "when the time comes" number? Otherwise known as the *oy vey* chorus? Will money, will titles? Nothing'll get us out of anything, but we keep swinging from tree to tree, don't we? Like the rest of the benighted human race. Chimps of a feather. Very good lobster, I must say. Nothing like forbidden fruit unless it's forbidden shellfish. Lord Morris of what are you going to be?'

Derek said, 'If I asked you to do something for me, Ad, do you think you could do it? Kensal Rise, I thought.'

'Not strapped for cash, are you? I can certainly spare you a fiver.'

'I've got a lot of properties, one way and another, all over the

214

shop. In the sun, by the sea . . . Which is why I'd like to have you accept one of them – '

'No,' Adam said. 'Thank you. Very much.'

'Hang about! How about this isn't for you, it's for me? And . . . the family. Think of your kids. Look at it that way.'

'The way it isn't, you mean? You've already made Tom a rich man, I gather.'

'Wrong. He's made himself one. By his own hard work. Anything wrong with that? You don't have to answer. And your grandkids, think of them.'

'I hate that expression. Almost as much as I hate "issues" and "unhelpful". Oh and "community" is coming up on the rails. This is going to be a close one!'

'Leave it out, Ad. How's Rachel?'

'She's been made a fellow of our college. Her Catullus book was a considerable *succès d'estime*.'

'Didn't sell, you mean? She had a baby, didn't she? Little girl?'

'And she's recently been approached about writing and fronting a TV series about Mediterranean islands that Alan Parks's company is producing. Just the gig she needs to land her a big-time job, like modelling lipstick.'

'What's her little girl's name again?'

'Still Melanie.'

'Including Melanie then. Working out now then, is it, the marriage?'

'Now and then. They live a life I never could, but you quite often have. Together and apart. *Odi et amo* in modern dress. Sleeveless and very cool. Is Carol still alive?'

'Still bouncing around. She weighs eighteen stone. Happy working at *Options* then, is he? Jonty.'

'You fixed it, didn't you? for him: the job.'

'All I know is, I bunged Lars a few thou, for your sake, and the future of humanity. And at the same time, yes, I did mention a certain bright young man. Give and take: the badge of all our race, that what you're thinking? In which case, fuck you, and not for the first time. What does Jonty do there exactly?'

215

'He's on the credits as a contributing editor. His main contribution probably being to flatter our mutual fiend Lars Waring. Thanks for doing what you did, Der. And, contrary to early reports, I do mean it.'

'Right, so listen, before you look at your watch again: I want to gift you a chunk of property.'

'Oh, Der, I really and truly do not want to be gifted. I don't want anyone to be. Gift is a noun.'

'You still put the ghost of Kennedy's Latin grammar like a wall between you and the rest of the world, don't you? You never even notice everyone else walking straight through it. There's this renovated *finca*, plus five hundred hectares, olive orchards at the moment mostly, I've got; south of Almeria, private beach unless anyone comes along. All I'm asking is you agree to become the titular owner.'

'How can I,' Adam said, 'when I haven't got a titule? Why? What's happened?'

'It hasn't. Yet. Which is the only time it's worth doing these things.'

'And what are they, these things?'

'Putting one's eggs in a variety of baskets. Because how long can it go on? The boom. I want to put a few things out of reach of . . . whatever might happen. Arm's-length time, and a little further than that, if possible.'

'Isn't that what the Dutch Antilles are for? Alternatively, what's wrong with Jersey?'

'Nothing crooked in this, Ad. I thought my brother might be one person I could trust, that's all, and do a bit of good to.'

Adam said, 'If this is some kind of compensation for the way you got Tom to come and . . . work for you . . .'

'Get out of here!' Derek said.

'I haven't cracked my claw yet. OK, if I take it with me?'

'You always want to be able to say what you like and hurt people and then have them glad to see you and think you're some kind of a bloody genius.'

'Pretty well covers it,' Adam said.

'Let's cut the crap. Nobody knows what the banks or the Spanish government or some local *ayuntamiento* – Valencia, in particular – might or might not do to property companies like A.O.M. somewhere down the track. Politicos smile and smile and then suddenly it's 1492 again.'

'You want to put some stuff in my name because you don't have a current wife you can do it with, is that love's new sweet song?'

'I'm talking about a spread that's worth not much more than five mill. Tops.'

'A peanut factory already.'

'Which you would nominally buy from us with a loan I'll make available to you that you don't any of you ever have to pay it off. Which will render it totally watertight from a legal-cum-accountancy perspective. Paperwork that thick, but my people'll take care of all that. And your accountant can check out if you want him to.'

Adam said, 'Listen, you couldn't just gift it to me, could you?'

'Crack that damned claw,' Derek said, 'and eat up. Bernice has got a baked Alaska melting out there. Have you thought about old age at all?'

'Not a lot. But I do watch the back of my hands and wait for it to put in its spotty bill.'

'Are you going to be all right, you and Barbara? Financially.'

'Don't sell me insurance, Derek, now, OK? I shall have a roof over my head. I have books. I have a pen; I have paper. That's all right enough. So I like to imagine. I was always afraid to want to make money, is the truth of it, Der, and have it look as if it mattered to me. I got what I asked for, and who wants that?'

Derek said, 'I dread it, Ad. Age.'

'Imitate Spinoza: don't think about it. You're still young. You have hair in the right places. And a Lamborghini or three, don't you?'

'Because what've I done?'

'The right things, obviously. You're going to be a lord already. Proves it.'

'Made a lot of money.'

'And a lot of women.'

'Some.'

'Into the hundreds?'

'Who's counting?'

'Into the hundreds,' Adam said.

'And you never know when it's going to turn out you've done it for the last time.' Derek must have buzzed again: the door opened and Bernice came in with a tray with a silver-covered platter on it. She put it on the marble shelf and collected the used plates.

Adam said, 'Thank you, Bernice. Delicious!'

'May I say something, Mr Morris? I've read a lot of your things. I particularly loved *An Early Life*.'

'My first book,' Adam said. 'I should probably never have written anything else.'

'That's what everyone says,' Derek said.

'That scene when you realise your friend is actually going to die . . .'

Derek said, 'That baked Alaska's going to be a vanilla puddle in a minute.'

Bernice removed the silver lid. The baked Alaska had not deflated. She cut wide slices with a sharp, warm knife, put them in front of Adam and Derek and then went out.

'Pretty girl!' Adam said. 'Is she one of your hundreds?'

'Granddaughter of a close friend of mine. Know your trouble, Ad? You're a moralist. And the thing about moralists is, they're always just a little bit sordid at the edges; ever noticed that at all?'

Adam said, 'Terrific pud, as Tammy Singer says, rather too often, on her beastly TV programme for oral voyeurs. Stomatologists? Good old Alaska.'

'I have heard that. Could well be the next place to be the next place we need to think about.'

'Tell you what, your lordship,' Adam said: 'I'll stick with Almeria.'

'It's no big deal, believe me. You don't want anything to do with it, more fool you. They all do it, and then some. The ladies and gentlemen you're afraid'll regard you as a conniving little Jewboy. Who do you think I got the idea from? A viscount actually.'

ii

After leaving Mount Street, Adam walked down to Berkeley Square and stopped at the bottom of Hay Hill while the light changed, and then changed again. He had no appetite to move. He stood there. A voice at his side said, 'Are you all right? Adam.'

Adam said, 'Rather a personal question, Terry, isn't it?'

'Only I noticed . . .'

'That I was "lingering shivering on the bank and fearing to launch away . . ."?'

'Not in quite so many words,' Terry Slater said.

'I know more Christian hymns than most Christians do, God help me.'

Terry said, 'Did you have some kind of a run-in with somebody called Mitchell Ambrose at all?'

'Said like a man about to tell me something I don't want to hear. Let me guess. He reviewed *Into Africa*. Am I right? Where? By all means don't tell me what he said.'

'It was in *West Coast*, but it was also posted on the net. It's very long and very − I have to say − '

'Do you? I doubt you do, but I'm sure you will.'

'Personal. What did you do to him?'

'I hardly know the man. He had a feud with a friend of mine, who died, is all I really know about him.'

'He regards you as "especially unqualified to write about Africa, and blacks and whites".'

'"Especially" meaning what exactly?'

'Because, so he says, you write from a − I think the word was "tainted" − perspective. Your major character being a descendant of people who won't admit they were deeply involved in the

219

African slave trade, which was, if I quote him correctly, "by far the biggest and certainly the most genuine holocaust".'

'Nice little nest of nuances in there,' Adam said, 'You know what, Terry? There's nothing to say about people like that. Even to contradict them is to go along with them some of the way. The part that says they're rational, civilised human beings. So: you've given up being a brilliant young publisher, they tell me, and become a brilliant young operator.'

'How did it do finally, the novel, saleswise?'

'After Innes Maclean also put the Caledonian boot in?'

'Must've helped. Do you mind if I say something?'

'I rather thought you had.'

'You know I'm an agent these days.'

'I don't mind you saying that.'

'Publishing, the way they do it at the moment, most of them, it's totally obsolete. I'm looking to build a client list of people who can command much bigger royalties than a measly – what do you get, ten per cent?'

Adam said, 'On a fine day with the light behind me.'

'There you go. Face it, the novel isn't an art form today, it's a commodity. Like books generally. It needs to be efficiently marketed, by people who can consult on content, oversee publicity and – key point – push distribution to the limit. The electronic book is only just around the corner. In other words, it's here. My clients have to be fully wired: on the box, on the net, they have to be – how about inescapable, when it comes to the public? Multimedia exposure is the *sine qua non* for success today. What was your last advance from Connie Simpson?'

'I don't suppose my sales'll cover it, whatever it was.'

'Ten grand? How old are you?'

'Shut up.'

'Exactly. You're famous, in a limited sort of way, and she doesn't have to pay you for a year's work what she pays a first-year, fumble-fingered secretary. Anything like. I'm looking to get my clients something like forty per cent of the take. Authors should be partners not peons. If you could be twenty-five again . . .'

'Got the snake oil with you, have you?'

'Do you want some coffee?'

'That won't do it,' Adam said. 'I've tried. If I was twenty-five again, what?'

'You'd be just the kind of under-sold, misdirected writer whose career I'd want to mentor.'

'How about "hone"?' Adam said. 'Mentor *and* hone? What I might have done with bigger tits! No call to help me across the road, OK? I was standing there because that's where I was standing. I was not waiting for nanny.'

Terry smiled and kept the smile there as he looked at Adam. 'I know what you're thinking.'

'More than I do,' Adam said. 'What?'

'What would Jason say? If you went with me.'

Terry's soft voice, and the measured amusement in the grey eyes, salted his words. He was wearing a grey-black Armani suit, white shirt buttoned to the throat, with a pseudo-clerical collar and no tie; a green tweed raglan was draped over his shoulders. Adam looked at his watch, but crossed the street with him. They walked towards the side door of the Mayfair Hotel.

'Excuse me . . . Adam Morris?'

A small woman, at once reduced and enlarged by a blue mackintosh and a woollen bonnet, stood under the awning of an adjacent newsagent, arms across her chest, hands hidden under her armpits. A brown Revelation suitcase, of a kind Adam had not seen in public for forty years, was on the wide pavement beside her. A carbuncular carrier bag was slumped on top of it.

'Yes.'

The woman coughed, twice, dryly, and then she said, 'It's Anna.'

'Anna. *Anna?* My goodness, so it is. Terry, this is my old friend Anna . . .'

'Cunningham,' she said.

'She's a poet.'

'Oh yes?' Terry also had a watch.

'A wonderful poet. Superfluous adjective. A poet is a poet is a poet. And she is. What're you doing here?'

'Same as everyone else: passing through prior to passing on.'

Adam said, 'The blight that man was born for.'

'A tag for all seasons,' Terry said. 'Listen, Adam, why don't we meet up and . . . ?'

'Anna, where are you . . . staying? In London?'

'Here's as good as anywhere,' Anna said, 'for the moment. I'm waiting to catch my bus.'

'But this isn't a bus stop.'

Terry had walked on.

'Go with your . . . friend,' Anna said. 'He looks as fresh as a fish.'

'Listen, I'll come back later, if you're still here.'

The coffee shop was dark and had only two rows of tables.

'I knew her at Cambridge,' Adam said. 'I thought she was dead actually.'

'And isn't she? Cappuccino or what?'

'Strong one, please. When did this happen?'

'Happen? What?'

Adam said, 'One minute you're a bright young editor and a composer of elegant brevities and a year or two later, you're Mr Ruthless, the fanciest literary pimp in London.'

Terry said, 'Do you want to keep this short?'

'Tammy Singer. Are you and she still . . . ?

'Tamara kept wanting me to go to more and more restaurants with her. I began to feel like her doggy bag. So I decided to move on. Must be better things to talk about. You, for instance. You went and wished the horror back on to Africa, in your last novel. But it's right here, isn't it? You know it and you daren't come out publicly and say so. England's the lion that's turned into Bush's poodle and thinks miaow is a roar.'

'I rather thought I'd indicated as much, the way Saul gets treated when he arrives home with Roy Carn.'

'Possibly. Only ironic undertones are a luxury no one clocks any more. I'm not thinking so much about what you said as who you thought you were saying it *to*. You've spent – what? – forty years satirising something grand and exclusive and supposedly high-minded that simply doesn't exist, not any more. In the hope of amusing, or even slightly vexing, an in–group of latter-day Bloomsberries that doesn't read anything much beyond the *F.T.* and *P.I.*, and doesn't go bull on culture either, if it ever did. The charmed circle illusion. You're still knocking discreetly on a cardboard door that's got "Come In and Help Yourself" written all over it.'

'Kafka did that one already,' Adam said. 'But I expect you're right. It was open all the time he was been waiting; and now they're about to shut it, being Franz's self-defeating point, the door. Are you writing a new novel yourself at all?'

'I've done a toothsome proposal. *Jacking Jack*. About Kennedy and women. The *New Yorker* are gagging for it.'

'Form queue this side, I imagine.'

'Talked to Jason Singer recently?'

'I've talked to him. Why?'

'I wondered how he was.'

'Since you made him Cuckold of the Year? Happy as Prozac, isn't he?'

'She made all the running.'

'But you did all the jumping,' Adam said.

'You don't actually know the half of it. Since I dumped her, they both hate me. From what I hear, they're now fucking each other like bastards, each of them secretly thinking it's me they're doing it to. Still with him, are you?'

'You're busy stealing his top clients, I hear.'

'No breaking, no entering,' Terry said. 'Samuel Marcus came to me, actually. On bended knee.'

'Sammy's so short, I'm surprised to hear he has knees.'

'He's a genius, is why you hate him.'

'No, it's just that he writes so loudly, I can't read him without earplugs. I keep hatred for best.'

'He's going right to the top, S.M.C.'

'No question. But then what?'

When Terry smiled, he narrowed his eyes but he did not blink, nor did he show his teeth. 'Your daughter,' he said.

Adam said, 'Do I follow you?'

'Profile tomorrow's ideal celebrity-intellectual-beauty and there she is. To the life. So: how do you reckon I should go about getting her? Be nice to her father, would that help?'

'Nice how?'

'Buy him this fortified coffee and . . . offer to represent him as well.'

'Not necessarily a credible move,' Adam said. 'Smacks of charity.'

'Better be totally up front, right? She's clever, she's beautiful and she's at least a third of the way there already. Even Samuel Marcus was admiring, in his way, about her Catullus book.'

'"As clever as she is seductive, Dr. Morris combines scholarship with salaciousness in an *aggiornamento* that graces ancient Rome with the lineaments of a Campden Hill boudoir." No one can lick Sammy for venomous drool. But then who'd want to?'

'Your Rachel deserves the big stage, is what comes out of it. So: will you introduce us and not – my big fear – blight my chances, and hence hers?'

'She isn't mine.' Adam was leaning backwards to see along the pavement to where Anna had been standing. 'She's a grown woman, she's got an address; call or write. You don't need me to do anything.'

'I only want you not to *un*do anything. She's still there, your bag lady. I can see her reflection across the street.'

'Here's your business plan, Terry. Call Rachel. You want my blessing, you have it. Only one thing do I ask, fervently: as soon as you get her – if you do – make sure she has a hermetically personal bank account for the millions you make her, one that plausible little cutey Jonty Logan doesn't have the key to, and I will press for your beatification. And here's the coda: never, ever say a word against her to anyone that I might get to hear about. Remember what was going to happen if the dons sighted Devon?

It can happen to you. My brother knows people who know people.'

'Your brother, did he ever think about writing a book? If he does . . . ringa dem bells!' Terry was checking the reflection in the windows again. 'She's still out there, your poet lady. Slip out the other way, through the hotel foyer; that's what I'd do.'

'I know you would.'

'You should write something on a subject that liberates you to say what you really think and feel, full throttle. You've reached the age. What've you got to lose? Haven't you pretended to be cool and ironic long enough? Come out with it, for God's sake, before it's too late. When did you last have sex?'

'Thanks for the coffee, Terry.'

Adam walked out of the coffee shop the same way he had come in.

'Anna.'

Anna coughed into her mitten. 'I never thought I'd see you again.'

'Just what the Grand Inquisitor said to that Messiah character. What're you doing in London?'

'I had an interview.'

'Interview? Really? For what?'

'There's this fund for smelly poets someone told me to apply to. It's got heaps of money from royalties from a rock'n'shock musical comedy they made out of the Book of Common Prayer or something like that.'

'And did they . . . disburse you any?'

'I was almost disqualified because I don't have an e-mail address. You can't be profitably stony broke any more unless you do. They let me off this once, with a stern warning. I'm to be notified; after they've deliberated.'

'That's what executives do, *un peu partout*, to keep the creatives in their now habitual cringe. Official decisions take longer to make than the works of supposed art they just might license. What are they going to deliberate about?'

'I had to show them a sample of my work in progress.'

Adam said, 'And what is it?'

'You can see it, if you want. You couldn't let me have ten pounds at the same time, could you?'

'Of course.'

Anna extracted her right hand from her left armpit. Her pale grey mittens turned black where they met the skeletal fingertips which took the banknote Adam was holding out. In order to reach into her suitcase, she did not seem to bend, but to shrink downwards within her bulbous mackintosh. She came up with a cardboard folder with unevenly aligned pages clipped inside.

'It's basically a dialogue. In verse of a kind. My kind. Entitled *The Sinners*. Between the Two Thieves.'

'The ones that were crucified with Jesus, might that be?'

'*He* only says two things. You know what they are.'

'Jesus? "Tomorrow, you will . . ."'

'Yes, ". . . be with me in paradise" and then at the end, "Lord, Lord, why hast thou forsaken me?"'

'I always wondered which bit of it was meant by "*sabacathani*", but I never dared to ask. And in your version they're why he says those things, I presume, the two thieves. Before and after hearing what they say to each other in the . . . interim.'

'What they say, to each other, *is* why. To each other; and, by implication, to Him. *My* implication, not theirs; they don't even know who he is. The point being, they're not sorry for what they've done in their lives; only for a few things they haven't. They've lived, they make Him realise, and He never has. He never could, because – am I not right? – He knew what sin was but he couldn't do it. He had to be good. That's how He comes to see how forsaken He is; the Word made flesh maybe, but never human. Won't take you long to read. Mostly monosyllables. I do like them. Less easy to fake things with monosyllables.'

'Yes and no,' Adam said. 'Are you no longer a Christian, does this mean?'

'No such luck,' Anna said. 'I have no hope, that's all.'

'I always thought despair was the sin against the Holy Ghost. That and pissing on the altar.'

'It's the only way left to take things as they are; and aren't.'

'What bus are you actually going to catch from where?'

'I live on my own. My bus is my bus and I know where to get it.'

'It's really a dramatic dialogue.' Adam had the folder open. 'But then you were once quite an actress. Do you know what Mike's doing these days?'

'Mike?'

'Clode. He's running the Cambridge Festival, among eight thousand other things. Perfect place to get it performed. Your little number. It's just occurred to me. Come the summer.'

'I shall be dead.'

'All of us may be.'

'But I've been promised,' Anna said. 'The man asked me to bring a friend when he was due to tell me my test results, but I had no friend to bring. Just as well. Friends get upset. Thanks for the dibs. Time you wrote a masterpiece, isn't it?'

'How're your children, Anna?'

'Haven't seen them in ages. I suspect they tell people I'm dead. I soon shall be, and then they can tell them the truth. That'll be a relief all round.'

'What does Simon do?'

'Oh yes,' she said, 'I expect you heard about that. He's probably an accountant, isn't he? You don't have to kiss me goodbye.'

He did though; and then he went back into the Mayfair Hotel and washed his hands and face.

iii

After tea that evening, Adam read Anna's twenty-two pages of ill-typed text. There were inked interpolations in handwriting which was taller and bolder than the print. Barbara sat in the lemon-coloured spoon-chair by the fireplace in the sitting room, reading *A Pleasant Stay*, the latest work of a lady novelist whose sublime, but plain, heroines (Alice, Gerda and Harriet among them) were always internally sadder, and wiser, after their sensitively described foreign holidays, although they spoke aloud only in nuanced platitudes.

Adam finished Anna's manuscript and held it out to Barbara. She put it on the floor beside her, finished the chapter she was reading and inserted the silken ribbon which the publishers had attached to *A Pleasant Stay,* a reminder of the polite tradition to which its author subscribed. 'She calls Florence "brown",' Barbara said. 'Would you call it "brown"?'

'I will now,' Adam said. 'This won't take you long.'

'She also calls it "Firenze".'

'Don't we all though, *signora*?' Adam sat in the armchair, under their Helleu drawing of Consuela Vanderbilt in a wide feathered hat, and picked up the latest edition of *Options,* still in its cellophane sleeve, from the lacquered Chinese table in front of the sofa. The article by Gavin Pope featured on the front was entitled 'Is Israel Necessary?' The accompanying cartoon, a parody of Chagall, showed a camouflage-suited Israeli, in a steel helmet, wearing an armband with a Star of David on it, holding a machine gun under his chin with one hand and about to play it with the violin bow he held in the other hand.

Adam reached for a pencil from Barbara's desk under the window on to the street and settled himself to annotate Gavin's piece. After reading and marking a few paragraphs, he resolved to say nothing about it to Barbara. He often did the same thing when he suspected that he had caught a cold.

When she had finished reading *The Sinners,* Barbara closed the folder and laid it across her chest and linked her hands behind her neck and stared up at the rose in the centre of the ceiling.

'So what do you think?'

Barbara said, 'It's . . . a paper crown of thorns, isn't it?'

'Clever you! That's exactly what it is.'

'Cleverer her. Much.'

'They don't even know who He is or what he's supposed to have done.'

'I got that,' she said.

'It's not anti-Christian, it's pre-Christian. And yet the words have been dipped in Christian usage, soured or blessed, depending how you look at it; she can't get away from that.'

'She doesn't try; that's where the irony comes from, isn't it, despite the seeming simplicity?'

'They're supposed to have been nailed to crosses, though, the two of them. They're a bit cheerful and articulate, in the circumstances, aren't they?'

Barbara said, 'You know that Dali crucifixion – '

'I thought exactly the same thing,' Adam said. 'The whole poem's a sort of down-to-earth addendum to his St John of the Cross number.'

'Is that exactly what I was thinking? In which case, wow! I meant that they are sort of up there, but not nailed, more suspended, in a graceless state of grace.'

'Licensed to say whatever they wanted to say because they had no hope. Just like people in heaven. If there are any. If heaven isn't good enough for them, it's too bad; there's nothing better to hope for. No upgrades in paradise. Gavin Pope is a two-faced smart bastard who ought to be up there with them.'

'You digress,' Barbara said.

'I do. Will it play, do you think, on the stage? Anna's little number. They owe something to the two tramps, don't they, her two characters, in the Beckett? I like the stuff they traded about Barabbas, what a nerve he had and what a *mensch* he was. It never occurs to them that Jesus might take it badly.'

'*Mensch?*'

'It isn't mentioned, but it's what she means. Barabbas is the real Jewish saviour, is how I see it; they remember his jokes, and his tricks, and his appetite for sex. And how he got away with it. How the *hell* did Anna imagine all that, and get it right? She doesn't say anything against anything, least of all Christianity, but her poem's like a bell that tolls the end of a mythology. Am I doing it too much honour? You should've seen her standing there in that mackintosh that went right down to her ankles. Looks like a scuzzy teapot in a cosy and she can write stuff like this! I'm thinking of sending it to Mike.'

'He can only say "maybe".'

'That's Mike. To think he almost married her!'

'He almost married everybody, didn't he? And did, quite a few of them.'

'The dog it was that lived. Is Anna's point, presumably.'

Barbara said, 'For me, her point is that God should be ashamed of Himself. The one thing He can never be. Only human beings know what shame is.'

'Hence He and His Son could never be . . . on the same team. Each, if they really existed, would have to be suspicious of the other. Through all eternity. The royal family in the sky. The deposit of the whole piece, for me, is the futility of the future and all the promises it's supposed to keep.'

Barbara said, 'I feel as if I ought to be taking notes.'

'And you're not? Do you feel like Chinese food at all?'

'I do feel very slightly like a noodle, as you ask.'

'I was hoping you'd resist that temptation.'

'Never been good at that.'

Adam said, 'And what is the bad news?'

'You're still not quite sure, are you?' Barbara said. 'Whether you really want me to love you.'

'Love is always having to say you're sorry. That can be tight under the arms sometimes, can't it?'

Barbara said, 'You do take a lot of trouble, don't you?'

'Do I? Yes, I do. To do what?'

'Hide things, don't you? What is it this time? Haven't got a sore throat, have you?'

'Sore head,' Adam said. 'Gavin Pope's written a furtively shitty article about Israel in *Options*. What's shitty about it is that it parades all the reasons why Israel deserves to be hated and why Jews shouldn't fall into the temptation, i.e. the trap, of feeling they have to defend it, no matter what Israel does, but then again . . . and what's typical is that, in the end, he very nearly smells of roses. Talk about Janiceps!'

230

'And that's why we're having Chinese?'

'That and the fact that I love you.'

'And in that order. *Janiceps?*'

iv

The next morning, Adam took the copy of *Options* into his room and shut the door. He braced Gavin Pope's article open by putting a tub of pencils on one side and a magnifying glass on the other and opened his laptop. After half an hour, he pushed it aside, reached for his notebook and set himself to analyse *Is Israel Necessary?* in manuscript, point by point.

When the telephone rang, he picked it up with a show of irritation. 'Hullo. That must be the Person from Porlock. Thanks for interrupting me.'

'I was hoping to speak to Adam Morris.'

'This is he.'

'Adam? Mike. You don't sound like you. How are you?'

'Are you buying or selling?'

'Don't get defensive. Don't get offensive. Relax. Take it on the chin. It's wonderful.'

'That's what Wittgenstein said, about life, but he saved it for when he was dying. What is?'

'What do you think? Anna's text you sent me. What was it Schubert used to say? Hats off, gentlemen, she's a genius.'

Adam said, 'Do you know something, Michael? I almost love you suddenly.'

'I always wondered what kept you. But let's not futz around. How do I get hold of her? Resist the desire to be anatomical.'

'Small temptation there. The only address I've got is this hostel in Lancaster.'

'Let me have it,' Mike said. 'I want to make her thing the festival centrepiece in July. Do you think she'd come?'

'She's expecting to die. But knowing you, you'll probably talk her into putting it off.'

'I've shown it to Harrison. And he agrees with me: it'd make a fantastic oratorio. You know what occurred to us would be terrific, as a supplementary element, if she'd do it?'

Adam said, 'Do me a favour, Mike: don't ask her for rewrites. Please.'

'That's a major part for a woman. Sticks out a mile. I've pencilled in The Virgin Mary. And what she feels about God. Could be the Magdalene though. Up to her. Both the guys could've had her at one point. The script's perfect as it is, but imagine – '

Adam said, 'Take a risk, Michael: settle for perfection.'

'To think I almost married her. I almost married her.'

'Don't imagine that she's anything like the Anna you knew, will you?'

'Well, I'm not anything like the Mike she knew.'

'Yes, you are though.'

'Who's this Porlock exactly you were expecting to hear from?'

'Big new production outfit, isn't it, with offshore hedge funds to burn on brave new ventures? I'm offering them my trilogy on the Protocols of the Elders of anti-Semitism, about this conglomerate of crooks and intellectuals that got together to blame the Jews for everything that they mean to do to them and then some. Poison dem wells, baby, and then market it as mineral water. Period piece, with flashes back to Patmos and places like that where the anti-Jewish propaganda machine first went public, big time. Pius the Twelfth is in it up to his pectorals. And T.S. Eliot and Henry Ford and Marty Heidegger and Ezra Pound and Ernie Bevin. Joyce, of course; Bill, not Jim. Huge cast.'

'*Trilogy?*'

'Like Sadie's *tuchus*: in two parts.'

Mike said, 'They'll never make it.'

'You don't know who they are.'

'Have you got a director?'

'Jake's the only man with the credentials. He's dovening to do it.'

'Sounds . . . Listen, Adam, on another topic, I've got this script . . . Ad?'

'What do you know? He just stepped out. He's a busy man, he would like you to believe.'

'All right it's crap, but this one's got a potentially great idea in it: thriller set in Shakespeare's Venice. Serial murders on the Rialto. No one else can crack the case, so they have to persuade, wait for it – '

'Shylock Holmes to come out of the ghetto and do the business.'

'You heard about it. That damn Shapiro. Think Porlock might be interested?'

'Sounds very much their kind of thing. Does Shylock have to be Jewish?'

'Seriously. I was told no one else had seen it. Would you at least take a look at it?'

'At most,' Adam said. 'I'm starting on a new book.'

'You always have to insist on being a loser. Soon as things go well, you're on your bike, the one with the flat tyres. You will come in July though, won't you? To Cambridge. You and Barbara.'

'People aren't necessarily going to like Anna's thing. Ask dubious you-know-who's like me and the Arch-bosh-shot of Cant will probably start shipping alms to the persecuted children of Hezbollah. Play your cards right, you could even get accused of blasphemy. Mary Whitehouse just might rise again on the first night. I can't promise the Four Horsemen of the Apocalypse but . . .'

'Do what you can, smartass. I'll make sure the cameras are waiting. What is it she says? "Life is too sweet and too sour to suit a God." Imagine that, with music. '

'Straight to number one. Just do her justice, Mike, will you? Anna.'

'Trust me for once.'

Adam said, 'Know something improbable, Michael? I do rather.'

He put down the receiver and sat there, not quite sure what he continued to find so moving. Then he picked up the telephone again and dialled a number.

'Lars? I've just been looking at this month's *Options*.'

'Good to hear you, Adam. I was hoping to talk to you about it. You must have been away.'

'With the fairies,' Adam said. 'It's that time of the year.'

'Do I follow you?'

'In truth, I haven't been anywhere too much, except the Fulham Road. No wonder you couldn't get hold of me. What were you hoping to say if you had?'

'Something Samuel Marcus Cohen said rang a bell with me. I hoped it might do the same with you. About the way in which technical improvements in communications work against the quality of what's then publicised in them. You could take this, so he argued, all the way back to Gutenberg, at the least. Perhaps even to the invention of script itself. Degeneration begins with progress.'

'Sounds like Sammy. You must've needed a big glass of water to swallow that lot. Or semi-swallow it. But then you're some regurgitator, Lars, aren't you, these days?'

'Are you tempted to pick up on it? I'm thinking especially about the cinema. How photography and sound get better and better and the movies get worse and worse, or so it seems to me. Am I wrong?'

Adam said, 'Gavin Pope.'

Lars said, 'I thought you might mention that.'

'And how did you think I might proceed?'

'We need to make people take a step back,' Lars said. 'Don't we? That's why we started *Options* in the first place. To play the gadfly part. Your phrase, I think.'

'No one can be on top form every day. Whose idea was it?'

'To have Gav write for us?' Lars said. 'Yours, wasn't it? Where would I be without you sometimes? You were in at the birth, Adam.'

'I didn't have in mind for him to have a go at Israel. I never had in mind to play midwife to a gadfly with a swastika armband exactly.'

'You're joking, of course.'

'Of course. And here's where the laughs kick in. How about I do a profile of Gavin Parks?'

'You mean Pope.'

'Now you're talking,' Adam said. 'So how many words by when did you say?'

'Adam . . .'

'Still here.'

'I hope you consider me a friend.'

'There is a waiting list,' Adam said. 'But I can put you down.'

'Because you do have this tendency to have vendettas with people who're basically on your side.'

'Trust certain people to play safe when it comes to enemies, is that your blunt point? Because who *is* on my side exactly and which side is it? I favour the left. Or do I? Goodness me! Perhaps I don't.'

'Now you know why I didn't mention Gav's piece to you in the first place.'

'Or the second. When did this "Gav" thing start? I always call him Gavin, but if Gav's smarter, I'll change my tailor.'

'Your son-in-law always used to call him that, apparently, when he was his student. I picked it up from him.'

'Should you see somebody?'

'Jonty thought Gavin's was a damn good piece. Once he'd done a few trims on it. But he did wonder if you would.'

'You haven't answered my question. Three thousand words on the modern Vicar of Bray. Bishop even. Archbishop, why not? Pontiff? By definition already. What do you say?'

'You've lost me.'

'This article of mine on Gavin the quondam progressive – '

'*Quondam?*'

'Look it up, Lars, you're named for people who were quondam, aren't you? The old folks back in Veii. Gavin as the quondam progressive who's working his way not only upwards but also backwards. Britain now has more historians than entrepreneurs. Then again, they *are* entrepreneurs. The past is their future and they're mining it like bastards, with big advances. The intellectuals've run out of ideas for the future, but they can always sex up the past and sell it off in chunks to TV. All our front-men are back-men these days, Gav *en tête*. Something along those sour, sly-booted lines.'

'If I didn't know you as well as I do, Adam . . .'

'You don't. Or you wouldn't have printed a cod anti-Semitic article whose author wouldn't dare to come out in his true colours, even if he had any.'

'Is that it?'

'I want to have some fun with Gav. Is it. What do you say?'

'Have a shot at it, by all means.'

'No, I want to have a shot at him. As soon as you promise you'll print it.'

'No editor can promise to print something he hasn't read yet.'

'What about Mandy's piece the other month? Got that on sale or return, did you?'

'It got us a lot of attention in the wider press. Mentioned on *Today* as well. I sometimes pay for things I don't print. Every editor does.'

'Not wearing epaulettes by any chance are you, Lars? You do pull rank a lot these days. So commission me. Second lieutenant will do. I did put money into your bloody mag, remember, so I'll only be getting back some of the pennies I put in your pot.'

'Reminds me: we're thinking of refinancing as a matter of fact.'

'Is that the rattle of your collecting box I can hear? Trot round the Middle East with it, why don't you? I hear that certain princely persons in flowing robes and custom-built Rabans have been known to give fat subsidies to ex-ambassadors willing to turn eastwards five times a day. A few sovs can straighten a man's bat no end, I'm told, so why not a second innings involving legal pundits and editorial hot-shots with flexible minds?'

'I do still want you in the mag, but I'm not convinced you'll be doing yourself any good grinding the same old axe.'

'I can wrap it up with some general observations that amount to a *clin d'oeil* at Sammy boy and his *Logick der Forschkin.* Or I could quote extensively from Chaim Hussein el Loco, who won't say a good word about Jews but loves Israel. He wants the I.D.F. to invade Stamford Hill and build some settlements.'

'Adam, let me give you a piece of advice.'

'Any time. And I can give you a piece of my mind in return.'

'Think again, frankly.'

'All right, possibly; but don't call me Vittington, OK?'

'It's not as if Gav was being *serious* about Israel and the various ways in which people – '

'Yes, it is. Because a certain fake meta-patrician flippancy is the form that seriousness takes with facing-both-ways British intellectuals who have access to all the fancy mags in London, yours and what used to be Innes Maclean's not least. Yes, there are quite a few of the Chosen among them, I grant you, before you tell me so. But only the ones who go along with the Perish Judah crowd at the same time as saying that "*As a Jew*, I particularly wonder when the Israelis will learn to stop distrusting their neighbours . . ." i.e. agree to stretch their necks for Hamas's recently sharpened blades. Peace in our time can come only when Israel consents to be butchered to make a Top Story this hour. Am I exaggerating?'

'Did I say so? But aren't you?'

'What about the bit in his article where Gavin says, and I quote, if I can find it, and I can, because here it is, "The suggestion that a Jewish cabal lies behind the Anglo-American (i.e. American) decision to invade Iraq was uttered aloud by a senior Scottish Jeremiah but, whatever its exaggerations, it owes something to the flagrancy of some Jewish advocacy. Dual loyalties may be an old charge, but . . ." Gav's cute little "but" in there says it all, Bryan.'

'I rather guessed you might not be laughing at the bit about loyalties.'

'You left it in all the same though, didn't you? "Only joking" is what bent umpires always say as they raise their finger to flannelled fools who still believe they're impartial. The British keep telling us they love justice, but what they really love is judging.'

'You talk as if being British was something distinct from you. How would you like it if Gav had said as much in his article?'

'There's a simple test, and you know it: anyone who advocates that Israel pulls back to its 1967 frontiers, in every particular, is also advocating that it be rendered indefensible, prior to its getting what Jews always deserve. If that's an incentive to peace, pull the other one, or – to put it politely – go and fuck yourself before you ask anyone else to do it.'

'Needs work,' Lars said, 'that way of putting it.'

'Try this then: I'd like my money back. That I put in your mag. That you got out of me by false pretences, although I would never say so. How do you like dem apples?'

'I don't think you should say that, Adam.'

'I'm supposed to have shares.'

'You do.'

'So buy them back off me.'

'We still haven't broken even. Remotely. Result: they're not worth haggling about.'

'Nice choice of terms, Lars.'

'I'm trying very hard to be patient. I hope you know that. Very. Because I really do not understand the effect I seem to be having on you.'

'No? Then I'll tell you: you're like a grey rag to a bull.'

v

At the end of April, Adam and Barbara locked the new locks and closed the new grilles on the doors and windows of 15, Tregunter Road. Once they had re-opened the shutters at *Écoute s'il Pleut* and lit the boiler, Adam felt the surge of liberation which distance from London always conferred on him. In early May, they drove the Mercedes on their annual excursion to the nursery, three kilometres short of Villeneuve-sur-Lot, where they bought white and salmon-pink geraniums, petunias and begonias and *Impatiens de Guinée* and another three containers of the yellow–and–rust lantana plants which Adam hoped, every year, would outlast the next winter and which never did.

After cauliflower soup, *steak-frites*, salad and a *demi carafe* of red, in a little hotel-restaurant in Saint Sylvestre, they walked the length of the village to the market where the stallholders were packing up. They bought the last box of *mouffliers*, which had been kept for someone who had failed to return, and then resumed the homeward journey.

It was a road Adam drove no more than two or three times a year, but that was often enough for it to seem familiar. There was little traffic between the villages. They were on a long curve, with trees on the left and low fields on the other side when, instead of veering right Adam took a lane between two tall plane trees and drove up a tight slope which ended in the forecourt of an unoccupied farmhouse. 'Bugger!' He turned the car round and went down again to the main road. 'No idea how I came to do that.'

Barbara said, 'You were probably dreaming.'

'To hell with Plymouth Ho,' Adam said. 'No, I just didn't . . . see straight, literally.'

'Dare I say, perhaps you need glasses for driving?'

'I've never needed glasses for driving.'

'See what I mean? You also work too hard.'

'What else can Dobbin do?'

'For a change you could always dig Norbert's manure into the vegetable patch, dredge the leaves and stuff out of the swimming pool, and prune the roses, not too short this time.'

Adam said, 'Tell you what: I'll take romance.'

'Can you see OK now?'

'To tell you the truth, I have more trouble reading than driving.'

'So you do have trouble driving?'

'Shall I call you Gav? Now that you're a Q.C. *Gav*!'

'I always thought you liked him quite.'

'So did I. I was wrong. Smooth is not necessarily good. Hyper-smooth *non plus*.'

'Careful here, because there's the level crossing and then – '

'I can see,' Adam said. 'Think I can't see?'

They spent the rest of the weekend filling the garden and the pots on the patio with the plants they had bought. On the Monday, Adam had intended to start a new novel, but he found himself compiling elements for an autobiography which he had the idea of setting out alphabetically; an egocentric encyclopaedia. After eleven o'clock, Barbara called to him that she had made some coffee. He went out first to check the post.

'The fat one's from Spain. Has to be *El Gordo* itself. I shall have to do what Derek wants, I suppose. Why is it, Ba, I almost – but only almost – want him to be setting me up? I don't really think he is, but I can hardly bear to even read this stuff. Look at it; reams of it.'

'Then don't. Get Bernard to. What are solicitors for?'

Adam said, 'What does that say, Ba?'

'Three million euros, doesn't it?'

'I really do need new glasses. One minute it looks like three and then it's thirty and then . . .'

'It's three million,' she said.

'That he's supposedly lending us. Three million!'

'Only on paper; isn't that what he told you?'

'That's the whole thing,' Adam said. 'On paper is on paper. And once it's on paper, it's on paper. Meaning I owe him . . . we owe him . . . three million for a property which we don't need, we'll never live in and – remind me why I ever . . . ?'

'You're repaying him with his own money, isn't that what's meant to be happening? He's only trying to do everyone a favour, isn't he? Your family.'

Adam said, 'You're not in the family?'

'I didn't say that.'

'You really don't think you are, do you? Forty years. *Fifty*. Jesus.'

'I don't want anything from Derek and I'm not getting anything. Why should I?'

'He's buying us, innit? He has to do it. He doesn't mean any harm, I truly don't think he does, but – What happens if I – ? I don't want to say it.'

'Who does?'

'What?'

'Want to say "die".'

'And it turns out there's a piece of paper showing that technically I owed him three *million* euros.'

'Ask him.'

'Or, even worse possibly, heaven forbid, *he* dies and some lawyer, some accountant, someone . . . How can you have a deal that isn't a deal because somebody says it isn't?'

'Should I know?'

'Presumably because he can transfer funds to cover the loan that'll kick in if they have to. I don't know. I make it sound worse than it is. But I still don't want to do it. And if I don't, he's going to think that I care whether he's shafting Juliana. If he is. No, I don't. At all. What does that say there? Is that five thousand or what is it?'

'Fifty. Thousand.'

'I thought it was. *Quarterly*, is that?'

'Do stop.'

'I can't sign something I haven't even read. My father said I never should and it's the one thing he ever said that I tend to stick to.'

Barbara said, 'If you don't want to do this thing, don't do it. And while we're at it, don't do *anything* you don't want to, from this day on. *Please*.'

'I'm taking it all too seriously. Is what Derek would say.'

'And what I'd say is, you take everything too seriously. And what would you say?'

'Boo to a goose, wouldn't I? If it wasn't a big one. How about we put roses in that crater where that Julie Brisson died on us? Pink floribunda?'

241

'Too late for this year,' Barbara said. 'Do you want me to talk to Derek?'

'Why should you? Yes. Or would you sooner yellow? You can plant container roses all year round, can't you? Funny: people don't call any more like they used to.'

'You always used to curse when they phoned all the time.'

'But that was when they phoned all the time. What's going to happen when it all dries up on us, Ba? And you're reduced to loving someone who's withered on the vine.'

'You said yourself: we've got more than enough to live on, haven't we? Forever.'

Adam said, 'But then again, how long is that? One or other of us is going to be left alone. Do you ever think about that?'

Barbara shook her head. 'And I don't want to.'

'So do I.' Adam said. 'I don't want it to be me and I don't want it to be you. Who does that leave?'

A week later, Adam proposed that, since it was a fine day, they should go into Caillac for lunch. They planned to go to the garden centre for some bedding plants after they had eaten. Adam parked the Mercedes in the tree-shaded *place* adjacent to the memorial to sixteen citizens of the town who had been executed by the Germans. They lunched on *pâté* and *magret de canard, pommes Sarladaises* and flat apple tart and then walked towards the main square for coffee.

Adam said, 'How're you feeling?'

'Fed. Very. Are you OK?'

'I think so,' Adam said. 'Not particularly actually. Perhaps that's why I asked. I hope not, but I do feel somewhat strange. In fact, I think I'll just . . .'

Adam stopped and leaned against the warm stone wall of the Renaissance house where, five hunded years earlier, a young citizen of Caillac wrote a bold essay attacking the willingness with which men, even those of supposedly independent circumstances, so regularly volunteer to be servile to tyrants.

Barbara said, 'Adam . . .'

'I'm OK. I think. I just need to . . .' As if practising slow-motion prostration, he slid slowly down and lay, full length, on the cobbles under the elaborate doorway of the old house.

'Adam. *Adam.* Darling . . . what's happened?'

'Don't worry. I just . . . feel better down here. Very . . . tired suddenly. I'm OK. Miles away and still here. Odd.'

A man in painter's overalls came across to Barbara. *'Quelque chose ne va pas?'*

Barbara was crouching down. 'Are you in pain?'

'Not at all. Not a bit. Just . . . don't want to move. Don't worry: if this is dying, it's not all that bad actually.'

'Please just tell me what you feel.'

'Nothing, in quite a large dose. "Unhinged" might be the word. I am hingeless and in need of a hawser. Message ends.'

'Voulez-vous que j'appelle l'ambulance?'

'Je veux bien,' Barbara said.

'No need. I'm OK. It's quite nice down here. Very comfortable cobbles these. Not too much give.'

'Adam, stop. Stop. Please. The ambulance is coming.'

'I just seem completely . . . exhausted. Too much gardening probably.'

'Just don't go to sleep, that's all. Adam, please.'

'Food's not as good in France as it used to be. Must be the euro. Where are you, Ba?'

'Here. I'm here.'

'So you are. So am I. Keep it that way, shall we?'

The workman brought a rolled-up coat and put it under Adam's head. Barbara put her check coat over him.

When he heard the siren of the approaching ambulance, Adam said, 'I'd really and truly much sooner go home. We can call Michel. Take me home, Ba, please. Listen, you'd better go and . . . because the car – '

'To hell with the car.'

'I only paid for us to stay till three-thirty. Go and put some more money in.'

'I'm going with you,' she said, 'in the ambulance.'

He lay there, comfortable on the stones, seeing the wide square in a new light, the horizon tall around him. The others were remote; even Barbara, whose calmness he admired more because he knew the fear it masked. The courage which he required of her made him smile, as if he were faking and she had been tricked.

The ambulance man said, '*Il a quel age, ce monsieur?*'

'*Soixante et onze ans,*' Barbara said.

'You're joking,' Adam said. 'Curious: it's very bright, your dying of the light.'

'Could you possibly be quiet possibly?'

They lifted Adam on to a stretcher and slid him into the tall ambulance. The drive to Caillac hospital seemed to require many quite steep changes of direction.

'This ambulance must have seen service at Verdun.'

'*Calmez-vous, monsieur.*'

'*Je suis bien calme.* I do feel bloody sick though. God, I do.'

Adam was taken into the vacant emergency room. The female doctor had him put on a high, plastic-sheeted gurney. He lay there, shivering in the warmth. While he waited to be examined, Barbara was excluded. She went to the Place des Martyres de la Résistance where they had left the Mercedes and drove it back to the hospital.

Adam had been covered with a blanket. The female doctor was consulting a senior colleague on her *portable*.

'What does she think?'

'She wants to do tests. Heart, lungs. What else have I got? I ate too much. I threw up. I want to go home. Is what Caesar would say in similar circs. *Ceteris paribus.* Was it OK, the car?'

Barbara said, 'We got away with not paying for all of ten minutes. How do you feel now?'

'She hasn't got the faintest what it is. Dr Morris does though: a severe attack of lunch. I threw up, vigorously, while you were . . . And now I feel much better. Pretty well normal, actually. They want me to stay overnight and see this – I don't know – consultant, I suppose – '

'You should. They're all looking very serious.'

'You know the medical profession: the longer the faces, the

longer the bill. Part of the training. I'm in favour of doing a runner. You saw *The Great Escape*. This'll be the low-budget version. I've never ridden a motorbike; never will, I suppose.'

'You'll never be Steve McQueen either,' Barbara said. 'Why do we have insurance if all you're going to do is run away?'

'So we can get away from a better class of care. I threw up. I feel better. *Écoutez, docteur, honnêtement — grace à vous — je suis tout à fait rétabli. Je veux bien rentrer chez moi tout de suite . . .*'

'*Il y a quelques formalités, monsieur.*'

Adam said, '*Ah, oui, bien sur. Moi, j'aime bien les formalités, surtout en français.*'

Adam signed the documents which were put in front of him and then he and Barbara walked, slowly, to where she had parked the car. 'I'm not going to do it, Ba.'

'What's that?'

'Sign those papers of Derek's. I'll tell you something else I don't think I should do: that's drive the car.'

'You're not well. You should've stayed in the hospital.'

'I'm fine. I just don't think I should drive. Nothing to do with just now. I wasn't going to tell you, but I did notice, while we were driving into town . . .'

'What?'

'I had this slight tendency to see double.'

Barbara said, 'I think we should go back to London. And have someone check your eyes.'

'There's an optician in every bloody village in the Perigord. Two usually. I can see fine when I don't have to. Like watch out for those two cars.'

'There's only one.'

Adam said, 'I knew that. Probably cataracts. Nothing operation these days, cataracts. Have it done when we next go back. Jesus, we've only just got here. I've got work to do.'

A few days later, they went to see Monsieur Prentout, the optician in St Cyprien. He tested Adam's sight with a sequence of lenses, none of which amplified or improved his vision. When Monsieur Prentout shook his head and announced that no new glasses were going to be any help, Adam wondered whether the man was properly qualified.

'*Je regrette, monsieur, madame, je ne peux rien faire pour vous. Je vous conseille d'aller consulter un ophthalmologue. Aussitôt que possible. Franchement, je crains que vous ayez des graves soucis.*'

They seemed to walk back to the Toyota through a different village. Adam said, 'Guy's some hick optician; what does he know?'

Barbara said, 'We're going back to London. You pass out in the street. You can't see straight. The man says he can't help you. We're going back to London.'

'It's probably psychological: all about not wanting to sign Derek's bloody documents.'

'We'll take them home with us, have Bernard check them over.'

'There's nothing wrong with them, I'll bet you; that's what's wrong with them: no reason not to sign them except . . . What do you think's wrong with me, Ba? I do feel very . . . slow, to tell you the truth.'

Barbara said, 'Shut up, will you? I do not want to cry while I'm driving.'

'What was that line Edward G. had, in *Little Caesar*? "Is this the end of Rico?" My name isn't Rico. Lucky, right?'

'You die, I'll kill you.'

Adam telephoned Derek that evening, after Barbara had made reservations to fly to London the following afternoon. Derek was not immediately available. He called, just before midnight, from Cape Town. Adam said that he hoped he would forgive him, but he was unable to sign documents that he didn't fully understand. 'Blame dad. Sons always do.'

'Nothing to forgive,' Derek said. 'Read them when you have time and if you've got any problems, we can talk about them.'

'I'm going to get someone else to read them actually. Better that way.'

'You don't trust me. You don't *want* to trust me, which is the weird part, from where I stand. But there you are.'

'Yes, I am. Truth is, I'm actually having some reading difficulties. Vision difficulties, to be honest. We're going back to London to see someone. It's not serious, but there it is.'

'See who? What's wrong exactly?'

'Is what we're going to find out. I'm fine, but I'm not fine, OK? It's basically a diagnostic problem.'

'I'll tell you who you ought to go to.'

'I know who to go to and that's where I'm going. Please don't tell me it's psychological.'

'Why ever would I do that?'

'Because I hope it is,' Adam said.

vi

'You do indeed have cataracts,' Dr Paxton said. 'Everyone of your age – '

'I was afraid you might say that,' Adam said.

' – has a tendency to those. However, that doesn't fully explain your symptoms. My turn to be afraid, I'm afraid. So: how are your physical reactions generally?'

'To what?'

'Slower? Has your wife noticed any – ?'

'What?'

' – marked changes, shall we say? Do you find you're . . . less energetic, more tired than usual?'

Adam said, 'Why do I feel this overwhelming desire to lie to you? Yes. Normal, I suppose. But then, normality stops being one's friend, doesn't it, at a certain point? This double-vision thing is the one that really bothers me. I can hardly read or write straight. And if I can't do those, what am I? Nobody I want to be.'

Paxton was a sandy-haired, paunchy physician in his middle years. He had been recommended, for his diagnostic skills, by Adam's G.P. He had the calmness of a capable gardener. He worked the corner of his mouth with his thumb as he considered Adam. 'How often do you find you have to shave these days?'

'I've always been a bit lazy in that department. Affectations of bohemianism. Twice a week maybe. Could that be sinister?'

'Suggestive, perhaps. How about . . . sexual activity? Are you still – having relations?'

'Sounds like Christmas,' Adam said. 'Relations. We love each other. My wife and I. Rather against the odds that, I suppose, but there we are. It's not quite as it was when we were in our twenties, but what is?'

'Body hair. Any noticeable diminution on that front?'

'Getting greyer and, now you mention it . . . yes. You know what's wrong with me, don't you, Dr Paxton?'

'No. But combined with your difficulties seeing, I have my suspicions.'

'And is it . . . treatable, what you suspect?'

'We shall have to see, and fortunately we can. The appropriate scan'll tell us soon enough. If you could come back tomorrow morning, we shall see what we shall see.'

Adam said, 'If it's what you obviously think it is, is it . . . serious?'

'It needs to be taken seriously, let's say. It's not something I'd advise leaving for longer than is necessary.'

As Adam walked in the sunshine to Russell Square underground station, he recalled that the French used to describe a condemned man as '*l'intéressé*'. Carrying the quiet freight of Paxton's equable apprehensions, Adam found London brighter, more interesting and more menacing. In his frowning vision, oddness and the ordinary almost, but not quite, coincided. Everyone who came towards him converged from distant duplicity to singular, deceptive proximity. He walked, like a rehearsing ghost, through a world that had no notion of his fear. The indifference of other people passed for a reprieve from a sentence that had yet to be handed down. He sat in the train like a secret agent, enlivened by the fear of detection and by affectations of indifference. It was a silly achievement to choose to act in a way that excited not the smallest remark.

He found it comforting to sustain the same performance on his return to Tregunter Road. To pretend that he was unalarmed by Paxton's insistence that he have a scan transformed fear into subterfuge. He impersonated the self-sufficient adult he would have liked to be. The following morning, as he prepared to honour his appointment, he recalled the image of Sidney Carton, as played by a great British actor. With what exemplary insouciance he ascended the steps to the guillotine, in black and white and a rather silly hat!

Barbara said, 'Do you want me to come to the hospital with you?'

'And wait around? I'll take some boring award-winning book, with the largest pissable print, to cheer me up. I shall be fine. My guess is, Master Paxton knows what it is and . . . whatever has to be done. Or can be. I shall be less of a sadster, as they say, if I'm on my own. I mean it. Far, far better that way.'

'Call me as soon as they tell you. Promise. Whatever it is.'

'I will,' Adam said. 'Especially in that case.'

After his scan, Adam had to wait an hour or so for the results to be printed and brought to Paxton's office. He walked round The Queen's Square, distinguishing, as if it were a mental exercise, between the trudging laity, going into the various hospitals, and the brisker medical persons, who carried plasticised credentials on tapes around their necks and seemed to parade with an officious, silent swish. In his fancy, their doubleness classified them as Adam's Eumenides. After walking, yet again, to Russell Square and back, he reported to Dr Paxton as if to the headmaster.

Paxton was in grey flannels and a sports jacket. He was wearing a tie with badges on it. Adam chose to be reassured by the physician's sportive datedness. Paxton slid the X-rays on the bright screen against a side wall. They seemed to be lightly starched and made a professional sound.

'Can you see that in there? Just above . . . that's your nose. The heart-shaped dark patch?'

'Heart of darkness, shall we say? Probably not. Yes, I can. What is it?'

Paxton said, 'That's the tumour.'

'The tumour. And is that . . . my brain?'

'No. I'm glad to say not quite. It's the threshold to it, you might say. The tumour is attached to the pituitary gland. And that – down there – is the optic nerve. The pituitary gland and the optic nerve share premises. Normally, there's usually plenty of room . . .'

'But . . . ?'

'The tumour, as it gets bigger, presses down on the nerve with the consequences for your sight which you've experienced. If it continues to grow, you'd find yourself, eventually . . . unable to see at all.'

'I.e. blind. And how long is "eventually" likely to take? Is there anything to be done? He asked casually.'

'I'm sorry?'

'An old friend of mine, who died not long ago, used to have this adverbalising habit . . . doesn't matter.' He cleared his throat. 'This tumour, can it be . . .'

'. . . excised? We have to hope so,' Paxton said. 'The good news being – '

'The good news! It comes by second post, it seems.'

'Do you still get a second post?'

'No,' Adam said, 'we do not get a second post. Lucky to get a first one. The good news is what?'

Paxton was frowning at the bright X-rays. 'These particular tumours may be large, as this one looks to be in your case, but they are at least accessible, and often benign.'

'As benignity goes, this one seems fairly unfriendly. How often is often?'

'One can't be sure, of course.'

'Malignancy is possible.'

'We can only wait and see what the biopsy tells us. Once Mr Powell's done his stuff.'

Adam said, 'If all goes well, should I be able to read again normally, and drive, and . . . boring things of that kind?'

Paxton said, 'Let's just say that there's a very high percentage of recovery when things are done properly, which is the way that Mr Powell prefers to do them.'

'Does he cut a hole in my head, or what?'

'No new hole required. He does the whole thing by going up one nostril.'

'Not in person? I know, I know. Good. Fine. When?'

Barbara was watching Sky News for the fourth more or less identical time, when the telephone rang.

'Hullo.'

'Hi, Barbara? Alan Parks. Have you heard the news?'

'No.'

'About Samuel Marcus Cohen?'

'I haven't heard the news about anyone,' Barbara said.

'Don't you watch? He got it, the little bastard.'

'Between the eyes? High time. Got what?'

'You can't guess? You're living in a parallel universe. The Big One, of course. Next stop Stockholm. Which is why I was hoping to enrol Adam. Is he there?'

'Not at the moment.'

'Only I'm doing an hour's special, tell him, on the man and his *oeuvre* and his nerve and — I need Ad at B.H., Thursday nine o'clock ack emma, armed with his unique brand of lethal bouquet. We can send a car.'

Barbara said, 'Adam can't make Thursday, I'm afraid. He's busy.'

'Can he not move things around? It's a crowning moment. Dame Joyce Hadleigh will be there to receive the wages of spin.'

'No, he can't,' Barbara said.

'Are you OK, Barbara? You sound . . .'

'I'm very well, thank you. I'll tell Adam you called.'

'Few are chosen and he can still be one of them.'

'Someone at the door,' Barbara said.

She put the receiver down and refused to cry. She picked it up again and called Rachel's number in college.

'Dr Morris.'

'Rachel, it's your Mum.'

'Mum, are you OK?'

'I'm fine. Darling, it's about Adam.'

Rachel said, 'What? Mum, *what?*'

vii

There was a white-faced clock facing the bed in Adam's hospital room. On the afternoon on which he was admitted, when he looked across at it, he had to screw up his face to be sure where the nervous electric hands were pointing. He knew there were two of them, but he saw four. That night, when Barbara had left, he turned out the light, but he did not sleep. The male nurse on duty, who wore slip-on shoes with wooden heels that clacked on the linoleum of the corridor, seemed to be both busy and slovenly at the same time. He came in in the morning and asked Adam, in what seemed an accusing Scots accent, whether he had had anything to eat or drink, apart from water. 'Condemned man,' Adam said, 'no breakfast. What kind of a deal is that?'

The nurse was not there to be amused. He threw a flat, floral garment on to the bed. 'Get that on you. They'll be coming in a minute.'

Adam was interested to find that he could not summon any emotion, apart from curiosity. They came, they helped him, although he needed no help, to transfer from bed to trolley and then they wheeled him to the lift and down to where the anaesthetist was waiting. Adam wondered if he should feel ashamed that he was pleased that Mr Jacobs was, he assumed, a Jew. He had counted down from ten only to five before he lost consciousness.

Presently, a voice was saying, 'What's your name?'

'Adam Morris.'

'What year is it, do you know?'

'Two thousand and three. Hasn't changed has it?'

'Oh, Ad,' Barbara said, 'don't. It's a routine question.'

'The tough ones are coming, I presume.'

'How do you feel?'

'Enlarged. Antigonus the one-nostrilled. Am I OK? Did he do it?'

'It all went fine, so he says. Nice smile, your surgeon.'

'He can still be a rogue. He's good, I think. How are you?'

'Fine.'

'What's your name?'

'My name is Adam Morris.'

'She has to keep asking.'

Adam said, 'If you say something often enough, you begin to wonder if it's true. Imagine waking up and being someone else. Rudolph Rassendyl. Did it work though, Ba, what he did? Am I going to be able to see straight again?'

'*Again?*'

'All right,' he said. 'All right. Thank you for being here.'

'Where else would I be? If you say Claridge's, I'm going.'

Adam said, 'What's your name?'

'Barbara Morris.'

'Glad to hear it.'

Adam spent a sleepless, dry-mouthed night, breathing as well as he could through the nostril which had not been bloodied by the passage of Mr Powell's 'hockey stick', the term the surgeon had used for the crooked instrument with which the tumour had been gaffed and extracted.

As milky morning light filled the room, Adam took a deep breath and looked across at the clock on the far wall. It was seven thirty-four. The makers of the clock, he could now see, were called Tempus Limited. Small print advertised their name in the bottom half of the clock face.

Two hours later, the registrar came in. 'Mr Powell thought you might care to know that, very much as he expected, there is no sign of malignancy, and no reason to expect its recurrence. He managed to remove what he called "most of the tumour". Experience suggests that means all of it.'

Adam said, 'Very nice of you to let me know.'

'He'll be in for a bow later, I daresay.'

'That's showbiz.'

Barbara arrived with several brown paper bags and a twin-bladed amaryllis that bulged from its black pot. She put them down and held on to Adam's foot. 'Not too early, am I?'

Adam said, 'Tempus and company.'

'What?'

'Look. At the clock. The makers' name.'

'So it is.'

'*Mein Führer,* I can read; as well as walk.'

She came and put her arms around him. 'Don't ever do this to me again, not ever.'

'And the good news . . . no malignancy. Dry the starting tear. Dear God, what a slightly very nasty thing is the human imagination.'

'Meaning what? Or have I guessed? Something perverse and . . .'

'Facetious?'

'. . . disgusting I was going to say – in you is almost very, very slightly disappointed.'

'My name is Adam Morris. Are you ashamed of me?'

'Someone has to be.'

Half an hour later, there was a knock on the door. Barbara looked up expectantly, but it was a messenger from Fortnum and Mason with a basket of fruit and drink and a supplementary box of smoked salmon, bagels and cream cheese.

'Had to be Derek. How did he find out what was going on?'

'Rachel possibly? I asked her to talk to Tom. He wanted to come to London.'

'No need, now I'm not dying.'

'Enough. I mean it.'

Rachel herself arrived soon after eleven o'clock. Her train had been delayed at Royston and then again just outside Liverpool Street station. 'Only me. You both look . . . you look OK. Are you being brave or . . . ?'

'He's all right. He can see straight. Any minute now he'd sooner be reading.'

Rachel sat on the bed and lay across Adam, her hair against his face. He felt the heave of her emotion, but she made no sound. When she sat up again, she turned away. Her face was wet. She shook her head. 'You would, wouldn't you,' she said, 'do this? This famous tumour of yours . . .'

'It's lost its reputation. Downgraded to a topical storm. It meant no harm apparently.'

Barbara said, 'I'm going to see if they can put some of this stuff Derek's sent in their fridge. He's rather overdone it.'

'They do,' Adam said.

'You sure put us through it,' Rachel said. 'Now that I know you can read again, I can give you this. Offprint of a tribute to Bill I did for the college mag. I kept finding things he'd said that I didn't, on reflection, wholly agree with. Odd. I also kept imagining him smiling. I had to pipe the cream on, which I duly did, I hope. I never realised quite how ambitious he was until I went through the *opera omnia*. Not that there's anything wrong with ambition, is there?'

'Don't look at me,' Adam said. 'As if anyone would, with all this stuff up my nose. Ambition and the need for money often share the driving on the intellectual's course through life. Yes, I have said it before, and now I've said it again. Apart from that, what else is going on?'

'Oh yes,' Rachel said, 'this Terry Slater character called me.'

'I have to confess: I did somewhat encourage him. None of my business to stop people making you rich and over-rated.'

'Guess what he said before he said anything else much.'

'He admired my work?'

'Would it be all right if he sent me his novel to read.'

'Clever.'

'I thought so,' Rachel said. 'Writes well. Am I wrong?'

'Clever of him. Are you going to go with him?'

'Go with him . . . ?'

'In the honing and mentoring department.'

Barbara looked through the spy hole in the door and then came in.

'I'm going to meet him. I suspect I really shouldn't, but . . .'

'. . . on the other hand – '

'He seems very . . .'

'And I have no doubt he is.'

'. . . very *now*. So the question is like, what do I really want?'

'Well, you know what the oracle says: "The person who asks the question" . . .'

'". . . is in the best position to answer it." But she can't.'

'Is often the catch. So drop it. What are you going to do meanwhile?'

'Whatever I do, or don't. And you'd better bloody well be there to see me do it, or not. Both of you. I'm very tempted by this Mediterranean thing your friend says he can set up. The fates of different islands, I love that. Melos, Thera, Samos, Sicily – that could take a year to do on its own – Crete, Malta, Corfu; no end to it. I don't know what the college'll think. It means being away at least one term.'

'Call it research. Not that you have to. Better still, ecology. Colleges love having celebrity dons these days. Looks good in the three-colour brochure.'

Barbara said, 'What does Jonty think?'

'He's totally for it. Says I can do some back-of-the-book pieces for *Options* as I go along.' She looked at them both. 'You mustn't worry about him and me. He's him and I'm me and . . . whenever the twain meet, that's when they meet. He's getting very good, well, better with Melanie, when he is. I wish I knew your secret, you two.'

Barbara said, 'How about there isn't one?'

'No?'

'That's how we manage to keep it,' Adam said.

viii

Adam had to stay in London until the wound ceased oozing and he had had a 'field test', which proved that his sight was back to normal. A month later, he and Barbara were clear to return to *Écoute s'il Pleut*. Things were largely as Barbara expected: the vegetable garden was thick with weeds; the roses all had black fly; the swimming pool was green with algae. Bees were nesting in the *grenier* roof and the Mercedes had a flat tyre, although it had been locked in the garage ever since they left. Adam said, 'Imagine what it would be like if we didn't pay someone to look after the place when we're not here.'

Before he resumed work on his encyclopaedia, he read and rejected everything he had written, so effortfully, in the weeks before their visit to Monsieur Prentout. On the Saturday after their return, they went up to St Cyprien to take him a bottle of Marqués de Caceres. Adam had bought several cases when they were in Catalonia the previous year.

The optician adjusted a customer's glasses and then handed them to her to try again.

'*Vous étiez très gentil avec nous, monsieur,*' Adam said. '*J'en suis très reconnaissant.*'

'*Normal, monsieur.*'

'*Heureusement, après une intervention chirurgicale, on a été complètement guéri.*'

The optician's customer said, '*C'est pas mieux. Du tout.*'

They went out into the narrow street. Barbara said, 'He hadn't got the smallest idea of who we were, did he? That'll teach you.'

'Sometimes a man has to do what he doesn't have to,' Adam said.

They went to the garden centre, to find replacements for the sorry plants which had not been sufficiently watered to survive their absence, and arrived back at *Écoute s'il Pleut* to hear the telephone ringing. Adam ran to open the *porte d'entrée* and get to the telephone before the answer machine kicked in.

'*Allo, oui?*'

'Dad? It's Tom.'

'Tom.'

'How are you?'

'Back to . . . I'm fine. Are you OK?'

'I am,' Tom said. 'Look, sit down OK? Because . . .'

'What's wrong? What's happened?' He covered the receiver as Barbara came with an indented plastic tray of plants. 'Tom.'

Tom was saying, 'OK, so listen: it's Derek.'

'What is?'

'Happened early this morning. On the motorway to Barcelona. He side-swiped a lorry, or vice versa, in the Lamborghini. He was doing a hundred and eighty.'

Adam did sit down. Barbara stood beside him, a hand on the top of his head. 'What're you telling me exactly, Tommy?'

Tom said, 'He's not dead. He's not dead. He's in the hospital in Madrid. But it's not good.'

Adam said, 'Right. So – what's his . . . his condition?'

'He's in intensive care, obviously. The car turned over, and over. Seat belt, roll-bar, just about saved him but . . . He's pretty badly banged up. They say they've got him stabilised; whatever that means. The worst thing is . . .'

'Well, come on.'

'They discovered that the impact ruptured his kidneys. Both of them. I mean that's the most urgent . . . problem.'

'Ruptured meaning what?'

'They can't save them. And he can't live without at least one. No one knows I'm making this call. Least of all Derek, obviously. Juliana does though. And she said I shouldn't. He's on life support, but . . .'

Adam said, 'How long can he last without a kidney?'

'Short term, they've got him hooked into the usual gear.'

'Long term . . .'

'Is the issue. He needs . . . a transplant that won't be rejected, even without a lot of drugs. Because he's very weak. Broken shoulder, broken ribs, broken femur, all kinds of stuff that would be bad enough, if it weren't for this.'

Adam said, 'I think I now understand, don't I, why you called, and why Juliana said not to?'

'I asked them if I could give him one of mine, but the match isn't reliable enough between an uncle and a nephew; not in this case, anyway.'

'As against brothers.'

'Is what I've been told,' Tom said.

'Now we know why we have two kidneys. Spanish drivers need us to. What do I have to do now?'

'*Have* to do? Nothing. Nothing. Because remember, what was the line? If you use the spare, you don't have a spare.'

'Are you sure I'm not too old?'

'You're not. I asked. I'm sorry, but I did. Otherwise this is a wind-up. Which it isn't, sadly.'

Adam said, 'Then there's not a lot to talk about, is there?'

'Dad, no one could blame you – '

Adam said, 'No. But then blaming myself is my strongest suit. I'll wear it to come to Madrid. And to hell with Almeria forever, incidentally, if you know what I mean; or even if you don't. Anything else?'

'One thing there is, yes,' Tom said. 'I love you, dad.'

Adam said, 'Tell me exactly where we have to be when and we'll get straight in the car.'

'I'll talk to them and call you right back.'

Adam put down the receiver, blew out his breath, and looked up at Barbara. 'Thank God I changed that tyre.'

Barbara said, 'One question . . .'

'I know the answer,' he said. 'My name is Adam Morris.'